VENETIAN COUSINS

STEPHEN CARROLL

Venetian Cousins

ANDRE DEUTSCH

First published in Great Britain in 1995 by
André Deutsch Limited
106 Great Russell Street
London WC1B 3LJ

The right of Stephen Carroll to be identified
as the author of this work has been asserted
by him in accordance with the Copyright, Designs
and Patents Act 1988.

Cataloguing-in-publication data for this title
is available from the British Library.

ISBN 0 233 98901 3

Printed in Great Britain by
WBC, Bridgend

To A.M.
and in memory of his friend
the Hon. H.U. *who vanished in 1956*

CONTENTS

Prelude   1

But I hate things all fiction . . . *there should always be some foundation of fact for the most airy fabric — and pure invention is but the talent of a liar.*

BYRON

Prelude

HE STORY OF my own destruction began in a seedy hotel in Venice not quite overlooking the Grand Canal. According to my mother my conception itself had been a miracle, but, as she later said, in a city that was wedded to the sea anything could happen. In any event, whether inspired by the winged lion of that maiden city or too much Frascati I don't know, but one egregious phocine torpedo must have struck home, exploded, and *ergo sum*.

I hope you will excuse this extravagant beginning. I wanted to start with a bang.

Many people have been conceived in Venice. It has always been a city for love. Some say it stinks, that it is vulgar, decaying and stuffed with trippers. They are quite right, of course; many people don't care for Venice. We all have our ways of judging those we have recently met; if you don't like Venice the odds are against our getting on.

If by chance you haven't visited the city where I was conceived please allow me to offer a little advice. You must arrive by water. Then you must climb any tower that can be climbed. When James and I emerged into the air at the top of the Campanile at San Marco that first time we were deafened by the bells swinging wildly above our heads. And then we looked down over the red rooftops and the churches, the canals, and across the water to San Giorgio. Venice – surely the most beautiful city in the world. James, James, James, is there some trace of your spirit left on the Venetian air? Do you still hear those bells ring as I do?

This is a true story. Well, true with a touch of fairy. I have had to make changes, to shuffle, to haze, to blacken; here a little and there a little, as it says in Isaiah. Even changing a name presents the fastidious author with a dilemma. An honest man is anxious not to wander too far from the truth. Let me start with my own name. My mother maintains that before I was born I was going to be called Mark, since the accident happened in Venice. Instead, she named me after a more sceptical saint. Call me Thomas . . . Thomas Lamb.

I have taken a six-month break from earning my living. What do I do? Well, if you want to know, I don't do anything, or to be more precise, I am between careers. Until the end of June of this year I practised as a barrister of the Middle Temple in London. If from time to time I seem pompous, please forgive me; it's the result of years of training. After Christmas I will be starting work as a lecturer in a law school, somewhere in the south of England. I was never a successful barrister. It has been said that I spent too much time at the wrong kind of bar and there may be some truth in the allegation. It would certainly be true to say that I failed to suck up to the right people; my pride is very fierce. There was also the question of Netta; things had gone wrong. Perhaps this long vacation is my equivalent of joining the Foreign Legion except that I want to *remember*. In any event, I needed a break. Before I start my new life I want some time off in order to plead my own cause, and, it should be admitted, to do a bit of prosecuting, and a bit of judging into the bargain.

I shall miss the Law Courts in the Strand, and I shall miss walking through the Temple on a cold November morning. I shan't miss much else about my old profession. The Law Courts is a magnificent building, a vast Victorian-Gothic pile concealing a maze of corridors in which I still get lost, in spite of twenty years of almost daily visits. After hours, the cathedral-like hall is sometimes used by members of the Bar for badminton. Think of moonbeams piercing the stained glass windows and catching the white feathers of the shuttlecock in flight. Ah, the Law! the Law!

I am setting down this account of *a life in being* at Steinpass in the Austrian Alps where there is a castle, a lake, and of course the mountains. It is quiet here, and comfortable and I take my meals at the nearby hotel. And there are plenty of ghosts to keep me company.

I have always been conscious of place and although I am not yet certain where these meanderings will take me there are three places which, for me, have a special significance. I have mentioned Venice and Steinpass. The third is the stretch of

Sussex where I spent my childhood. Imagine an angel descending from heaven, inserting the needle of a giant compass into the spire of Chichester Cathedral and describing an arc with a twenty-mile radius to the north, taking in a sweep of the Downs between Chanctonbury Ring in the east and Harting Hill in the west and including the rivers Rother and Arun, the castles of Amberley and Arundel, and the great houses of Petworth, Parham and Goodwood. I could also mention the Sainsbury's emporium, the Happy Eaters and Burger Kings, the major roads, the housing estates. I think it fair to let you know that I prefer to exclude such places from my thoughts so far as it is possible. There are plenty of contemporary writers only too willing to celebrate them.

I must cast off the years and go back: back to Sussex, back to childhood, back to the days when this particular wanderer was *en ventre sa mère*.

PART ONE

*Childhood
and
School-time*

CHAPTER 1 · *Trailing Clouds*

Y IMPENDING ARRIVAL was not the cause of unalloyed pleasure to my parents since they were not married at the time of my conception and in those days it was still a scandalous thing to produce a bastard. A marriage was therefore arranged at which I was very much present although unaware of the fact. I like to think of my mother wafting up the aisle like a hot air balloon to the strains of *The Wedding March*, to be joined with her reluctant bridegroom, but this would not altogether accord with the facts. They slipped away and did it quietly – 'like a couple of thieves', as Uncle Frank, that old hypocrite, was later in the habit of saying.

My mother, Dorothy Phelips, had a twin sister called Mary. One day the sisters were visiting the National Portrait Gallery in London when they came across Aunt Mary's future husband gazing at a portrait of Wordsworth. A hasty courtship ensued. It must have caused a stir in the village when Uncle Frank, who was thought to have had no dealings with the fair sex, had suddenly, at the age of forty-four, married a girl more than twenty years his junior. She brought with her an easel, three trunks of clothes and her newly pregnant sister. I went along for the ride. There is a story, which I was told much later by the doctor who became Netta's stepfather, that the reading in church, the Sunday after our arrival on the scene, included the passage *to every man a damsel or two*.

By all accounts, my mother and aunt had been beautiful girls, and no doubt the fact that each was a duplicate of the other added to their combined appeal. I first remember them as a pair of tall, slender, girlish women, who moved with a liquid grace. Their clothes were the sort you see in Augustus Johns, and I now think of them emerging from the vegetable patch or fruit cage with a lap full of potatoes or a colander of raspberries, or perhaps one of them is resting on a spade while the other leans back, hands on hips, laughing.

The domestic arrangements were rather unusual. My first

home was a caravan at the bottom of Uncle Frank's garden. My father, Toby Lamb, had chosen not to live the bourgeois life. He had, it seems, honoured his obligations to my mother and myself by giving us his name and also by paying for our simple dwelling. Then he buggered off. Oh yes, he did drop in now and then. His visits were always unannounced, since he was not one to be tied down. He used to come and go at irregular intervals, seldom staying more than a night at a time, and disappeared from my childhood finally – O unreliable word – when I was seven. His visits were the cause of great excitement, and all my early feelings of sadness or disappointment are linked to a father who, right from the start, played hard to get. Fathers, if you want to be worshipped by your children, vanish.

I believe that however hard I try, I shall never be able to shake off my father entirely. I have never been a man of action and perhaps my only way of hitting back is by character assassination; the battle with Father is cerebral only. All gods are false. We invent them because we must have them. How real is my father, and how much the invention of his only begotten son?

Coniston, Uncle Frank's house, is not a house of any particular distinction. It was built in about 1912 by Uncle Frank's grandfather, a local builder, along with Windermere, Grasmere, Ambleside and Thirlmere, and Uncle Frank had inherited it four years prior to his marriage, on the death of his mother, who had pampered him until the end. Villagers still talk of having heard him asking his dying mother to bring him a cushion. His 'pianist's hands' had prevented him from mastering the simplest domestic tasks and as a result his life had lapsed into squalor even before his mother had gone down into the pit. You might think it strange that a studious bachelor of mature years should have taken on a young wife, let alone her pregnant sister, but Aunt Mary was capable of cooking and sewing on a button, and, I suppose, of turning a trick or two in the bed of Uncle Frank's desire. No doubt the arrangement was an improvement on a diet of cornflakes and the pleasures of solitude.

The caravan was at the bottom of the garden. I was Prince

of the tin palace. It was a simple home but quite adequate in every respect except respectability. The usual offices were to be found in an outbuilding to Coniston known as the wash-house, and Mother and I usually shared our meals with Uncle Frank, Aunt Mary and James, who first saw the light of day some six hours before I did.

James and I were cousins. He was proud of having a birthday first. Those six hours had divided the calendar and his birthday preceded mine by a day. We started off like our mothers, *twins almost in genius and in mind*.

Father had given my mother his name. Lamb. Not a bad name: a name with literary, religious and culinary associations. My mother, however, left us in no doubt that she came from a better family than my father. *His* father had not hunted his own pack of hounds. After such a sententious proclamation she and my aunt would dissolve into laughter. Our family history is clouded in obscurity; there were no extant grandparents on either side. As for Uncle Frank's family, well, the less said the better. I discovered the English national sport at an early age: class. Make the most of it, *mes enfants*, for tomorrow looks grey.

Why had our mothers thrown in their lot with Father and Uncle Frank? This was not, of course, a question that troubled us as children. Children accept their estate as being the right one, whatever it may be. Certainly our mothers had both been pregnant when they married and they were short of cash. I am not privy to any other factors in the equation, although one generation back takes us to *madness*.

Our maternal grandmother had been mad. Our mothers were farmed out as children. They hardly knew their mother and had never met their father, who, they were told, had died hunting. When they were still away at school, they heard that their mother too had died. She had been a rich woman and had seen off three husbands before she expired. The last two had been possessed of double-barrelled names, Wyndham-Vaughan and Bowman-Kaye. For years Mother and Aunt Mary wore white silk pyjamas which had belonged to their two stepfathers, and which bore the initials embroidered in stylish maroon thread of the two unfortunate men who had gone before, which proved that they had allowed themselves to be dressed by their wife. What underlings they must have been. Grandmother left her entire estate to a dogs' home. Our mothers had no money of their own and no invisible means of support.

Since our mothers were minors, their headmistress took matters in hand and saw that proceedings were instituted against the executors. Counsel's opinion was taken. There was irrefutable evidence of insanity; if the testatrix could be shown not to have been of 'sound mind memory and understanding' at the time the will was made it could be overturned. However, in the process of pursuing their investigations, the solicitors were unable to find any reference anywhere to her first husband, Archie Phelips, the man our mothers believed to have been their father, and concluded that he had never existed. He was the fox that never was and had been invented by our crazy grandmother. Our mothers were therefore presumed to be illegitimate children who, at that time, could not inherit on an intestacy. In other words, even if a court had declared the will void, they stood to inherit nothing. The trustees of the dogs' home settled the case by giving them a paltry sum which saw them through school and art college and enabled them to study in Venice for a year, and three enormous trunks containing their mother's clothes.

Those three trunks were kept in the loft at Coniston. It was a favourite game of our mothers to bring down one of these into the garden and to take out the clothes one by one. How they delighted in trying on the long gloves, silk dressing gowns, long scarves and (yes, I remember) undergarments. Most of the clothes had never been worn and some still had little labels attached with string showing the price, which was usually in guineas. Even Uncle Frank, an unfrolicsome indoor man by nature, went alfresco in order to join in the fun. Do I really remember seeing the two of them putting on the lingerie for him, or have I imagined it?

Uncle Frank . . . just his name embodies so many confusing and conflicting feelings. How can I sum him up? A big bald bespectacled nervous man whose ears and fleshy nose sprouted hairs. A man who blustered and fumed and shouted and bullied. A man who loved Wordsworth and wild flowers.

A mean uncomfortable man who enjoyed losing his temper. A man for whom I thought I had no love.

On the way to the village church, where he was organist for thirty years, he would teach us the names of the trees. Sycamore Hornbeam Ash Elm Oak Elm Elm Yew. That's how they went.

Neither Coniston, nor the village in which it stands are idyllic. The village is scrappy like many Sussex villages. It is bisected by a main road that leads to the sea and in the summer it is sometimes impossible to cross the road for traffic. On our side of the road stand the five Lakeland houses, a dozen or so 1930s-built bungalows, the Black Horse, a car-breaker's yard, and a disused nursery. On the far side, a dead-end lane leads to the old village, consisting of some flint cottages, the village shop, the Red Lion, the Norman Church (as the sign at the end of the lane proclaims it to be), the Georgian Rectory, and the Manor House, formerly the seat of the noble and oddly named Blancs. A quarter of a mile beyond the Manor stands Blanc Hall, a romantic, if heterogeneous pile started by the family in the seventeenth century and added to in every century that followed. When I was a child Blanc Hall had been occupied by Sir Richard Blanc, an ancient and decrepit hermit, who was rarely seen in the village. To the south of Blanc Hall is the railway line with its dangerous crossing. If you live in the city you may not be aware that there are still plenty of villages like mine in England, sandwiched between trunk roads and motorways. You just have to look for them.

I T WAS THE garden of Coniston, as well as its peculiar ménage, that made it remarkable. The garden – half an acre of roses, hollyhocks and plums; a jungle, an Eden where initiations and rites took place and strange rituals were enacted.

My first memory? The huge step from the caravan down into the garden. My father seated on his umbrella-stick encouraging me to take my first voluntary leap into the unknown. And what was the umbrella-stick? I suppose I should explain. During the war Father had been injured fighting in Burma. He had been shot in the leg while leading an assault on a position held by the Japanese. I liked to picture the scene – Father, a dashing young officer, raises himself from the ground, and gives the order to charge with a wave of his gloved hand.

READY MEN . . . CHAAAAAAAARRRRGH!!!

The bullet that hit him passed through the thigh, shattering the femur, and as Father fell, he just had time to say 'Carry on' to his brother officer before passing out. That was the end of the war for Father. Six months later a homeward bound troop ship carried him back to England and Oxford where lectures alternated with treatment at the Radcliffe. Infection had set in, and never left him, and he had constantly to change the dressings on the leg since yellow muck oozed from the wound. Sometimes a splinter of bone would emerge from the blue-red gaping hole, he would call out in triumph, and I would be invited to inspect the expelled fragment. You could see the bullet hole on each side and a long scar. Naturally, all this added to Father's glamour. The fact that the bone had shattered left the damaged leg, as he called it, two or three inches shorter than the other one. Hence the use of the umbrella-stick. Father's prop, which was a shooting-stick complete with base-plate and a crook-shaped handle like an ordinary walking stick, was also an umbrella. It was heavy and very strong and doubled as a sunshade, rifle and Samurai sword. Father liked to emerge from the shrubbery waving it like a Japanese officer or to creep up on us holding it like a machine gun, giving a *rat-a-tat-tat*. We spent a lot of time looking out for Japs.

In the summer-time James and I lived in the garden with our mothers. Uncle Frank went to work in his big black car and when he returned went indoors straight up to the room where Wordsworth, his beloved poet, awaited him. At seven-thirty he would clump down the stairs for dinner after which he played the piano for exactly one hour. What happened next was a mystery, since James and I would have long been in our beds. In our infancy Uncle Frank featured very little. He was like his car, a big shadowy presence with which we had little direct contact. When we were old enough to dine *en famille*, he sometimes read to us from a tattered red book called *The Poetical Works of Wordsworth*. This was frequently the cause of mirth. The attack was usually led by our mothers, and always resulted in the rout of Uncle Frank, who retreated upstairs proclaiming, 'I'm a solicitor. I'm an important man. My grandfather built this house. I'm not going to be treated like this.'

Coniston is, I suppose, a typical house of its kind; a bit of timbering and stained glass, bay windows, a heavy front door, and the best position of the five Lakeland houses on rising ground. From the windows of the Holy of Holies, as Uncle Frank's study was called, you can see in the far distance, over the roofs of the houses on the other side of the road, beyond the paddocks and fields of the coastal plain, the line of the South Downs, and in one corner of the horizon a landmark, made famous by that idiosyncratic Sussex writer Hilaire Belloc, which seemed to me, when I was a little child, to be at the world's end, on the line that divided earth from heaven. Halnaker Mill. 'I'll take you there one day,' said Father a number of times. He never did. He never will.

*

Gentle Jesus meek and mild look upon a little child
Pity mice and plicity suffer me to come to thee
God bless Mummy Daddy Aunty Mary Uncle Frank
Cousin James and all kind friendsand
helpmetobetruthfulandkindforeverandeveramen.

Ours was not a religious household. Prayers were part of the prelude to sleep. How well I recall listening to the voices of my aunt and mother as they chatted into the night when I was supposed to be asleep, and how well I remember the sound of the rain beating on the tin roof. And in the morning the dawn chorus. Blackbird, thrush, wood pigeon, wren.

And the tin bath we used in summer, the tin bath where I first saw the naked female form. Netta, standing and gently splashing the water with one foot. Netta, my Aphrodite of the bathtub. Why, I asked my father, had our friend from the Manor not got an appendage like other people? Father pointed his umbrella-stick at the missing organ, laughed, and explained. Some kind of theological discussion must have followed. There's a small brown photograph taken at this juncture, of James, aged three, looking up at my father to ask what would happen if a bomb went up and hit Jesus. Father jabbed his umbrella-stick heavenward and replied, 'God would work a miracle, ha-ha-HAAA . . . AHH . . . AAATISHOOO!' Father had the loudest sneeze in the county. It could be heard as far away as Halnaker Mill.

I had a grudge against God from the earliest time. Do you remember that my mother had planned to call me Mark, because I had been conceived in Venice? Well, on the left side of my neck and face I have a birthmark, which is roughly the size and shape of a human hand. So you see why I was christened Thomas. Even Mother's sense of humour didn't run to Mark. As an infant I wasn't aware of it, of course, not until Netta pointed it out. She asked if I had been slapped and when Father announced that I had been born with it she looked very solemn, nodded and declared that I had been slapped by God. Netta has always had a great sense of justice. She was a born fighter, but I was like James's afterthought, a watery *doppelgänger*. He was a beautiful child. When we fought or raced he always won, and yet he never bullied me. I always looked up to him and he looked after me. When I was called Strawberry Face or Scarface at the village school, he (and Netta too if she was there) came to the rescue; summary trial and execution of the offender immediately took place. James was a golden lad with his big frame, crop of golden curls and broad smile. He was a born hero; I had to write this.

I say I felt no jealousy or resentment towards James but something comes into my mind. The two of us, alone in the house one winter's night. The sitting room at Coniston had a brick fireplace, and since Uncle Frank was infamously mean, this was the only source of heat in the house in winter. The mantelpiece served as a shelf where he lined up the household bills like certificates of honour. Perhaps he was sitting in the Music Room, dressed in hat, coat and scarf while he played the piano, while our mothers were in the caravan, which had its own stove and was really quite cosy, chatting and drinking their home-made wine, or had slipped out to Ninny's Tomb, which I later discovered was their code-name for the Red Lion, where they indulged their taste for barley wine and mischief. On the particular winter's night that I am struggling to remember, a hot coal had fallen on to the hearth. 'Pick up that bright star, James.' James was about to pick it up when he realised just in time and shook his head sadly. My first betrayal.

James and I must have been about six when we engaged Netta as a stripper. She agreed to show us her naked body in exchange for a handful of raisins. Ah, the innocence of childhood! For a few stolen raisins she took off her clothes in a most serious and business-like manner, after school, behind the caravan, when no one was about. She had just slipped off her knickers one afternoon, when Father appeared; he had a habit of turning up unexpectedly. Netta stood there, pale, beautiful and naked, her hands full of raisins, her chin lifted, and said nothing. Father looked at the caravan step where the open bag of raisins proclaimed her a harlot. 'Ha-ha. For raisins,' he said, and limped off, swinging his umbrella-stick. At Netta's insistence the show continued. Justice required it.

We must have got through bags of raisins that summer. I would keep watch while James filched a few handfuls and stuffed them into his pocket. She did it for raisins, only for raisins. Blackjacks (four a penny), pink shrimps (two a penny), sherbet fountains (2d), palm toffee and licorice pipes (of inestimable worth) left her unmoved. Ah, Netta, do you remember? Do you tremble when you see a packet of raisins? But I am forgetting. Netta chooses never to tremble.

Unlike her Swedish mother, the Valkyrie, who was as blonde as Wagner would have wished, Netta had hair that was almost black. She has always been beautiful, but has never shown much interest in the fact. It is as if her looks have been a kind of inconvenience to her. She has never shown any enthusiasm for clothes or hairdressers. Her beauty is something she happens to be wearing. When she stripped for us behind the caravan she did it without a trace of coyness; she wasn't that kind of girl. She always refused to be worshipped. I suppose this is why, in the end, we went our separate ways.

Netta's mother, Birgit, as we children were obliged to call her, was not easy to get on with, unless you happened to be a complete underling; she and I have always been on excellent terms. For one thing, she was constantly engaged in works of construction and destruction. Anyone who had seen her wielding a sledgehammer would be wary of picking a fight. And I can assure you that no man in his right mind would pick a fight with Netta.

The Manor, where Netta lived, was about ten minutes' walk away, beyond the school, the church and the rectory. From the outside it looked like a typical Sussex manor house built of brick and flint under a red-tiled roof. Inside, however, things were different. Birgit had gutted it. Chimney breasts alone divided kitchen from living room and living room from library. The walls were bare flint, hung with her own canvases, most of them abstracts. There is a fine triptych of Birgit, Birgit and Netta as Madonna and child, and Netta aged about three on one wall of the sitting room. She had also made a lot of the furniture. The kitchen, for instance, sported an elm refectory table and eight beechwood chairs, all of which she had made in the barn. The carver was a magnificent throne and might have come from a castle. From here the matriarch presided. Netta's father had fled long ago. Birgit liked to relate the story at dinner parties: Netta's father had returned from his work in London one night and had been unable to get in by the front door, since it had been completely covered with rubble ejected from above by Birgit during the day. He had gone round to the back door to find that it had been bricked up, got a ladder, climbed in through an upstairs window, packed a suitcase and left, never to return.

Interest was added to Birgit's ménage by the appearance of strange-looking painters and potters, and even of a visionary-looking poet, who wandered around for a while; she had planned to set up an Artists' Community, as articles in the local newspaper proclaimed it, but usually the aproned sculptor or bearded playwright stayed for only a short time before departing. Our mothers were artists themselves, and while they could not be said to have formed part of Birgit's household, they were frequent visitors. The doctor often called in too, although, at that time, he had a wife of his own.

The Lady of the Manor did not attempt to appear ordinary. For instance she drove a hearse. It was useful for carting about her work for she went in for bulk. Sculpture and things. Environmental art. And it was useful for carting us about too. It certainly made people stare when the gate was flung open and we three children fell out of the back. Imagine wandering up the dead-end lane of a Sussex village and seeing the black beast hurtling towards you with a Valkyrie at the wheel. BLAH-BLAH. BLAH-BLAH.

At the first whiff of spring Birgit would organise expeditions, and we children would be carried off by her in the hearse to some high and remote spot from where we would walk for half a day. It was on one of these spring walks along the downs, somewhere between Bignor and Eartham, that I saw the spire of Chichester Cathedral and Halnaker Mill at the same time – Halnaker Mill, symbol of all that was unattainable and far off.

T IS THE summer of Netta and the raisins. I am six years old. I wake early in the caravan. Mother is still sleeping. I get dressed and tiptoe out on to the dry August grass and go to the wash-house to perform my ablutions. I can just reach the tap. I go into the house. Uncle Frank and James are in the kitchen; Uncle Frank likes an early breakfast. He is instructing James in the art of boiling an egg.

'You put the egg in the small saucepan and half an inch of cold water. Then you put the lid from a smaller saucepan so that it slips inside. Turn on the electric ring. As soon as it starts to bubble properly, switch off. Wait until the bubbles stop. Result – a perfectly boiled egg, using the minimum of electricity. When you boys have to pay the bills you'll appreciate the advice.

'Now the tea. Measure out the water by the cupful and pour it into the kettle. That way you avoid waste. Tea bags are more economical than loose tea, because you can dry them out and re-use them up to six times. Then you cut them open and the leaves can go on your mothers' roses.'

While Uncle Frank is making the tea, James is drawing a face on the boiled egg with a biro. A frieze of hair around the bald crown, a Hitler moustache beneath an amorphous nose, a chin dimple and a pair of specs. Result – a pretty fair impression of Uncle Frank.

Uncle Frank doesn't mind this at all. In fact he rather likes it.

Aunt Mary appears after half an hour, leaning liquidly against the door frame in her white silk pyjamas. She puts the kettle on and, using fresh tea bags, since she is not easily intimidated, makes tea. She fills two pottery mugs, a legacy from a departed member of Birgit's Artists' Community, and slips out of the door into the garden.

Uncle Frank reads to us from *The Prelude*. At the moment he is going through it at breakfast time, a page a day, and he ticks off each page and adds the date. The book is filled with

ticks and dates, in red and blue ink and in pencil. Today we
have

> need I dread from thee
> Harsh judgements, if the song be loth to quit
> Those recollected hours that have the charm
> Of visionary things, those lovely forms
> And sweet sensations that throw back our life,
> And almost make remotest infancy
> A visible scene, on which the sun is shining?
>
> One end at least hath been attained; my mind
> Hath been revived, and if this genial mood
> Desert me not, forthwith shall be brought down
> Through later years the story of my life.

It is a Sunday. We help our mothers, who are wearing
long loose skirts and loose blouses in faded colours, to get
the stall ready in the front garden, and James and I carry
out the two signs FIGS PLUMS JAM and put them in the
hedge so that they can be seen from the road. Our mothers
are in high spirits. Aunt Mary brings out her easel and puts
it on the lawn at the front. She knocks off another picture.
She sells quite a few paintings to passers-by and at the local
exhibitions. So does Mother. You can't tell their pictures apart.

James and I are excited because we are going to the sea.
BLAH-BLAH. Netta and Birgit arrive somewhat later than
planned and we tumble into the hearse. Uncle Frank does
not come. He returns from his labours at the village church
and goes straight up to the Holy of Holies. He prefers to
study.

We know Netta's mother is called the Valkyrie but we must
not say so. We have to call her Birgit like everyone else. Today
she is in a state of dudgeon. She has been having words with
the Rector's wife (her neighbour) about the things she has on
her front lawn. The Rector's wife says she's fed up with having
her view obstructed by a lot of junk, but the Rector's wife knows
nothing of art. If you give that woman half a thumb she will
take your whole hand. You have to fight the bourgeoisie tooth

and nail. The woman is as dull as dishwater and would like to see all artistic endeavour thoroughly spannered.

The seaside! Sun, sea, sand and wasps. An argument with the people in the next dune. They are listening to *Family Favourites* on a transistor radio. Birgit sends them packing. We play in the sea and make sandcastles. James and I have pointed red spades; Netta has a square blue one. We are late back. Uncle Frank is pacing about. We are late for tea.

Our mothers set up their stall again later to catch the returning day-trippers. James and I play in the garden. Through the open windows we can hear Uncle Frank at the piano. The women are in prankish mood, and for a joke put a price in the window of the Westminster which Uncle Frank has parked in the drive. A man looks at it and wants to take it for a run. Uncle Frank is playing some of Schumann's *Kinderscenen*. It is beginning to get dark. Almost time for bed. Mother and Aunt Mary say they must call the owner. There is some shuffling before he comes to the door. The women giggle together while Uncle Frank fumes and blusters. He explains that the women are mad. There is an altercation before the man retreats.

'You shouldn't do this sort of thing. It's most embarrassing. I'm a solicitor. I'm an important man. I shouldn't be treated like this – ' he pulls at his socks, 'My grandfather built this house' – and turning to me, he bends down and, pushing his nose within an inch of my face, shouts, 'And what are you sniggering at? What do you contribute?'

Uncle Frank was much given to rages. He seethed and boiled and spent time stoking his temper so that there was usually plenty of notice before an explosion. The pulling up of socks and reddening of the face would be followed by a period of hissing and scowling. Then the sock pulling would be done with more and more vigour as the hissing and scowling increased. Sometimes he would begin to talk to himself and various set speeches followed in which the words *sponger* and *parasite* featured. Once a decent head of steam had been built up these would be spat out in a kind of muted shout. Even the best of audiences will tire of a production which it has seen too often and Uncle Frank was not one to stay around when it became clear that his reception was not worthy of him. He would then abandon the stage with a slamming of all the doors he had to pass through on his retreat to the Holy of Holies. If things were really bad he would drag some poor object, perhaps set aside weeks before for the purpose, to the top of the stairs and hurl it down with the cry of SPONGERS so that it would land with as much thunder as possible. And so it was on this particular summer evening, which is how the wooden hatstand came to be broken and how the spongers and the parasites came to be gathered together at the foot of the stairs to mock the man who called himself the provider, and who liked to say *he who pays the piper calls the tune*.

'What a man!'

'An *important* man.'

'A *learned* man.'

'A man with *letters* after his name.'

'Supreme of heroes – bravest, noblest, best!'

At the very end of the garden at Coniston, beyond the fruit cage and behind the caravan, was a disused nursery. In spring the field was full of daffodils. This always set Uncle Frank off and we would be treated to a reading of the famous poem. In accordance with family tradition, this would be accompanied by bouts of giggling from the women and cloud-like gestures from James and myself.

One of the beautiful things about spring was the daffodil-picking, which was a ritual introduced by our mothers. It was always carried out after dark, which may have been because we were committing the tort of trespass, as I seem to remember Uncle Frank pointing out. We would wait for a fine night and a good moon, and together with Birgit and Netta, would go off down the garden, through the fence at the bottom and into the field beyond. There we picked at random from amongst the vast crowd of budding flowers and returned home with our arms full, the cold stems sticky in our hands, having made no visible impression on the star-studded field.

It still flashes on the inward eye: a full moon, a cold night, stars around us in heaven and on earth and that slightest and most delicate of scents. Spring.

Although Uncle Frank took no part in the commission of the offence, he allowed his grandfather's house to be filled with booty, and, to give him his due, it was one of the few festivals which gave him real pleasure. At the sight of so many of Wordsworth's beloved flowers he beamed like a benevolent ugly sister. It was on the night of the daffodil-picking one year, when I was seven years old, that an extraordinary event occurred.

We had been back at the house about ten minutes, and the women were bustling about finding jugs and vases for the flowers. Uncle Frank, who had, everyone agreed, been in the foulest of moods, had cheered up and was now presiding as Master of Ceremonies; this was his night of the year. There was a knock at the front door, an unusual enough event, since our usual visitors were already with us, and the doctor, for instance, would have come the back way. James ran to open the door and Netta and I followed.

'Uncle Toby!'

Standing outside with the full moon behind him, leaning on his umbrella-stick and wearing his academic gown, was Father, who looked to us as exciting as Dracula himself. Father never came to the house; even as small children we were in no doubt that Uncle Frank hated him. 'Hello James, Thomas, Netta. How are you all? I must come in,' and in he hobbled with us in his wake.

There was a banging of vases and a gasp from all three women. Even Birgit, the Valkyrie herself, was silent. They looked at Father and at each other and at Uncle Frank and at us. Uncle Frank's face had turned the colour of a ripe Victoria plum but he said nothing.

'I'm sorry to intrude on your family gathering, but there was no one at the caravan and I haven't much time. I may be away for quite a while, you see, and naturally I felt . . .'

'Oh' from Mother.

'Oh' from Aunt Mary.

'I'm going away tonight, out of the country.'

Mother and Aunt Mary swayed like a couple of reeds and began to giggle. 'I suppose this is something to do with Henry?' said Mother. It was the first time I remember hearing any reference to that name.

'How lovely the daffodils are,' said Father, turning to Uncle Frank and adding 'fluttering and dancing. Ha-ha.'

Uncle Frank went an even deeper shade and pulled up his socks. His teeth began to show and a familiar hissing noise had started up.

'I've deposited a little money in your account,' said Father, addressing my mother, and taking a sweeping bow, he wrapped his gown around him like a cloak, turned and hobbled out of the room. We children followed him out of the front door. I know he rubbed my head with his hand, said he was sorry that we hadn't yet got to Halnaker Mill and promised to write. Then he limped off to his car, jabbing his umbrella-stick at the moon. 'That's my old enemy,' he said, 'the moon.'

I heard the engine of the car start up. The headlights burned brighter and he reversed away from me into the road. Then he was gone.

Much has been written about the telescoping of time, of how because of a trick of imagination some seconds last longer than others, and they do. After a few of these seconds I went back into the house with the others to find that everything in it seemed intensified and strange.

Mother and Aunt Mary fussed about, trying to seem normal. Birgit made some excuses and left on her own, since Netta insisted on staying. Uncle Frank hissed and spluttered his way out of the room and clumped up to the Holy of Holies. There was much shuffling of daffodils, a host of loaded glances and some nervous tittering.

Perhaps half an hour elapsed before an unfamiliar sound was heard coming from upstairs.

'It's coming from my room,' said Aunt Mary.

'*Your* room?' said my mother. 'You mean you're not sleeping with Frank? You mysterious creature. When did this happen?'

'I moved out on Sunday, while he was at church . . .

His snoring. And he has fits. He bounces about in the bed. What's that noise?'

'It's soaring,' said Netta.

'Oh, I forgot you children were here. *Sawing* is what you mean.'

Sure enough, the muffled sound of sawing was coming from upstairs. For a while we listened amongst the daffodils as the sound came and went and then, like the conspirators we were, crept into the hall and up the creaking stairs. Aunt Mary led the way, followed by Mother, Netta, James and myself. We paused outside the room. The edge of the door was lit up but there was no sound. My aunt quietly turned the handle and peered around the door. A second or two of silence followed, before she giggled and we all shuffled in to inspect.

Uncle Frank was lying on the bed at a low level, like King Arthur in the barge. The mattress had been removed and was propped up against the wall like a drunk, and the bedclothes were piled on the floor in an untidy heap. In one hand he loosely held an old and jagged saw which trailed from his half-open hand on to the floor. Uncle Frank lay there for all the world to see as if he had been cloven through the helm and would be drifting off to eternity at any moment.

The women giggled, gently at first, then uncontrollably. Uncle Frank had been trying to saw the bed in half. This had been the cause of the strange sounds we had heard from below. A little gash in the wooden frame showed he had not made much progress. Lying prone and clutching his rusty Excalibur, he lifted his weary head and said, 'I want you to come back.'

'Come back?' said our mothers in unison.

'Come back to my bed,' and the wheeling brand clattered to the floor.

I didn't see Father again for ten years. During that time we must have heard from him about once a year, sometimes at Christmas, or sometimes a week or two after my birthday. Post was of course delivered to the house, and if Uncle Frank happened to get to the post first, there would be trouble. Father's cards, with their exotic stamps, postmarked Innsbruck,

Venice or Bombay, were received with much excitement, but they disclosed no pertinent information. One read: *I'm sure you would like it here in Bombay where there are elephants in the streets.*

In many ways it's easier for sons whose fathers are dead or in limbo. The image remains untarnished.

Uncle Frank went to the church to play the organ for his own pleasure about once a week, usually on a Saturday, and I would often go along. On one such occasion I was wandering around the church while he played, when a cadaverous form leapt at me out of the gloom.

'I did not mean to startle you. I am Sir Richard Blanc; the last squire. If you are interested in the memorials I will gladly show you around.' What appealed to me in particular was that Sir Richard treated me, at the age of seven, exactly as an equal.

'Let us begin the tour,' he said, as if talking to a visitor from abroad. We might have been part of an eighteenth-century engraving. *Travellers inspecting the ruins of . . .*

'This is a memorial to my great-uncle, who disappeared in search of the Magnetic North, and this is a memorial to his father who perished in the Zulu War, and this' – and he pointed at a familiar marble slab which read *In memory of Sir Percival Richard de Vere Blanc Blanc* – 'is to commemorate my great-great-great-uncle who was named Percival *Blanc* Blanc because *his* father' – and he pointed at the next memorial – 'was obliged to change his name from Blanc to Urquhart in order to inherit a fortune. Ah, yes, the old name struck back, and these were his twin daughters Rose and Lily who died of consumption . . .'

'My mother and Aunt Mary are twins.'

'They are?' and he looked at me with a peculiar sideways look. 'I have a list of twins. May I ask their names?'

I told him their names, married and maiden, and he solemnly repeated the latter. 'Mary and Dorothy Phelips. Thank you. Thank you *so much.* May I ask where they live?'

I gave him the address. He was thrilled by the news.

We went outside and hurried across to the far side of the churchyard. 'This is the grave of my parents. If you will please excuse me for one moment,' and he knelt down and picked up a jar of dead flowers. I walked a few paces and gazed out over the meadow where some cows were grazing. Once I glanced back to see how my friend was getting on, and I observed that he had changed the water in the pot and replaced the same dead flowers. I gazed more intently ahead.

'Do you find you can identify with that?' he said. I thought he meant the countryside in general and nodded. 'You can empathise with a cattletrough? Oh, how I envy you. It must be wonderful to have such *peace of mind*. Ah, a feather, a white feather, an *owl's* feather. How marvellous. I have a collection of feathers.'

After our first meeting, we regularly met at the church on Saturday afternoons. I was even invited to Blanc Hall where I was shown collections of stamps, eggs, butterflies, medals and lead soldiers. Sir Richard was fifty-eight years old. As far as I was concerned he might just as well have been a hundred and fifty-eight. He was certain that he would not live beyond the age of sixty. 'I am *fifty-eight* years old,' I remember him telling me. 'I shall not live beyond the age of sixty. I have a list of people who died at the age of sixty. There's Gustav Holst whose ashes are interred in Chichester Cathedral, Admiral Collingwood, Lord Nelson's second-in-command, Sir John Stainer who only had one eye, *possibly* Sir John Franklin, who disappeared, and there's John Byrne Leicester Warren, third and last Lord de Tabley and . . . oh, I could go on . . .'

'Do you have any other lists, Sir Richard?' I asked.

'I have a list of composers who died in Venice. I have lists of one-eyed people, people with one arm . . .'

'One-eyed people?'

'Yes, it begins with Hannibal. Then there's Lafcadio Hearn who lived with a mulatto, Lord Alfred Douglas who was bitten by a dog, General Wavell and Lord Nelson and General Carton de Wiart . . . Those two are on two lists . . . they each lost an eye *and* an arm. Not many people have that kind of distinction . . . and I've got a list of people who disappeared . . . There's Ambrose Bierce, who vanished in a cloud of dust in Mexico, there's Maurice Macmillan, who disappeared while walking on Mount Olympus . . . and the Honourable Henry Usher, Lord Castledown's heir who disappeared off the Sussex coast only last year . . .'

We always parted in the drive of Blanc Hall with some ceremony, handshaking (he had a ferocious grip) and many farewells.

The name *Henry Usher* must, somehow, have seemed familiar, because I remember relating the conversation to my mother, who always asked me to repeat exactly what had been said at our meetings. His name registered with her, and I recall my mother and aunt speaking of it with some concern one night, in the caravan, not long after, when I was supposed to be asleep.

Incidentally, Sir Richard, the last squire, died at the age of sixty. I had grown fond of my friend and I missed him. Blanc Hall remained empty for several years before the developers moved in and converted it into *Luxury Apartments*.

CHAPTER 4 · *School-time*

From Ha'naker Mill or Graffham Down
A wanderer looking for the sea may sight
Rising from the invisible town
Piercing the heat haze, the spire of Chichester.

ET US GO forward now to the summer holidays, say
ten years later. James and Netta are home from their
grand schools. James was at Eton (Uncle Frank used
the excuse of school fees whenever he didn't want to spend
money); Netta was sent to a convent in Suffolk. I went to the
local grammar school.

It's perfect August weather. The combine harvester has
been out since dawn cutting the barley in the big field. James,
Netta and I cycle to Chichester, where we plan to look in the
bookshops and in the Cathedral, and Netta wants to buy some
jeans.

We sit on a bench in the shade of a lime tree with the
green roof of the Cathedral and its magnificent spire behind
us, and picnic in the Bishop's Garden amongst the marigolds,
roses and hollyhocks.

This is the day when I begin to compose my poem
Chichester Cathedral, which will win me ten shillings in a
competition run by the local paper. It will have twenty-one
verses. Here's the last:

A drifting ship in a phantasmal sea
Buffeted by storms and Sussex weather
Indifferent to God and to eternity
The towering Cathedral journeys on.

Back for tea at the Manor; James puts on the kettle, Netta
produces bread and butter and I pour the tea . . . THUMP
THUMP . . . the sound of footsteps on the oak floor above
us . . . CRASH. A scream or two . . . LAUGHTER (bass and

contralto) . . . HA! (sounds of struggle) . . . OW . . . BITCH
. . . more laughter. Deep cooing. Then perhaps a sound not
unlike the song of the cuckoo, sometimes frantic, sometimes
with more regular pauses between notes.

'Oh, that's Birgit and Martin,' says Netta, looking up
from her tea. 'It's the bedsprings.'

Then from above, shouting and laughter, cuckooing, grunting and gasping before a marked silence falls.

'Any chance of some more bread, Netta?' says James.
'The strawberry jam is delicious.'

'Your mother made it. Would you like some too?' I nod.

Once more life begins to stir above our heads. The creak of
floorboards, the sound of pipes and plumbing, a heavy tread
on the stairs and a huge bearded figure appears, draped in a
white towel, shakes his massive head, grabs a bottle of wine
from the refrigerator and disappears. It is as if a mythological
scene has been enacted.

Martin is Birgit's regular boyfriend and he stays quite a
lot, although he has a family of his own somewhere near
Folkestone. Martin is a likeable fellow and is usually as merry
as Jove but Birgit's other boyfriends keep clear when he is
around. He is known as the Blacksmith and makes sculptures
in metal which are exhibited far and wide.

Birgit invites James and me to stay for dinner. We have
one of her excellent bourguignons and she presides over the
meal from her magnificent throne. There is plenty of wine
and Birgit in particular is a little under its influence.

James and I admire Birgit and love to hear her talk.
She is our idea of an intellectual, a sort of one-woman
Bloomsbury group, and we revere her. She is a socialist,
an anarchist, a free-thinker, an autocrat, a reactionary, and a
magnificent woman. You can ask her about anything and she
always tells you what she thinks on religion, sex, art, politics,
anything.

The next day is going to be a big day. It is the opening of
Birgit and Martin's first joint exhibition. MANWO: PAINTINGS
AND SCULPTURE BY BIRGIT BACKMAN AND MARTIN DALY
proclaim posters around the village and even further afield.

'Martin,' says Birgit, 'it's no good sitting here drinking.

We have to cover that bare wall. We must finish the painting.'
They take the rest of the wine with them.

We youngsters follow them to the barn ten minutes later.
Birgit is slapping some yellow paint across a big piece of canvas already painted rose taupe. The effect is startling. Martin
is working on the stretcher.

'I'll just blow some red spray paint on that side,' she says.

My eyes wander to Birgit's series of four paintings, *Airstrip
1*, *Airstrip 2*, *Airstrip 3* and *Airstrip 4*. £200 each, according to
the price list pinned up on the beam.

'Do you think you'll sell them?' I ask.

'I don't want to sell them. I like them. That's what I
always do if I like a piece, I price it too high. It gets them
used to paying. Then they see this,' and she nodded towards
the rose taupe with yellow adornments, 'for £50 and they
think it's a bargain. You see.'

Airstrip 1, *Airstrip 2*, *Airstrip 3* and *Airstrip 4* are big canvases
looking like windows and it is as if you are seeing stretches of
motorway through Venetian blinds open at different angles. In
Airstrip 1 the blinds are wide open and by the time you get to
Airstrip 4 they are nearly closed.

'And that,' says Birgit, 'that piece by Martin, *Mother and
Child*, is one of the most sensual sculptures I have ever seen,'
and she looks at Martin as if she is about to eat him.

I examine the work. It is life-size and constructed of
jagged fragments of metal welded together. 'Yes,' I answer,
'I see what you mean.' Even in those days I was a liar.

A few days later, while the exhibition is in full swing James,
Netta and I set off on our bikes for a picnic by the sea. Just as
we leave the Manor we see a bald-headed pedestrian rounding
the corner. Uncle Frank is on his way to church. We stop for a
few moments. He is in a jolly mood and tells us he is composing
a poem, and has got as far as the title, which is to be *Blanc Hall,
a venerable pile*, and even as far as the first line. He declaims:

'At the end of a gently sloping lawn two lofty cedars
stood. I can't think what to put next.'

Being the poet of the family I suggest, 'Their leaves
were made of greenery and their trunks were made of
wood.' Everyone laughs, even Uncle Frank.

We go on our way, swim at Climping and lie in the dunes afterwards (no doubt I lie with my good side towards Netta). I have really begun to fancy her and can't stop looking at her. I begin to think how lovely it would be if I could stick my hand inside her bikini bottom. I wonder what sex would be like with her (with anyone). Oh yes, I want to kiss her and simply to *get on top of her*. But alas, I know such yearnings are unworthy.

We return to the Manor laden with strawberries bought at a roadside stall. Netta is just getting the cream out of the fridge when there is a gentle tap on the door.

The doctor's grinning head appears. 'Is Martin about? Your mother in, is she?' He grins. 'Been swimming, I see.'

James and I decide it's time to go home. As we cycle into the familiar drive of Coniston we observe that the telephone, trailing several yards of brown flex, is in the middle of the lawn. A touch of domestic Magritte. Had Uncle Frank's attempt at poetry not met with success? A mood? It is after all Sunday, and no bill would have arrived. I let James go in alone and head straight for the caravan. Mother is in the garden. I mention the telephone.

'Oh my dear – a terrible row. We had a telephone call – your father – he's back. Why he couldn't have written I don't know. He wants to see you! Uncle Frank must have ripped it out. He was certainly having a good fume.'

She puts her hand up to her mouth and laughs but I can see she is nervous.

CHAPTER 5 · *London*

O N THE APPOINTED day I went straight from school to catch the train to London, and using a borrowed *A–Z* found my way from Victoria station to Father's club. I was impressed with what I saw as I cut up the back of Waterloo Place, passed by the Athenaeum into Pall Mall and mounted the steps. I took a deep breath, pushed my way in through the heavy mahogany door and announced my business to the porter: I was here to see my Father.

I strode manfully across the black and white marble hall and found my way to the gallery, where the porter had told me I would find the object of my quest. I had not set eyes on Father for ten years and had built up a picture of what the meeting would be like. I had prepared a speech which was intended to be firm yet conciliatory. I had been somewhat neglected. Father had shown scant interest in my welfare. He had kept my mother short of funds and I had been educated at state expense. However, he was my father and I was his son. The past was the past and we could start anew. That sort of thing.

Alas, my preconceptions collapsed when I found that my well-travelled progenitor was sitting at a table, laughing and chatting with James. My confusion was obvious and apparent, not unexpected, and enjoyed. 'Ha-ha, I believe you two have met. I'll order you a sherry . . . Yes,' to the waiter, 'three more dry sherries. Yes, large sherries.'

The rest of the day is a blur. Looking back, I know that after the first shock, it was one of those occasions that seem to have been completely happy, and in spite of the solemn grandeur of our surroundings and the pin-striped old gentlemen about us, we had a pretty riotous time. I studied my father's face closely and recall how it refocused from the face I remembered as a child, and became again something that I had always been familiar with and would always know. There were some gold fillings in his teeth which showed when he laughed – otherwise all was the same. And there was the umbrella-stick slung over the back of his chair.

The news was that Father was now working as a temporary master at Eton. This explained James's presence and was to be a closely guarded secret, since under no circumstances was Uncle Frank to know. He would have blown sky high. A pact was sworn; we would tell no one.

James by this time was already over six foot and with his golden hair neatly trimmed looked a distinguished and handsome young man and seemed very much at ease. He beamed a great smile at me; I always felt safe when he was around even if I was just a little jealous. Father announced that we were to be joined by another guest, and shortly thereafter a face familiar from newspapers and television appeared.

The man concerned was a well-known politician, an old-fashioned Tory and one-time Cabinet Minister, and I am sure you will understand that I cannot paint a fuller picture of him or his identity would become clear. Some of you will doubtless see through my smoke screen and know to whom I refer when I append the name Nicholas York, for that is what I shall call him. It turned out that he and Father had shared an apartment in an Indian palace. They were old friends. My father moved in such circles.

Father introduced me. I stood up. 'How do you do, sir,' I said.

'Not *sir*, please, dear boy . . . Nicholas. So you're Thomas. I've heard a lot about you. Toby, why didn't you say your son was so charming? The trouble with Toby is that he talks about himself the whole time, don't you, Toby? We're not dining here, I hope. The food's worse than school. Why don't we toddle off to Prunier's? The walk'll do us good.'

'Oh yes,' said James. 'You'll like Prunier's.' He'd been there before.

About half an hour later we arrived at the famous restaurant. It may sound odd to you, but this was the first time I had dined at a restaurant of any kind, good, bad, or indifferent. Prunier's fitted comfortably into the first category. I had lobster. They say you always remember the first time. Madame Prunier, thou shouldst be living at this hour.

Nicholas was fun. There was no trace of condescension or of his being a man of the world talking down to schoolboys, although of course he did show off. Most of the time he was showering sparks like an arc-welder. He was a brilliant mimic, impersonating Winston Churchill, Harold Wilson, Father and other notable figures. The name *Henry Usher* kept cropping up in conversation, and I remembered that I had heard it before. The old squire, Sir Richard Blanc, friend of my childhood, had mentioned it, as had my mother and aunt. But at Father's club that night, I could not then have guessed how significant the name was to become. 'What that boy needs is a good whipping,' said Nicholas, addressing the handsome, golden-haired youth opposite him, in an impersonation of Henry's drawling speech.

After the meal, all four of us limped off to find a taxi. Father was in front waving his umbrella-stick, with Nicholas following, walking with one foot in the gutter, the better to imitate Father, and with James and me behind. We hailed a taxi outside St James's Palace, and I got to the station just in time for the last train home.

I planned to tell Netta about my evening, but only her. Mother said very little on the subject when I saw her in the morning (by this time she slept in the house and I was truly Caliph of the Caravan), limiting herself to polite and even sarcastic questions about Father's leg. In fact I was piqued at her apparent lack of interest since I was feeling rather smug.

Full of my story, I couldn't wait to see Netta. I was so pleased with things that I kissed her for the first time. We were drinking wine on the floor of the library and looking at art books. Suddenly I attacked. She was not at all taken aback, which is what I expected, and actually gave a sort of wriggle so that I found myself on top of her, and she permitted me to stamp the clumsy imprint of a kiss on her mouth. It was more like a declaration of war than lovemaking, but as I lay there breathing in the scent of wine from her virgin lips I felt that life had begun.

CRASH. The mad artist and Martin were back from the Black Horse. Our intimacy was, perforce, ended, and I leaped off my companion just as Birgit barged in with 'Hi. Don't get

up – we saw the light – don't be embarrassed. We don't want
to spanner your fun.'

At this, Martin appeared, in the process of uncorking
a bottle of wine, and roared with laughter. They were too
involved in their own affair to worry about us and went
thumping and laughing up the stairs. It was not long before
the familiar sound of the cuckoo was heard in the land.

After the initial strike into foreign territory, nothing more
happened on that front for several months. Netta and I
resumed our state of *intimacy without physical contact*. But
I think I already knew that I loved her.

I saw Father again during the Easter holidays, at the Opera;
I remember James kept the tickets hidden in a pair of
wellingtons in the garage. As we would be too late to catch
the last train home we were to sleep the night at Father's flat.
The official story was that we were staying with a schoolfriend
of James.

We sat in the front row, right behind the conductor.
'Damn the man,' said Father, 'I can hardly see what's going
on with him waving his arms about in front of us. That's
what they mean by *restricted view*. Henry would have had
him removed.' The spare seat next to me had been reserved
for Nicholas York, who didn't turn up.

During the second interval we climbed the magnificent
staircase and admired ourselves in the enormous mirror while
Father explained what would become of the great lover during
the final scene. We were facing the mirror and about to go
down to take our seats when Father grinned at his reflection
and said, 'He'll be dragged off to hell, just as you will be if
you don't behave yourselves. Henry and I will be waiting for
you.'

In those days, Covent Garden was still a fruit market
and the delicious smell of oranges used to waft into the
building where it mingled, not unpleasantly, with the Dior
and Chanel of the ladies. Red plush and oranges, and an opera
about the virtue of women. And then we surged out into the
orange-scented air, and headed down to Maiden Lane to dine

at Rules, all mirrors and pictures. 'Edward VII used to dine here,' said Father, 'and so of course did Henry.'

Nicholas appeared just as the beef was being carved, explained he'd been stuck with Crossman, tucked into the beef with considerable enthusiasm, signed a blank cheque which he pushed under Father's plate, and departed without further explanation.

Later, when Father was ready, we three survivors picked our way through the lanes to his car, a somewhat dilapidated Humber Hawk in two-tone maroon and beige. He drove with the driver's window wound right down and his black and white Magdalen scarf thrown over his shoulder undergraduate-style.

The flat turned out to be in Brixton in a 1930s block. We filed into the dismal corridor and Father pressed the button for the lift which arrived with much clanking and banging. He pressed the button for the third floor. Nothing. 'Blast and damn,' he said, opening and shutting the door once again. Up we went and out into another gloomy corridor. There was much fiddling around with a bunch of keys as we made our way to the door, and further fumbling as Father undid no fewer than three locks – two mortices and a Yale. The curious smell of other people's dwellings. Father's: coffee, Brasso and bleach. To the right was the bathroom into which he promptly disappeared. He switched on the light, leaving the door open, placed one foot on the lavatory seat and lowered his trousers, and unwound a length of bandage from his damaged leg. 'Go into the sitting room. Light the fire. Pour me a sherry, James, from the big decanter.'

To the left a small room, very cluttered, with a door leading to another equally small. James turned on the light. The general effect was cramped and dusty with heavy gold wallpaper and lots of pictures. The old gas-fire lit with a bang. Above it was a large oval painting of a jowly middle-aged man, full-lipped and sneering, in curling wig and armour. 'Clotworthy', came the voice from the bathroom, 'is one of Henry's ancestors. Henry's in the photograph in the other room, under the swords. He's the one with a dent in the head. Fell off a motorbike.'

We found, beneath a pair of Samurai swords hung with a ragged Japanese flag, a framed photograph of a tall, well-built

man of about thirty wearing a flying jacket and motorcycling
boots. Under his blond hair is a perceptible dent. He stands
in a field, with hands crossed, holding a flag in one hand and
beaming a great smile. 'Brands Hatch,' said Father.
'He doesn't look much like Clotworthy. Did you meet
him at Oxford?' I ventured.
'Henry is dead. Pour me another sherry, James.'
Before we left for home the next day, we had learned
quite a lot about Henry. Father had met him in India during
the war, and they had worked together in Canada ('Henry did
a bit of teaching'). We were shown a photograph of three
men on a balcony wearing turbans, who on closer inspection
turned out to be Father, Henry and Nicholas ('We stayed in
a Maharajah's palace in India'), and another of Henry as a
youth with a gun over his shoulder outside his ancestral pile
('Henry's father is a viscount'). There was one of him sitting
astride a motorcycle ('We used to whizz up on the Vincent
for lunch at Woodstock') and also in the tattered album were
photographs of Japanese soldiers looking younger than us, who
had been killed by Henry and Father ('This one's rather sweet,
don't you think? If I hadn't killed him I might have taken him
home as a houseboy').
I think the exhibit that pleased us most, however, was
a Japanese pistol, complete with holster and leather belt
punctured with bullet holes and stained with blood.
'A patrol of Japs appeared from nowhere. There was
nothing we could do except fire at them. Henry had the
Sten. Luckily it didn't jam. They have a habit of jamming at
the worst possible moment. I got rid of my three-eight after
that – they were so heavy and inconvenient in the jungle.
Little holes, aren't they? I keep this in good order. It's a nice
pistol. Of course Henry took over when I was shot a month
later . . . I was leading an assault on a hill called Peach. Henry
had taken his platoon around the side in a flanking movement.
The Japs hadn't realised we were there. Then the Colonel came
crashing up. "What's holding you up? Don't you know we're
on our way to Tokyo?" The Japs woke up and started firing.
"You'll just have to charge. We can't have the whole battalion
held up for half a dozen Japs." I told the daft old bugger that

Henry was attacking from the other side but, no, we had to charge. I was halfway up the hill when I felt something like a pneumatic drill going through my leg. Henry emerged from the shrubbery and I more or less collapsed on him. I just had time to say "Carry on, Mr Usher," before I passed out. Henry shot the fellow, I'm pleased to say. I've got a picture of him here somewhere. They took me back to hospital in Ranchi after that. I was stuck there six months before they found a ship to take me home. I didn't see Henry until after the war – met him again in Piccadilly, quite by chance, in the entrance to the Regent Palace. I was on crutches, ha-ha.'

At some stage, Henry had disappeared. He had vanished into the mist.

'Henry is dead,' repeated Father, who wore his friend's gold watch with its black face and the gold cufflinks and signet ring bearing Henry's crest (a warhorse astride a tower). 'It's official.'

CHAPTER 6 · *Rambling Studies*

SOMETIME IN AUGUST our exam results arrived. James got the two passes he needed for Oxford. Netta had also applied, but had failed the entrance exam, and in the event she was forced to settle for the same provincial university as me, a fact which brought joy to my treacherous heart.

We had arranged a party with a number of friends to coincide with the arrival of our results. What we used to do was go down to the sea at Climping, a long stretch of sand between Littlehampton and Felpham, light a fire and cook up some gritty sausages, and fun it was too, particularly once night had fallen and we could bask in the glow of the bonfire. I was feeling rather pleased with life and when a tall and nameless nymphet suggested a paddle, I nodded, and we slipped away from the others down to the water. I can still remember the smell of her neck as we lay in the dunes while one of the party strummed his guitar.

When I got back to Netta after half an hour's absence she pretended she didn't mind. She didn't know that nothing much had happened and that I was still a stranger to the pleasures of the fateful cleft.

James and I were planning to go camping with Father in France. It had been Father's idea. Strict secrecy was to be maintained; even our mothers were not to know. Since I had not, at that stage, set foot on foreign territory, this was to be a great adventure for me, a voyage of discovery.

I spent the evening before quitting England alone with Netta. She was having driving lessons at the time in the hearse which boasted a Rolls-Royce engine and, like its owner, had been built to last. Netta's determined face peering from the windscreen of this leviathan was one of the sights of the county. On this particular evening neither she nor I had passed our driving tests, but Netta wasn't concerned with formalities. Whether we had Birgit's permission to take it out on the road I can't remember but take it we did. Netta's driving was of the determined sort. I fear I must have displayed a lack of nerve as she swung the beast round a sharp bend and was told, 'Birgit says you have to accelerate round corners.'

Somehow we got to Climping and parked the hearse in the pub car park and went inside for an illegal drink. We were both seventeen. We walked on to the beach. Blue blue jeans and dusk falling, and me on the verge of my first trip abroad, alone on the beach with a beautiful girl, *with Netta*, who was both familiar and yet strange, and here we were, holding hands.

We took off our shoes and paddled a mile or so along the edge of the sea. It's very shallow at Climping and at low tide you can walk halfway to France before it's deep enough to swim. I suppose she'd been piqued by what had happened the week before, and at some stage we went whooping and splashing into the sea quite naked. We were blessed with stage effects since, although it was not yet dark, a half moon had come up over the harbour breakwater at Littlehampton. We ran into the warm water kicking the spray as we went and as soon as it was knee-high dived in. Oh Netta, the dying light on your wet skin, your shoulders, your breasts. The fateful cleft now hidden beneath its wedge of dark hair. Netta standing four square and naked in the lapping water, self-conscious and beautiful.

We ran back, rubbed ourselves dry with our shirts, and talked as moonlight took over from sunset. For me this stands out in my memory as a night of mythical significance; the death of innocence. When young you can't wait to bury it, and when middle-aged you spend all your time trying to bring it back to life.

And later, when I was back at the caravan alone, I wandered around my little tin home, which I often did before sleeping, looking up at the stars, and feeling a sense of wonder and peace that I don't think I've ever been able to recapture.

The day pricked out for our departure was a Saturday and Uncle Frank was up and about early, unlike our mothers who didn't stir themselves in time to join us for breakfast. Uncle Frank had a sense of occasion; there was more than a

streak of Polonius about him. Remember that neither he nor
our mothers knew that our travelling companion was Father.
Uncle Frank boiled eggs for us and made toast and asked
James to read to us from the Poet. He read from *Tintern
Abbey*, and I shall never forget his fine sensitive face setting
itself for the task. His blond hair and noble brow seemed to
belong more to the Romantic age than to the nineteen-sixties.
James's sort of good looks were much older than *Brideshead*,
as old perhaps as Byron or Scott. Yes, Young Lochinvar, that
was him. Anyway, Young Lochinvar glanced at me, grinned
a conspirator's grin, and got down to it:

> And so I dare to hope,
> Though changed, no doubt, from what I was when first
> I came among these hills; when like a roe
> I bounded o'er the mountains, by the sides
> Of the deep rivers and the lonely streams,
> Wherever nature led; more like a man
> Flying from something that he dreads than one
> Who sought the thing he loved.

And as he read on in his splendid boyish voice, and I
watched his face, a more beautiful version of mine, take on
a genuinely serious expression as the strength of the poem
made itself felt, I too became aware, for the first time, of the
power of words.

> – I cannot paint
> What then I was. The sounding cataract
> Haunted me like a passion: the tall rock,
> The mountain, and the deep and gloomy wood,
> Their colours and their forms, were then to me
> An appetite; a feeling and a love,
> That had no need of a remoter charm,
> By thought supplied, nor any interest
> Unborrowed from the eye.

In fact, I was so impressed by this poem, which I must have
heard before at least a dozen times, that I asked Uncle Frank

if he would lend me a *Wordsworth*. He did better than that. Uncle Frank went upstairs, found a battered copy and handed it to me with affection, although it was probably affection for the poet and not the wanderer who, if he had only known it, was about to decamp with his greatest enemy, my father.

Old Wordsworth, as we at Coniston were in the habit of calling him, is right when he speaks of things *fastening on the heart insensibly*. That's exactly what he'd done with me, thanks to the much-derided Uncle Frank. You have told me countless times, difficult old man that you are, that I shan't be getting anything out of you. You're wrong, as I'm sure we would both be pleased to admit.

BLAH-BLAH. BLAH-BLAH. The klaxon summoned us to depart, Uncle Frank waved us off, and we were soon hurtling towards the station with Netta at the wheel of the hearse and Birgit beside her in the passenger seat. They didn't stay to wave us off, and from the deserted platform we watched the black Behemoth disappear in front of its own smoke and the smoke fade away five minutes before our train arrived.

Once at Dover I waited up on deck for the cords that bound me to Albion to be loosed. Father, too, who had picked us up in the Humber at our secret rendezvous, was impatient for the off. 'At last,' I remember him saying, as we looked down at the quayside.

Father was wearing his baggy army shorts, which didn't quite cover the bandage, and was armed with his faithful umbrella-stick. Over one shoulder was his black and white Magdalen scarf and over the other he carried an old army bag filled with maps and dressings. 'Fresh air, breathe it in.' I was feeling pretty chilly after twenty minutes at sea and was relieved when Father suggested that we should go below.

'What a lot of common people there are,' he said, casting his eye over the queue at the duty-free shop.

'What about your sherry, Father? You said you couldn't live without it. We'll get it for you,' I said, all filial piety and devotion.

'AARRGH! The leg is a bit sore today.' The umbrella-stick went on before, proclaiming Father's majesty, and the ranks of the common people divided; some looked alarmed, others merely curious. 'Yes, if you could get just three large bottles of dry, unless you'll be wanting any, of course. We don't wish to run foul of officialdom, damned babus – no, make it a half-dozen. I'll be on the upper deck. James, you come with me. I'll need you to set up the deck-chair.'

Back on deck

> Lightly equipped, and but a few brief looks
> Cast on the white cliffs of our native shore
> From the receding vessel's deck, we chanced
> To land at Calais

and we were soon rumbling down the ramp into the town.

'So, Thomas, it's your first time out of England. Escaping from the bosom of the family at last.'

'Not entirely, Father.' It was the first time I'd ever got the better of him. We drove sedately through the busy town with me as navigator and James in the back.

'The first time I went away', said Father, 'was to Vienna in 'thirty-eight. It was an exciting time. I was there when the Führer marched in. He came within a few yards of me. No, I didn't give the Nazi salute. I touched my hat as any decently brought up schoolboy would for a Head of State. When I got off the train I'd been conned into giving my return ticket and almost all my schillings to a man who claimed he was a refugee. He took my address and promised to repay me, but of course never did. I lived on goulash soup for a month. Now do we turn off here?'

I fumbled with the map. We went straight on. 'I think the turning was back there, Father. I'm sorry.'

'You're so damned unreliable. Haven't you got any sense of direction?'

'Sorry, Father, I was listening to you.'

'Henry always said that I could do the fastest three-point turn he knew, apart from his own, of course. He drove a taxi in Montreal for a time. He loved uniforms and brass bands. He wanted us to join the Salvation Army. We once got caught up in a procession in Regent Street,' and he broke into the opening

lines of *Onward Christian Soldiers.* 'Henry had a simple streak
– like you, James.'

That night, we camped inside the walls of a yellow castle.
The town was called Phalsbourg and it was in Lorraine, or
Alsace – my geography has always been poor. Wherever it
was, it made a good impression on an insular schoolboy. I've
always liked castles. We put up the two tents, newly purchased
from army surplus, each consisting of two wooden poles and
a sheet of canvas, and sat for a time while Father had a few
sherries.

'Oh no, we didn't camp until we got into Burma, and we
didn't use tents for long there. They were too much trouble.
Sometimes my batman built a little frame, using four Y-shaped
bits of wood, about six inches high, on which he put a couple
of stout bamboo poles with slats across. Trouble was, if you
moved you were likely to fall through. I had a hammock which
I used to sling between two trees, but it was more bother than
it was worth as you were always afraid that your gun might
get caught in the netting and go off. No, it was mostly a case
of sleeping on the ground, two men to a blanket, though I did
have an inflatable pillow. I didn't like using my boots.'

Next day Father woke us with tin mugs of tea. 'Fresh air
is the best cure for a headache,' he said. 'You boys shouldn't
drink so much,' and before breakfast we walked through the
dewy morning air to the washroom. As I had lived in a caravan
all my life there was nothing new about it, except that we were
in France. 'In India I had a magnificent bungalow with its own
thunderbox,' said Father. 'A sweeper appeared discreetly whenever it was used and left some cedarwood incense. Headache
still troubling you, James? Fresh air will soon fix that. We'll
go into town and buy some croissants for breakfast.'

The following night was spent in the Black Forest. There
was a café at the campsite and we dined there. 'Oh, India in
the war was marvellous,' said Father. 'The barracks were about
a mile away, and we cycled in. They had wood fires at night.
The bearers wore mess costume: immaculate white and white
gloves too. I remember there was a time at breakfast when the
adjutant was served by a pair of black hands. That sort of thing
didn't go down too well at Wellington. At dinner we would

drink to the King-Emperor. There was a full band, of course. James, do get that fellow to bring some more wine. Yes, the Nilgiri Hills were a paradise. I was very shy and for a week I hardly said a word. Then I met Henry. He was sitting next to me and he said something that started me talking. You may know how difficult it is for some people to stop once they get started . . .'

A propos of nothing a coarse-looking German of about Father's age, having finished his meal, got up, gave us a nasty look, spat on the floor and walked out. Father didn't even notice. 'Well, suddenly there was an ominous silence . . . everyone had finished the soup and I hadn't even started mine . . . you know how it is, you don't know whether to send it away or swallow it at lightning speed. I did both, took a quick gulp and signalled the bearer. Henry was rather amused. Kindness was not one of his strong points.'

Before going to bed Father took us across the road to a bar which he said was a whorehouse catering for the nearby US army base at Freiburg: they were always good for trade. But we didn't strike lucky. We saw a rather glamorous girl with a poodle crossing the road as we went in, but nothing more.

'I used to go by bus to the cinema at Ooti sometimes,' said Father as we made our way back to the tents, 'and once, when the film had ended, I found I'd missed the bus back to Wellington. The manager asked me to be patient and retired to his office. After ten minutes a bus full of rather indignant Indian gentlemen appeared from the Wellington direction. The manager had telegraphed ahead of the bus and it had been turned back for me. I'm sure they were only too pleased once they saw who I was.'

Father was very mysterious about our destination each day, and we navigators would be given the minimum of information; we had no idea where our pilgrimage would lead us. Somewhere near Verona the Humber overheated. 'Damn and blast these wretched garages. I had the thing serviced. What's the matter with this damned country . . . England, I mean.' The three of us fumbled about under the bonnet. Father, always ham-fisted and impatient, cut his

knuckles when the spanner slipped, and jumped about for a
minute like a ballerina. James took out the thermostat and we
got back into the car.

'Is your hand hurt badly?' said James.

'I didn't let a broken arm and a sprained ankle stop me
from crossing the Irrawaddy,' said Father. 'I'd fallen out of
a tree. I was carried across in a litter borne by four bearers.'

'Plastered?'

'Ha-ha. We might have been attacked at any moment. There
were Japs everywhere. More bearers followed behind with my
record collection . . . I couldn't have fought without Beethoven.
I had the complete symphonies, all in seventy-eights. Damned
heavy, they were, and the old wind-up gramophone. Carrying
that lot a hundred yards was enough to cripple a man . . . Ah,
here's the church. I want to show you a picture.'

The picture, above an arch at the end of the nave, turned
out to be a Pisanello. *San Giorgio e la principessa*. Is it still my
favourite painting? Possibly not, but I always stop off to see
it when I pass that way. It means half a day extra since they
opened the pass across the Brenner. No later artist would have
shown the princess and the saint divided by a horse's rump.
The quattrocento was an age when impropriety was of a different kind. But you can't forget those faces. His for instance.
It has nothing to do with heroism or his being a saint. See
how he turns away from the princess who has been offered
to him as a prize for slaying the dragon. Why does he reject
her? Because he's afraid of her, that's why. And why does this
picture interest my father? Your guess is probably as good as
mine. And outside the fragile city with its elegant castle the
hanged men, meticulously drawn, lazily swing.

ENICE. I REMEMBER driving over the long bridge linking the industrial mainland with its chimneys, oil tanks, gasometers and yellow smoke, to the old city, and not thinking much of it. We parked several flights up in the multi-storey, under the neon CAMPARI sign, where Father gave the keys to an attendant. The man was a convivial sort and we carried on a discussion in our different languages for some minutes. He loved motor vehicles and particularly a customer's Velocette motorbike, which, we were to understand, was a *bella macchina*, and got so carried away in his praise for the thing that he started it up and invited James to have a go. While an enthusiastic conversation was going on between James and the attendant a contrapuntal monologue was issuing from Father. 'Henry had a Vincent, a Black Shadow. Used to whizz up to Oxford on it when Nicholas was due to address the Union. He'd stay at the Eastgate or out at Woodstock. You could lock the steering. "Look, old man, no hands." It was most exhilarating.'

While Father reminisced, James had growled off on the Velocette with the attendant shouting and gesticulating by way of encouragement. Roaring back on the *bella macchina*, James beamed his great smile. 'Come on,' said Father, as James and the man congratulated each other, 'we've got a lot to do. We can't spend the entire day discussing motorcycling.' James shrugged his shoulders and we trudged off with the baggage ahead of Father, who urged us on to a vaporetto with his umbrella-stick.

So it was that I found myself chugging along the Grand Canal for the first time. We got off at the Rialto, walked over the bridge and through the busy market on the far side before turning into a dingy and foul-smelling alley. Without notice, Father stopped and pressed a doorbell. After a few seconds the door opened and we entered a seedy hotel. Father booked us in, explained that he was staying elsewhere, and arranged to meet us at eight that evening on the terrace outside the Monaco. No, he wasn't staying there but in a little palazzo which belonged to a friend of a friend. Then he explained to our landlady at some length that he had stayed in this very *pensione* in the far-off days of his youth, asked her if she remembered one or two characters, explained the reason for his limp, demonstrated the uses of the umbrella-stick and left us alone.

We were led into a dark and close-smelling room by the landlady who turned on a glaring light, advised us as to the time of breakfast and the distant whereabouts of the facilities and went about her business. Like all tourists, the first thing we did was to open the shutters and look out. Three floors below was a fruit market and at a diagonal you could see the glittering water of the Grand Canal only twenty yards away, churned up by the bouncing motorboats, and on the far side a palace of astounding beauty and grace. Ah, Venice, city of my conception.

Five minutes later James and I were closing the front door behind us as we went to explore the *streets without end and churches numberless*. We bought a map at a paper stall as instructed by Father, and set off on a tour of the city: wandering through an alley smelling of licorice and bread, past countless jewellers and tat shops, shops selling ancient-looking lingerie displayed on plastic legs ('There must be a lot of one-legged can-can dancers in Venice,' said James) and shops selling metal cups and shields ('Awards for gondola races?'), little craftsmen's shops ('Knocking up antiques, no doubt') until we found, set in an almost deserted square, a huge building ('The Frari church') which sprouted weeds and even saplings at odd corners from its crumbling brickwork. We paid a few lire to an ancient friar and went inside. In a space which seemed as big as Victoria station there were perhaps half a dozen people. The impression it gave was of vastness and simplicity, the plain brick walls marked here and there by huge, though dwarfed, memorials of helmeted warriors and long dead dignitaries. We wandered around guided by the shades of Titian, Monteverdi and Canova.

Out of the gloom into the dazzling light; James led the way

with his map, and off we went through a maze of alleyways, some allowing a glimpse of the Grand Canal with its palaces, and some blind; past seedy decaying buildings plastered with graffiti, both political and amatory, and places with names like San Toma and San Pantalon, until we got to Accademia where we crossed the Grand Canal. What a view! People drifted down the steps towards us:

> The Italian, with his frame of images
> Upon his head: with basket at his waist
> The Jew; the stately and slow-moving Turk,
> With freight of slippers piled beneath his arm!

Next: empty squares and dark alleyways hung with washing and canaries, until, ah! there it was, on the Grand Canal, of course, the Hotel Monaco, where we were to meet Father later; much later. Then along the waterfront with its bridges and spluttering vaporetti, the fretted Palace of the Doges and the amazing Piazza, San Marco itself, so oriental and extravagant ('We'll save that for later'), the café orchestras ('and that is Florian's, where the world's greatest buggers have taken tea') fluttering pigeons, more bridges and narrow streets crowded here with tourists ('Keep looking for *Per Rialto*'). We observed

> Among the crowd all specimens of man,
> Through all the colours which the sun bestows,
> And every character of form and face:
> The Swede, the Russian; from the genial south,
> The Frenchman and the Spaniard: from remote
> America, the hunter-Indian; Moors,
> Malays, Lascars, the Tartar, the Chinese,
> And Negro ladies in white muslin gowns.

Ah! there it was, the famous bridge again. Back to the seedy *pensione*. Thank God James had been navigating. We had just enough time to wash and change before setting out once more to find Father.

Sitting beside him at a table by the water was Nicholas York. Father always liked to spring a surprise. With him all things were possible; we had expected some camping in France and here we were in the Maiden City. 'It's social death to be seen in Venice in August,' Nicholas whispered to me.

'But that means no one could admit to seeing you. No one who is anyone, that is.'

'Exactly. We haven't seen one another. Have some champagne.'

We dined alfresco under a huge moon overlooking the glimmering water with the white dome of the Salute over Father's shoulder. I allowed myself the indulgence of thinking that it was indeed the same moon that had shone on my swim with Netta only a few days before.

'More champagne!' We were a noisy crew.

'Of course, you weren't with us in Burma, Nicholas, so you won't remember, but one Christmas when we were going after the Japs – we were supplied by parachute – we were expecting a bumper drop which was rumoured to include some claret *pour les officiers* and beer for the men – we hadn't had a drink for months – when three Japanese fighters appeared overhead. It was the only time I saw any Jap planes the whole time we were in Burma, and they shot our Dakotas out of the sky. Henry was furious. Pass your glass, James. Do you know this young man was riding a motorbike all around the multi-storey car park this morning. He's a very bad boy, and it belonged to a complete stranger.'

'Ah,' said Nicholas, 'Henry would have said "what that boy needs is a good whipping," ' and he poured himself another glass.

'Henry is dead,' said Father. 'In 1957 they found a body washed up at Littlehampton –'

'Wittering,' interrupted Nicholas.

'But a positive identification wasn't possible. They didn't know about the tattoo, ha-ha. In a drunken moment he'd had himself tattooed. Yes, he had his left buttock tattooed with a ducal coronet.'

'Actually it was the family crest . . . a warhorse astride a tower.'

'Don't be such a pedant, Nicholas.'

'Henry was born a rebel. *Better to rule in hell than serve in heaven*, he used to say. He saw himself as Lucifer and his father as God. He was a romantic.'

'I told the boys about his Vincent. Do you remember me riding pillion in the High?'

'I certainly do. An alarming spectacle, especially when he let go of the handlebars. The most frightening thing that ever happened to me was when Henry drove from Bombay to Poona with me on the back of the Norton. I shall certainly never forget that! Do you ride a motorcycle, Thomas?' He leant across and refilled my glass.

A vaporetto pulled in at the stop a few yards away and a crowd surged off before it chugged away again in a splutter of fumes. The wash lapped against the wooden piers of the terrace, causing the tethered gondolas to jerk up and down in the water. I shook my head. 'Did you know Henry well?' I said, and I saw him give Father a look that I couldn't interpret. Nicholas hesitated. James took up the pursuit.

'We've seen a picture of the three of you on the balcony of an Indian palace.'

'Have you? I suppose I did know him tolerably well. We met at Oxford when I was due to make the first really important speech of my career. He came up on his motorbike with Toby. He was staying over at Woodstock if I remember. He liked the Bear. There was an incident at the Taj Mahal afterwards.'

'The Taj Mahal?'

'Oh, it's a restaurant in Oxford that was popular with undergraduates,' butted in Father.

'Oxford was divided in those days, purely on class grounds I'm afraid. The three of us were enjoying a quiet meal when one of the party opposite –'

'Common people,' interrupted Father with a theatrical air of disdain that James and I had christened the Clotworthy look, after that ancestor of Henry's whose bewigged and armoured likeness greeted visitors to Father's flat with a wrinkled sneer.

' – began to impersonate Henry. They were half a dozen or so –'

'Not a wise thing to do,' said Father in the Clotworthy drawl.

' – and one of them actually went so far as to call out in

an affected impersonation of Henry's voice, "Oh, I say" . . .
Henry just got up from the table and ambled across to them.
All he did was to put his hands on his hips and beam. They
bolted, tipping the table up in the process.'

'Rice and chapattis everywhere.'

'He sounds an amazing man,' said James.

'He was six feet four,' said Nicholas, 'and not a person
to cross.'

'Is it true his father lives in a castle in Scotland?' I asked.

'Yes,' he said, 'it really is rather grand. Did you know
that he was offered Scotland by Mosley? Well, he was, or
so the story goes. He jumped the right way, for once, and
declined the offer. He said the British public wouldn't stand
for uniforms – black shirts – and he was right. Henry was
told by a gypsy woman that he was born to rule in the East.
He loved to say that, didn't he, Toby . . . *I was born to rule in
the East, old man . . .*'

'And he did, too. He nearly got court-martialled for over-
disciplining the troops,' said Father. 'He was sent out to take
charge of a ramshackle lot called the Bombay and Eastern
Mahratta Railway Rifles. The NCOs were all ex-booking office
clerks and of course completely useless. Henry ran the place like
an eighteenth-century Prussian drill sergeant. The trouble was
that although the government had authorised their call-up, it
hadn't authorised their pay, so Henry had a near mutiny on
his hands. Henry believed in immediate action and took the
law into his own hands, giving the ringleaders six cuts of the
swagger stick. Henry didn't believe in the normal channels.
Rules are for common people, he used to say.'

We drank a lot that night. We told Nicholas about the
journey, since he was laughing about Father's idiosyncrasies,
and how he always insisted on driving with the window down.
'At school Uncle Toby's thought to be quite mad,' added James.
'He takes lessons with all the windows open, even when snow
lies thick on the ground, wearing only his Magdalen scarf.'

'I hope he wears more than that when instructing the
boys,' said Nicholas. 'Henry told me your love of fresh air
nearly got you killed once, Toby, on a train . . .'

'Yes, we were on a train in India. Have you boys heard of

Dacoits? No? Such ignorance. Bandit tribes. Ruthless killers. Shave themselves from head to foot and cover themselves with grease. When a train is at a station they climb down from the trees on to the roof, and then slip through any open window they find. I was travelling with Henry. It was the middle of the night. Suddenly I heard Henry's voice, "Put on the light, old man, I've got something interesting here." I turned it on. We had a carriage with two bunks and a washroom off. There were three windows, two with grilles and one with glass. You were supposed to lock them from the inside, but I'm sorry to say that I hadn't. Henry was holding the fellow around the neck in a stranglehold. An evil-looking knife was on the floor. "He was about to slit your throat. You're lucky I'm a light sleeper." A few minutes later the train crossed an enormous river. Henry dragged his companion to the washroom, I heard the door open and slam shut and Henry came back alone, wiping the grease from his hands.'

'You mean he . . .' I said.

'What else could he have done? We didn't want the train held up. Besides, the fellow would have got a couple of years and would have been back at his murderous trade. Who knows how many lives Henry might have saved by that one act? Anyhow, we went back to sleep. In the morning I awoke to find the point of the blade an eighth of an inch from my nose. Henry had thoughtfully placed the knife on my pillow during the night, so that when I opened my eyes it was the first thing I saw. I've got it at the flat on the kitchen wall. I use it for carving.'

We took a gondola that night. 'An exquisite form of transport,' as Nicholas described it. I commend it to you, particularly if your funds are limitless. You enter a long black narrow slit of a boat, curled at either end. The single oar slurps gently in the water and you are propelled deliciously along in a series of rhythmic thrusts. Gondola: from the Greek kuntelas, according to one book I've seen. I wonder if there's a connection.

Under the Bridge of Sighs a photographer snapped our picture in a blaze of flash and tossed us the ticket. I'm sure the News of the World would have liked that picture

a few years later, when Nicholas was front page news –
Father lolling back and stroking his chin next to James,
and opposite, a mirror image, me almost in the arms of
an urbane, sometime notorious and now all but forgotten
Nicholas York.

I think there were few people in Venice more intoxicated
than us that night, and this, no doubt, is how James and I
managed to get ourselves invited back to the palazzo. I wish
I knew where it was. I have searched for hours on end, and
must have passed it a hundred times, wherever it may be, but
I know I shall never find it again. I remember the gondolier's
gull-like cries as he spun us round the corner of the narrow
canal and pulled up by some slippery steps covered in green
weed where we had difficulty getting Father out of the boat.

'You boys wait here,' he said, and the two men disappeared
inside. We heard the lapping of the gondola as it faded into the
night, and the tapping of Father's umbrella-stick on the stone
steps inside, then a distant cry of pain as Father stubbed his
toe, followed by the familiar sound of his laugh.

Two or three minutes went by before we heard a woman's
voice from the balcony above our heads. 'Please come up.'

We obeyed, and soon found ourselves in an enormous
room lit by dusty chandeliers, furnished with a grand piano
and harpsichord and with theatrical costumes draped over the
chairs. We could now see the person who had invited us in
– a well-groomed woman of thirty or thereabouts – and two
elegant creatures in ball gowns.

'James and Thomas,' she said, 'may I introduce you to
Giorgio and Rinaldo? They work in the theatre. Together
we make these clothes. They try them on for me and soon
we will make music for you.' I could not place her accent,
but she was not English.

A huge figure appeared before us, clad in *tricorno*, cloak
and white carnival mask, and provided us with champagne. We
were not introduced. Giorgio and Rinaldo sang arias by composers of whom we hadn't heard, and the lady accompanied
them on the harpsichord. The three men had wandered out
to the balcony where we could hear them laughing, and after
a while the masked giant returned to refill our glasses, and left

us again with a sinister theatrical flourish. In our intoxicated state, James and I took this as normal behaviour, the sort of thing that you would expect to find in a Venetian palace at midnight. The lady was charming, and paid us a lot of attention, asking us about our schools and our extraordinary family.

Then Nicholas sat at the piano. He was in splendid form, singing and accompanying himself:

> On a tree by the river a little tom-tit
> Sang 'Willow, titwillow, titwillow!'
> And I said to him, 'Dicky-bird, why do you sit
> Singing Willow, titwillow, titwillow?'

By this time, Giorgio and Rinaldo had joined in with their beautiful voices, both singing counter-tenor, but by the last verse it was the mysterious stranger who was leading the singing:

> He sobbed and he sighed, and a gurgle he gave,
> Then he plunged himself into the billowy wave,
> And an echo arose from the suicide's grave –
> 'O willow, titwillow, titwillow.'

Eventually, when we were very drunk, Giorgio and Rinaldo, who had changed out of their costumes and now wore jeans, walked us back to San Marco. The café orchestras had packed up hours before, and after we had said goodbye to our conductors, we staggered back to our humble *pensione*. I remember telling James, somewhere by the Rialto, that it was not, after all, social death to be *epicene* in Venice, even in August. It brought joy to my drunken heart when James had to ask me to explain.

The noise must have started a couple of hours after we got into bed; sleep so rich and deep that it had taken me, at any rate, far beyond the realm of dreams, and then suddenly, almost without warning, I was rising up, up, up to meet the clattering and thumping, the calling and shouting of the dawn chorus of market traders. Our room was at first still pitch dark, but the glimmering square behind the closed shutters showed that the time for sleep was over. When my eyes had come to terms with the dazzling light of day, I saw once more the Canal, and the oblique view of the palace that I now knew was called the Ca' d'Oro. In the foreground was the market. Never before had I seen from my bedroom such a display of bright fruit and vegetables, and all around, on the flagstones, the litter of empty boxes and tissue paper. A few yards away wooden boats, red, green and blue, were unloading supplies, and all the time there was noise; calling, chanting, singing.

And on our side of the canal, the Pescheria, the roofed and pillared fishmarket, and visible on every side fish – bright silver, shining red, deep blue, black, hydra-headed, cut open like water melons or writhing and wriggling in buckets, or staring with enormous fish eyes from marble slabs, and again, the stallholders calling, singing, chatting and wrapping. Everywhere seemed to teem with life,

the Babel din,
The endless stream of men and moving things

We had the day to ourselves. Father was busy and had instructed us to meet him for dinner at the Monaco again. How did we spend the day? My memories of Venice are confused, I've been back so many times, but I think we must have found our way to San Zanipolo, a cathedral as big and empty as the Frari church, where, no doubt, we sat outside at a café looking up at the bronze statue of Colleoni, that magnificent equestrian Clotworthy, high on its pedestal; and we must have taken a vaporetto to San Giorgio Maggiore, from where we would have looked back at the skyline opposite – the Salute, the Campanile, San Marco, the Doge's Palace – surely the most beautiful man-made vista anywhere. No doubt we spent most of our time wandering aimlessly, hardly knowing we were lost. I remember that we went to the top of the Campanile. How could I forget that time when we clambered out of the lift and were deafened by the bells swinging wildly overhead as we looked down on Venice from the highest point of the city? James, James, James, is there any trace of your spirit left on the Venetian air? Do you still hear those bells as I do?

Father was alone when we joined him that evening. Nicholas was engaged elsewhere and Father was in a tetchy mood. Nothing was quite right. The food, which he had proclaimed first class the night before, was now disappointing and the wine dull (we didn't have champagne), and yet, to me, the moon seemed even brighter. Somehow this prompted me to ask Father about what James and I called his famous last words – what, I asked, had he meant when, after the daffodil-picking so many years ago, he had jabbed his umbrella-stick at the moon and said, 'That's my old enemy, the moon'? This set him off, and we had *So we'll go no more a roving* at full throttle, after which he launched into a tirade against Wordsworth, à propos of his other old enemy, Uncle Frank.

'Byron, now there's a poet for you, a man of action. You do realise we're only a few yards from the Palazzo Mocenigo where he lived. He had no time for yokels. Kept a bear in his room at Cambridge; they wouldn't allow dogs. He planned to enter it for a Fellowship. He kept a whole zoo here, swam the length of the Grand Canal and returned home to make love to a countess. The sort of life Clotworthy would have had. Not like dreary old Uncle Frank, though he's a worthy enough clot in his way, ha-ha.'

James was not amused by this. He had some old-fashioned views on loyalty to one's parents. Once Father had seen that James was not pleased with him he got worse. Wind him up and see him go. And this is when he made the fatal error, as he ranted about Byron and Venice and culture. I don't recall exactly how, but he let slip that it was not only me who had been conceived in a *pensione* near the fishmarket, but also James.

'But my father has never even been abroad,' said James. 'What do you mean, Uncle Toby, what are you trying to say?'

Father was aware that he had blundered and gave a

violent jerk in his seat. 'Oh, he must have been,' he said as his umbrella-stick clattered on to the flagstones. Thinking time. James retrieved it and stood holding it for a moment stretched out before him with a hand at either end, splendid as the great Lord of Luna himself. Father had turned a ghostly white and, struggling to regain his composure, said in a strained voice, 'Well, given the choice I'm sure you would prefer to have been conceived in Venice. I'm sure I would,' but James was staring hard at him. He knew.

Later that night, when James and I were in bed in our shuttered room and after we had put out the light and said goodnight he asked, 'Who do you think is my father?'

And I answered, 'It seems pretty obvious.'

'I suppose it means we're brothers. More than half, but not quite whole. I wonder if there's a term for it. Venetian cousins perhaps? It explains a lot of things.'

'Why Uncle Frank hates him so much, for instance.'

'How long do you think it went on? And did your mother know, do you think? Presumably she was *prima donna* then, although I'm not sure she got the best of the bargain. And do you think Frank knew about it, I mean that she was pregnant? Was he a complete dupe?'

'I know Hercules is supposed to have got fifty girls pregnant in one night, before he began his Labours. Do you think we were conceived on the same night? Perhaps all three of them were in bed together at the same time.'

'Not even Byron could have managed fifty in one night. Or do you think he could?'

'I wouldn't mind trying. Do you suppose he identifies with Byron because of the limp?'

'And his grand ideas ... And I bet this is the humble *pensione* where it happened.'

'Perhaps in this very room.'

'Uncle Toby would have insisted on a four-poster.'

So, on our last night in Venice, both James and I fell asleep knowing that we were both products of Cupid's illegal darts, and believing that Father, like Long John Silver, had made up for weakness in one limb with prodigious strength in another.

CHAPTER 8 · *The Alps*

EXT DAY WE headed for Innsbruck where Father booked the three of us into a run-down hotel in the old part of town. There was a beer garden behind it with a corrugated plastic roof and bustling waitresses in Tyrolean clothes. We dined here, on wurst, beer and song, and then followed our limping leader a few hundred yards to a cellar bar in the Goldener Adler where a hideous crone was singing and playing the piano. It was a smoky dive with a vaulted roof, and I liked it. The atmosphere, Father pointed out, was more Issyvoo than à la mode. 'What do you mean,' I said to Father, 'Issyvoo?'

'Haven't you read anything?' he said. 'Isherwood.'

'Sorry, Father,' I said, 'but you wouldn't pay for my education.'

'What are you two on about?' said James.

Father kept calling out for viertels and was soon telling us that in Adelaide or Toronto or Calcutta, Nicholas had been as drunk as a fiddler's bitch, a sign which James and I recognised by this stage: if we wanted to find out any more the last thing to do was to ask. He enjoyed nothing better than to give a little information and then to clam up with an air of Clotworthy disdain. Curiosity was a social gaffe of unforgivable proportions, especially about such a trifling matter as one's parentage. We just had to wait. Neither the wine nor the singing elicited anything further that night. When the reckoning was done and we had got up from our table, the Issyvoo dame called out after us, 'Goodnight, darlinks.' I looked back and saw she was making an obscene gesture with her tongue.

It must have been about midnight when we put Father to bed and went exploring. What James and I were looking for in the old square with its famous golden roof was evidence of *vice*. Round and round the cloistered arcade we wandered in a quest for ladies of the night – and a lonely pair of Englishmen we were, since all we found were some machines that sold

French letters. We each made a purchase but that was as far as we got.

In the morning we had a tour of the city, courtesy of Father, and followed him up through the golden square to the fine cathedral, and back again through the vaulted streets to the Hofkirche. What I liked most about this building were the huge bronze Gothic knights that lined it, any one of which might have dragged Don Giovanni off to hell. So impressed was I by these fantastic figures that Father and James went on ahead, and I found them outside in the cloister museum, happily playing with an old fairground machine which sported trams and maypoles and dancing Hitlers. James was as fascinated by this toy as I had been by the Gothic knights and continued to watch it with childish glee until our combined store of five schilling coins had been exhausted.

Father seemed to be in no hurry to leave Innsbruck, and it was not until after lunch, taken in the same beer garden where we had dined, that we set off once more in the Humber. Soon we had left the ancient town behind and were winding our way up from the populous plain into the Alps. The landscape took on a sterner character, and great cliffs of mountain hemmed us in on either side. Rounding a corner we saw an impossibly green lake and then suddenly on the other side, there it was – a Gothic castle perched on a crag, and below it a small hotel with a track at the side and a sign saying ☛ CAMPING ⚐⚐⚐. The car turned into the narrow track and we crunched our way over the gravel past a tiny onion-domed church, rumbled over a rickety wooden bridge, and after a few hundred yards arrived at the campsite.

Father switched off the engine. The doors slammed one after the other as we got out of the car. A few feet from us was a huge wooden trough under a tiled roof which sheltered a gushing waterspout. On the other side of the track I noticed a telegraph pole capped with a German army helmet. Cool clear air. The smell of pine trees. And so, for the first time, I entered the enchanted world of Steinpass.

ANMELDUNG!!
UM DIE ECKE ☞

said the sign facing us. Not an unattractive building. A former summerhouse. Carved into the woodwork on the side facing the yellow gash in the mountain was its name, VILLA MARIA, and under it, the words

Zur Herberge hier für kurze Zeit,
Die Heimat ist die Ewigkeit.

'This is our dwelling for a time; our true home is eternity,' translated Father, handing me the passports. 'Take these to the office, and register. James, find somewhere to make camp. I'm going to change my dressing.'

The villa housed some of the staff from the hotel. At one end was a door leading to a shop and café. I opened the door of the café and peered in. A woman of about thirty dressed in peasant costume, with blonde hair in bunches, stood behind the counter. She was small but, in spite of being so advanced in years, pretty. She greeted me in a formal but friendly fashion, holding herself very erect as short women do, and giving almost a little curtsey as she held out her hand for me to shake. I handed her the passports, and although I could speak no German and she only campsite English we exchanged pleasantries and blushes. After a few moments Father added to my embarrassment by hobbling in. He immediately took over, conversing with her in staccato German and prodding his umbrella-stick at me in deprecatory fashion. He gave her the works, showing her the stick in all its glory and getting her to sit on it in the shop. As always, the conversation progressed to his wound and we had the usual sounds of gunfire and laughter, before returning to find James who had erected both tents, and had put the kettle on the camping stove to make our tea.

No doubt we had an exploratory tour before sherry time outside the tent. We rarely dined like campers, and took advantage of whatever culinary splendours were on offer, which in this case meant a stroll up to the hotel. I sometimes had the feeling, when travelling with Father, that he had been to the places we had visited before, and there was no room for doubt in this instance since the elderly proprietor and his wife and their son hurried down to greet Father with considerable ceremony. That was the first time I met Erhard, he of the lugubrious brown eyes, who I was to get to know so well on subsequent visits. Dear Erhard, who loves Steinpass with a sad and lonely devotion.

We dined in the charming old-fashioned dining room: the furniture, panelling and shutters were all of pine, painted duck egg blue. After we had eaten, Father, wanting to talk with our hosts, suggested that James and I retreat to the café at the campsite.

I had had plenty of spare time on our holiday to look at Uncle Frank's gift of *The Poetical Works of Wordsworth*, and foolish though you may think me, I confess it influenced me greatly. I had seen Venice through the eyes of the poet and here, high in the Alps, I felt I had at last reached the landscape of his soul. I had learned huge chunks by heart, and everywhere his words came to me out of the elements themselves. Perhaps this was little more than an extension of the sort of thing that causes a small boy to emerge from a cinema with six-gun blazing, but that's how it was.

'Stolen boat?' I said to James. He nodded and we turned towards the lake.

It was indeed a beauteous evening, and before returning to the campsite, James and I turned off the main track and walked down past the byre with its lowing cattle and warm dungy smell, beyond the little onion-domed church, and under the new bridge that bears the date 1893 on its flank, to the lake.

By this time night had fallen. The boathouse was locked, and to get in James had to climb over the roof. I heard him clamber into a boat and the plop and splash of the oars and saw the prow appear through the darkness. James put in at the bank and I got on board and pushed us away from the shore.

It was an act of stealth
And troubled pleasure; nor without the voice
Of mountain echoes did my boat move on;
Leaving behind her still, on either side,
Small circles glittering idly in the moon,
Until they melted all into one track
Of sparkling light.

Once we were out of range of the hotel lights it was very dark. The Pleiades and Cassiopeia shone brightly overhead. The black shapes of the mountains were reflected in the lake which itself had seemed as black. The water was as still as ice except where our boat had cut a passage through, and here the waves took with them the reflex of the stars, making them shimmer and fragment in our wake. From the middle of the lake I could just make out the castle, set in an arc of mountains high above the hotel, and to one side the white trail of a waterfall plummeting down to another, as yet unknown and high arched bridge.

Within a few minutes we had returned to the boathouse. Certainly we had been as quiet as the lake itself and had spoken no word. Our guilty pleasure having gone undetected we were in high spirits and as ready for mischief as any pair of naughty schoolboys.

I opened the door of the café and looked around as we went inside. There she was, through the cigarette smoke, standing behind the bar and chatting to a customer. James ordered beer. She indicated a table where we sat down and after a few moments brought over our drinks. She seemed rather severe and I felt disheartened; where was the friendliness of this afternoon? I looked around. Antlers on the wall, a postcard stand on the bar, with pictures of the castle and the lake, a glass-fronted cupboard lined with different kinds of schnapps. James ordered again, and when she brought the beer invited her to join us and, in pidgin German, offered her a drink. She gave a little curtsey of thanks, fetched herself some wine in a green-stemmed glass and sat down between us. It's curious how things can sometimes go more easily when you don't speak the language. Gesture, mime and laughter can be a good substitute for conversation, and besides, Trudi, as we now knew her, had retired behind the bar at some stage and had emerged clutching a small Anglo-German dictionary, which enabled us to look up vital words such as *blushing* and *esteem*. At the end of the evening she was in no doubt that I was an ardent admirer.

Sometime before midnight James and I retired to our tent. We could hear Father grunting and snoring a few feet away. It was raining, and the canvas let in little splashes of water which, though refreshing on the face and hands, made our sleeping bags and the blanket beneath them unpleasantly damp. I slept soundly and in the morning, when I opened the flaps, the grass was steaming in the bright sunlight. I staggered out, shielding my eyes, and was in position long before eight when the shop opened. Lurking in the wood on the other side of the little stream with a good view of the café, I fancied myself invisible, and watched as she opened the door and came out to stretch herself like a cat in the morning sun. Within a few minutes a van had arrived and the baker was unloading trays of fresh white rolls, each marked with a cross. I had learned from Father that a thorough reconnaissance was advisable before battle and that dawn was a good time to attack. I was the first customer of the day.

After breakfast it was time for a stroll with Father, and he took us up the track that led to the castle. 'This is the old road,' said Father gesturing grandly. 'The bridge is Roman.' As instructed, we leaned down to look at the stream sixty feet below, and then crossed to the other side from where Father pointed his umbrella-stick in the direction of the source, high in the mountains. 'Note the wall paintings on the castle, the red eagle of the Tyrol and those soldiers. Sixteenth century. The track actually runs beneath the castle. As you see, it's far from being a ruin. The Mad King stayed here. Haven't you heard of Ludwig of Bavaria? Such ignorance. He used to set out from Neuschwanstein in the middle of the night. He'd get out of bed, summon his servants and order them to harness the sledge while he got dressed. Then out into the blizzard with bells ringing furiously. That's the way to travel, with outriders and lanterns, don't you think? No doubt you saw the picture of him arriving here in the lobby of the hotel. No? No powers of observation. It's not a bad painting. The humble proprietors have stepped outside in the snow and are bowing before the mad king who sweeps by with a negligent wave of his hand. I sometimes think I'm a little like Ludwig, don't you? Ha-ha. There was a portcullis at each end of the tunnel. Didn't you notice the grooves, Thomas? If you're going to be a lawyer, like your Uncle Frank, you'll have to learn to be more observant.'

We followed Father along the track which wound on into the mountains as he continued to point his umbrella-stick for our edification. 'This is where we'd set our mortars. We'd have complete control of the pass from here. There was a terrific battle at the end of the war as I expect you know, James. The Yanks were pushing up from Italy. I always thought the war in Europe was a minor skirmish compared to Burma. Ah, India, we could have held it, you know. The army was loyal. Difficult terrain here, as you can see,' and the umbrella-stick waggled in the direction of the new bridge, now hardly more than a speck in the distance below. 'Just now I feel like some lunch. ARRGH, the leg's been quite good so far, don't you think?'

And we sat on the terrace of the hotel, drinking wine from green-stemmed glasses, eating trout from the lake and listening to Father. We even drank a toast to him – To Father. Yes, James and I agreed, he was the father of us both.

After we had been at Steinpass three or four days, a phenomenal storm marked a change in the weather. The lightning was the most dramatic I have ever seen, lighting up the castle and the old bridge with brilliant flashes and causing the thunder to echo down the pass and to reverberate and crash round all the distant peaks. Rain fell in torrents. Over dinner we discussed plans. Father wanted us to move on to Vienna. I wanted to stay put. James thought I should have a free hand with Trudi. It was therefore agreed that they would leave me behind with one tent and most of the camping equipment and return in four or five days' time. You can have no idea of the terror and excitement that the thought of being left alone at Steinpass with Trudi gave me. Rain battered and peppered the umbrella as we trudged back to the tents.

As feared, all our bedding was soaked, and we slept in the Humber. Father was quite game about these things, although he was glad to clear off with James in the morning when it was still pouring with rain. I was left alone, bewildered among woods immense.

CHAPTER 9 · O World!
O life! O time!

ALONE IN THE pouring rain! I spent the day in the café with Trudi playing cards, and was quite dizzy with lust. Evening came and the rain continued. Sheets of pouring rain /// /// /// How could a woman with any heart turn me out in the middle of the night to sleep in a wet tent? ////////////////////// She didn't. She let me sleep on the floor of the café wrapped in a blanket from her own bed. And the following day the same thing happened. More rain. /// I helped her in the café, of course, stacking crates and washing up. There weren't many customers. People clear off in search of the sun when the rain starts. We played cards ♡♡♡. I read. The days pass most pleasantly when there's a current of lust in the air. Once more I was allowed to sleep in the café. I was acquiring squatters' rights, and, worn out with ungratified desire, I slept well. But when one morning I awoke to bright sunlight and steaming meadows it seemed to indicate that I might be cast out to fend for myself. What would Father have said? *Retreat or attack.*

Propelled by fear and excitement, I walked far into the mountains that day, right across the pass to the next village, where I had an omelette with cranberries and a glass of milk for lunch. Good sound bodybuilding food. There would be no retreat. It was do or die.

I needn't have worried. Trudi must have felt similarly concerned at the change in the weather since, at locking-up time that night, the key was turned and the bolts pushed home with me the right side of the door. I don't remember how the attack began, but the enemy was soon leading me across the forbidden corridor to her bedroom. I slept with her that night, and a busy time we had of it, although being young and untested, I failed to press the point and being a virtuous woman she must have felt unable to take advantage of a young Englishman, an orphan of the storm. And the packet of French letters burnt a hole in the pocket of my trousers as they hung over the back of a chair.

But as you might expect, the next night or perhaps the night after, I girded my loins for the attack and, for the first time, found myself voyaging in the warm and luscious waters of the fateful cleft . . . I pant, I sink, I tremble, I expire! *O World! O life! O time!* But alas after this initial triumph my enthusiasm knew no bounds, and no sooner was the transparent scabbard in place than it was tight as a swollen gooseberry and ready to burst.

My mistress of the campsite made sure I was off the premises before the baker arrived, unbolting the door and pitching me out at about ten to eight.

A bright sunny morning. The Humber! They were back! I couldn't wait to brag to James of my success. I reached into the tent and shook his foot. 'James, I've got something to tell you.'

'I've got something to tell you too, but not now. After breakfast.'

I went back to the shop and bought rolls, eggs and ham (Father liked ham and eggs for breakfast), got the camping stove going, and cooked up while they got ready. They had arrived back at midnight; I hadn't been there and my news was stale, it was obvious.

I heard about Vienna, with its broad cobbled streets, huge cathedral, Habsburg tombs, palaces and splendours, and about Grinzing. 'The number of restaurants we walked into at night – and out again,' said James. 'If the whole staff including fiddler, chef and cook's boy didn't rush over as soon as we sat down Uncle Toby would get up from the table and sweep out with a Clotworthy wave of dismissal and I just had to follow.'

After the revelations in Venice relating to his paternity James had been tense and anxious under his usual bonhomie. But now his mood had improved. He and Father were getting on well. I also noticed that James was wearing Father's signet ring, Henry's old ring. Father actually asked how I'd fared with Trudi, which was an indication of his extreme good humour; it was almost unheard of for him to take an interest in my affairs. 'I was hoping you would marry an Erzherzogin,' said Father, 'but no matter. I hope she didn't stand any nonsense. I must have a word with her.'

Soon James and I were out on the lake. I shall never forget the beauty of that morning. James was, at first, silent as he dipped the oars into the black water and headed straight into the dazzling sunlight. All around us mist was rising in tight grey curls, and as we changed direction away from the shadow of the great peak on the far side, the ripples left in our wake were suddenly bright as flying fish. The sky was all shifting cloud and in a moment the glassy surface of the water fragmented as raindrops bounced from it and sparkled in the sun like fireflies. All the while, on the far side, the Roman bridge with its white waterfall, the castle and the craggy ridge towering behind it glowed bright in the morning sun. 'Come on, James,' I said impatiently, 'what happened?'

'Oh, a couple of things. I picked up a tart in Vienna. They hang around one of the main streets – the Kärntner Strasse, I think it was. They were everywhere, standing in the shop doorways or chatting in twos and threes. I thought they'd all be old and raddled, but they're really pretty. We paraded up and down for a while having a look at what was on offer. I felt like a farmer at Chichester market out to choose a heifer . . . Look, do you want to row?' I nodded and we changed places.

I took up the oars, doing my best not to appear incompetent, but James wasn't watching me. His thoughts were of Vienna and his own adventures.

'Well,' he said, 'as we cruised up and down, as Uncle Toby called it, he poured advice in my ear about wearing a French letter and not being robbed and so on. I must say, he seems extraordinarily well versed in these matters . . .'

'Yes . . . Yes . . . Go on . . .'

'We found one who wasn't at all bad-looking standing in a shop doorway. She was wearing a white raincoat. Uncle Toby walked straight up to her and started to chat her up and found out where she was staying and how much it was – five hundred schillings for fuck she said, just like that, and a hundred for the room – that's six quid, and we walked round the corner to her hotel. It wasn't particularly seedy, it was just an ordinary hotel. The man at reception handed her a key and a French letter – so I've still got all mine – and all three of us started to go upstairs, "In case of trouble," Uncle Toby said, but the man got rather heated and called out, "Nur ein Mann, nur ein Mann," and took no notice of the Clotworthy wave, and he had to retreat to a waiting room where they had magazines, I saw afterwards. Nothing fancy, just the sort you'd expect to find at the dentist. I followed her upstairs. She unlocked the door and in we went to an ordinary hotel bedroom with only a bare lightbulb but otherwise okay and she just got on the bidet. Right in front of me. Just like that. You see, she wasn't wearing any knickers. Then she dried herself with a towel and came over to me. She undid my trousers and started to touch me up a bit and while we were standing there she got out the johnny and rolled it on. Look out, you're going into the bank ... Use the other oar. That's better. God, It's a beautiful morning. You know I'm really glad to be back here. I wish we could stay for ever.'

'Come on, James. What happened then?'

'Well, we got on the bed. There was just a sheet on it, no bedclothes of any sort – she didn't even take her clothes off – it wasn't in the least romantic. I put my arm around her and started to touch her tit ... I thought she'd like it but she didn't seem to. Then she said – she spoke American – "You work or I work." I didn't know what she meant and I found she'd got on top of me –'

'On top of you?'

'Yes, she'd got on top of me, and it was really rather embarrassing, and I asked her why she hadn't taken off her clothes. I mean that's the whole point really, isn't it? And she said it was another hundred schillings to take off her clothes. She said, "Five hundred schillings for fuck and one hundred schillings for no clothes." Well, I agreed and she got off and I went over to the chair where I'd left my trousers and I found I didn't have any Austrian money and I only had a ten shilling note which was embarrassing but thank goodness she agreed to take that until we got downstairs. I told her that Uncle Toby might want a go too – he had said he might if she was any good – and we got back on the bed the right way round and off we went again, with her sort of moving her legs behind my back which was a bit odd. Anyway in the end I stopped and she asked me if I'd come and she sat up and pinched the end of the johnny, smiled, and said, "Good fuck?" just like that. Then she said, "First time with girl? The first time it is work for the girl," and crossed herself. It's a funny thing but I was shocked to see she'd been sunbathing. I mean she had bikini marks, you know. She'd been lying on a beach somewhere with ordinary people, people who didn't know. I almost felt I should have done something to save her, like Gladstone, but I know that sounds daft. She was so matter of fact about the whole thing. Then we got dressed and went downstairs. I explained about the money and after checking that I hadn't been robbed he paid up. She asked him if he wanted to go up with her but he didn't and the three of us went out into the street. It was just like that scene at the end of *Casablanca* where the three of them go off to the airport. We said goodnight and that was it. I don't even know her name. Now what about your adventures? I'll row and you talk.'

I told James what had happened in his absence. When I got to the end of the story he said, 'There was something else I wanted to tell you. Oh drat, there's Uncle Toby,' and there he was all right, limping along the path by the lake in his baggy shorts, with his army bag slung round his shoulder. 'He seems to be trying to communicate with us,' said James with a wry smile, 'but I haven't finished what I wanted to tell you.'

'I think he wants to come aboard,' I said, looking over to the bank where Father was paddling the air with his shooting-stick umbrella.

'He'll just have to wait,' said James and I gave Father the wave of an idiot son and we carried on across the lake: the first act of wilful disobedience since my initiation into the rites of man.

'Father's come clean, has he? He's owned up?'

'Well, that's the point, he isn't my father. We got it wrong.'

'You mean Uncle Frank is, after all?'

'No, you fool, it's not Uncle Frank. You see I *was* conceived in Venice, like you, but my father is . . .' and he was beaming with pleasure, 'my father is *Henry Usher.*'

'Henry?' And James went on to explain, as the oars splashed gently into the clearest water I had ever seen, how Father had told him that when our mothers had lived in Venice after leaving school, they had lodged at our seedy *pensione*, and had met Father and Henry who were staying in an apartment rented by Henry's father, Lord Castledown. They had all been intoxicated with Venice, and when our fathers got back to England they had found identical letters waiting for them postmarked *Venice*, telling them the good news that the girls were in pod.

So, even if my father hadn't managed to sire us both, James too had been the product of an over-zealous tadpole that had outstripped its tribe, and the fruits of its labours had lodged ever after at Uncle Frank's grandfather's house. How strange the ways of fate! That it should have happened like this, that it had happened at all. So James was the bastard heir to a viscountcy. 'Will you be made a lord?' I asked him, half mockingly, half in envy.

'I would have been an Honourable if Mother and he had married, like Uncle Toby and Aunt Dorothy. I suppose he didn't want to be tied down. He sounds a sort of free spirit. As things stand, I'm a dishonourable because I'm a bastard,' and he laughed. 'My grandfather paid my school fees. That was always a mystery – Father, I mean Frank, being so mean, and all that *spongers* and *parasites* stuff. I suppose you can't blame him really. I still don't know if he thought he was my real father. Henry disappeared when I was about seven, as far as I can make out, so he could still be alive. It was here at Steinpass that Uncle Toby and he parted for ever, on the Roman bridge. He walked across the pass to catch a train from Bernwald. It's all very mysterious. I think he must have been in the secret service. See if you can find out anything. Here's the old reprobate. I'll pull in and we can pick him up.'

'Here you are, at last. Didn't you see me wave? I'm

so glad you can row, Thomas. It's nice that you can do something. Here James, let me have a go. I'll show you boys how to row.'

Father struggled aboard and got into position and then away we went, zipping about at great speed. I had to admit that he was a much better oarsman than me.

'So you managed to pass some exams,' he said out of the silence. 'Did you say, James, that you were going to Corpus? Pity it's not Magdalen. Did I tell you how Henry nearly got us sent down? Nicholas was at the House, of course – Christ Church, such ignorance! – and had a wager with Henry over some venison. Henry stayed late in my rooms one night and crept out armed to the teeth with rifles and daggers, shot a deer and carried it to a punt to make his escape. Somehow he got caught by one of the bulldogs smuggling it into Great Quad and, as ever, mentioned our names as if that would have made it all right. Nicholas was giving a grand dinner in his rooms the next night and Henry was going to cook it over the open fire; he'd already procured a huge cast-iron cauldron. "I'll show you how we do it in Scotland, old man," he'd said to Nicholas. Nicholas had to stand bail, and Henry was fined five pounds and got his name in the paper to boot. *Viscount's son in deer park prank.* That wasn't the last time his name was in the papers. And did you say, Thomas, that you were going to a *red brick* university?' I nodded. 'Tut tut. Where exactly? . . . That's in Nicholas's constituency. I must get him to keep an eye on you, and I believe Henry's cousin, Lady Eleanor Hopton, is the Vice-Chancellor. When I was your age, I went to India for the first time. A gypsy woman told me I was born to rule in the East.'

'I thought it was Henry who was told that,' I said.

'Sometimes I get us muddled up. Ha-ha.'

We stayed another ten days at Steinpass. Long enough for it to pass into my blood for ever. James and I spent the days on the lake and in exploring the woodland paths and mountain tracks. We climbed down beneath the Roman bridge and jumped from rock to rock so that we could sit under the waterfall for hours at a stretch.

'Twas sweet at such a time, with such delights
On every side, in prime of youthful strength,
To feed a poet's tender melancholy
And fond conceit for sadness.

At least twice every day we walked up to the castle. We saw no one. It was always deserted. There were two heavy doors to the castle, one on each side of the tunnel, and each time we went through we tried them. They were always locked.

After dinner in the hotel, Erhard, the son of the owner, would sometimes join us, and James and I would ask him about the castle. It was, as Father had said, hardly a ruin and looked habitable, certainly to one whose first home had been a caravan. It seemed amazing that so fantastic a place should have been abandoned. But when we spoke of it Erhard just shook his head.

And at night, after we had dined, and after James and I had left Father talking with Erhard at the hotel, we boys would stay late at the café, and when the time came for it to shut James would say goodnight to Trudi and to me and leave us. What nights they were! Trudi, châtelaine of the campsite and of my virginity, I salute thee across the years.

Father was most reasonable about my nocturnal exeats. Indeed he had solved a pressing problem on his first night back by supplying me with a further stock of French letters, all of which bore German writing and the word *Wien*.

During our last night together I told Trudi that I loved her. I did, a bit, but she answered, 'No, Thomas, you love the night.' She also told me that in the night all cats are black. How right she was. For me in the night all cats are Netta. In the morning, when the time had come for me to leave her bed for the last time, she made a point of kissing me on my birthmark.

Later that morning, when we had packed our things and were ready to depart, she presented me with a small bunch of wild flowers in an elastic band. A sweet gesture. A remembered act of kindness and perhaps even of love. I thought of pressing them inside the leaves of *The Poetical*

Works of Wordsworth, but when Father stopped the Humber outside the hotel so that he and James could say goodbye to Erhard and his family, I ran down the track by the side of the church to the lake and scattered them on the water where they floated until I had turned my back on them for ever. I knew I would never see her again. I was returning to my destiny and my destiny was Netta. Nonetheless, I thought this a fine and fitting gesture, as perhaps it was. Now I come to think of it she also gave me a lock of blonde hair which I kept for some years. What became of that? Dust and ashes, no doubt.

PART TWO

Further Education

CHAPTER 10 · *Rambling Studies* (*Continued*)

RETURNED HOME from the greatest adventure of my life with mixed feelings. I was desperate to see Netta for instance, both for her own sake and in order to confess, or perhaps I should say to *boast*. I had come back, I was home. And what was more I now felt myself to be a man. What a piece of work it was who hurried to Netta's door that day.

'Netta?'

'Thomas?'

In no time we were in the hearse and heading for the elusive symbol that to my child's eyes had seemed to divide earth and heaven, a place which, despite my ten shilling prize poem, I had only seen from afar. I had always wanted to keep it for a special occasion. That time had come and I now directed my young chauffeuse to drive us to Halnaker Mill. Lunchless we whispered along the Queen's Highway at two in the afternoon, knowing that no storm, no tempest, could stop the inevitable.

Twenty minutes later we had parked the black beast off the main road and were walking hand in hand up the slope to paradise. It was a day in late September, a day of dappled sunlight, when it felt warm in the sun and cold out of it. The hedges were a tangle of blackberries, rose hips, honeysuckle berries and yellow bracken. Clusters of elderberries hung down like bunches of grapes. The path was littered with acorns and hazelnuts. The clouds dropped fatness. Ripeness was all.

At the top of the hill, in front of the windmill, we turned to look on Chichester and saw the great spire rising from the heat haze, and saw too the tower of the madhouse which stands a mile to the north of the Cathedral. I had not thought of that. Halnaker Hill was deserted and the Mill, once in desolation, had been repaired. There was no door and we wandered in to the bare conical interior. The upper floors had not been replaced in the restoration and you could see through a few beams straight to the top. The stone walls at the lower levels bore the inscriptions of other lovers, though there was none to say *Netta ti amo* which my beloved allowed me to inscribe, laughing the while at the foolishness of my gesture. And then we stepped outside into the warm afternoon, where we made love on the grass. This too was more a gesture than anything else, an affirmation, and I remember looking across to the spire of the Cathedral and the tower of the madhouse and up at the white sails of the windmill and feeling a sense of immense relief, of the rightness of the thing. And I felt terrible too, terrible as an army with banners.

I had at last reached Halnaker Mill, symbol of all that was unattainable and far off. I was not to know that this was to be the finest period of my life, the days when the fruits of the earth were mine, a time when hope was superfluous. The weather was set fair and I just had to hold out my hands for them to be filled with good things.

When we got back to the Manor the doctor's Raleigh was parked outside and I didn't go in. I went back to Coniston, and since Uncle Frank was busy at his piano practice I slipped upstairs to the Holy of Holies so that I could see the view from the window, the view of Halnaker Mill which had meant so much to me. Was I already hankering for the past?

An hour later I was back at Netta's. We had tea and I told her more of my adventures. I confessed to her about Trudi. She was neither shocked nor impressed. Off we went again in the eight-miles-to-the-gallon hearse, this time to Climping, where we walked along the beach and swam naked and made love under the stars. I lift the tender curls of black hair from the honeyed column of your neck and kiss you. Netta, I love you. I love you, Netta.

Ah, Youth, that vaunteth itself and is puffed up.

Coniston: a Sunday morning. While Uncle Frank was at church, stirring up the congregation with *Dear Lord and Father* – appropriate, you may think, for James – the latter was ransacking the Holy of Holies while I kept watch below. Distant bangings and thumpings were followed by the familiar sound of James leaping down the stairs three at a time. He opened the door, threw something on to the table, and said, 'What do you think of this lot?'

As I thumbed through half a dozen well-worn porno-graphic magazines, I couldn't help feeling a little impressed. Uncle Frank had a secret life.

'And these?'

These turned out to be letters. 'This is from my father,' said James, handing me one written in blue-black ink and signed *Henry Usher*, 'and these are from my grandfather,' and he handed me a number of letters signed *Castledown*.

The next day we went into Chichester Library where we checked the reference books:

> **CASTLEDOWN**, 9th Viscount, Ireland, *cr* 1725, **Charles George Augustus Walter Melmoth Usher**, *cr* Baron 1693, late Capt. Royal West Highland Mounted Rifles; *b* 11 Aug. 1893, *o surv. s* of 8th Viscount and Lady Georgina Levinge (d 1926), *d* of 9th Earl Binstead; *S* father, 1904; *m* 1st 1919, Barbara (d 1935), *d* of late Maj.-Gen. James Scott-Bell DSO, DL (one *s* decd); 2nd, 1941, Fiona Barclay. *Educ*: Eton, Christ Church, Oxford. *Recreations*: shooting, fishing. *Heir*: none. *Address*: Keep Castle, Invernesshire.

James copied it all out, and the entry from the other red book too.

So Henry was dead. It was official. It was gazetted.

It was the signet ring that caused the storm to break. James had not, of course, been foolish enough to wear it since our return, but it turned out that James and I were not the only ones who had been snooping. He was out when Mother and Aunt Mary cornered me, out playing tennis with Netta.

'We want to talk to you.'

'Do you know how James got hold of this?' and she held out the ring.

'Er . . .'

'And he's been behaving oddly. He's rude to his father and to me.'

'Uncle Frank's things have been disturbed.'

'Oh?'

'It's your father, isn't it? He took you on holiday, didn't he?'

'We have a right to know what's been going on.'

'We must know what's been happening. Where did you go? Did you go to France?'

'Er . . . Yes.'

'When did you last see your father? He went with you, didn't he? Why didn't you tell us? We wouldn't have objected.'

'But we don't like this cloak and dagger way of carrying on. We don't like to be deceived.'

'Just tell us what happened. We know something's been going on . . . Just start at the beginning . . .'

'I . . .'

'Yes?'

'I don't know what to say.'

'You've seen your father. You've been to Venice.'

It was like being in a squash match with a couple of county players. I stood no chance. Surrender, or hara-kiri, or the longed-for miracle? The front door was opening . . . the longed-for miracle! The return of James. The relief of Thomas.

He saw what was up and immediately took over. 'Carry on, Mr Usher,' I might have said, collapsing to the ground in his arms.

'What is it you want to know?'

They started, the same technique, one-two, one-two. James stood there, hands on hips, looking grimly down on the two women. 'Very well. It's time the truth came out. I know your husband is not my father. You have kept it from me all my life. I have been deceived by you and I cannot forgive you. I will not forgive you if I live a thousand years. We know all about it, the squalid interlude in Venice. It strikes me you were no better than a couple of giggling adventuresses. Yes, I did look through his things, and the less said about it the better. You have deceived me about the facts of my own parentage. You led me to believe that he was my father, the man who constantly called me a sponger and a parasite. I now know that it wasn't him who paid my school fees. That's one mystery I've cleared up. If I'd known why your husband hated me so, perhaps I would have understood. Or perhaps he didn't know when you married him. Perhaps he found out later. Did the poor fool really think he was my father? Did he? Ah, here comes the unfortunate man.'

We heard the car on the gravel drive, followed by voices, Uncle Frank's and Netta's. Pin-striped Uncle Frank ushered Netta in with his usual attempt at gallantry. He saw something was up but Aunt Mary had barred the way to the stairs. 'James knows you're not his father.'

A reddening of face. 'He knows about Henry.'

Puce. A pulling up of socks. The big bald head lurched forward. 'I've done my best for you all these years, for all of you. I've taken you all in. You think you've been deceived. I've had to put up with it for nearly twenty years. I'm a solicitor. I'm an important man. My grandfather built this house and I'm treated like a fool in it.'

'To deceive me about my father was unforgivable.'

'Your father. You think he was better than me because his father was a viscount. Well, if you want to know, your father was ... a spendthrift ... a ... an incubus, a ... pariah ... that's what he was, *evil* ... And the same goes for *you*,' he said, leaning in my direction and all the while waving his hands about like the conductor of some mad musical work.

'I don't see what harm my father's done you,' I threw in, emboldened by the presence of James and Netta, my defenders of old.

'If you must know, your father is disgusting.'

'I don't suppose he keeps pornography in his room.'

Henry Irving would have been stretched to lean as far forward and wave his hands as dramatically as Uncle Frank at that moment.

'You've been snooping in my room, I know you have. I let it go for the sake of peace, but I've had enough. *I've had enough.*'

I felt Netta clutch my arm, like someone at the theatre at a moment of crisis in the performance. 'You', and with head craned, he took a lunge forward, 'are nothing but a lot of *spongers.*'

We saw the foam fly from his lips as he flailed around, like a man beset by a swarm of wasps. 'He's a *pervert*,' he said, lurching and pointing in my direction, 'a pervert. Your father is a *queer*.'

I laughed at this, but Mother didn't, and neither did Aunt Mary; and nor did James. I looked at Netta for support. She stood there four-square, her eyes glazed. She was enjoying herself.

'A *queer*, that's what he is. That's why I wouldn't have him in the house. I didn't want the place contaminated, and I've put up with it for twenty years. For twenty years I've been sheltering the produce of a pervert, and what's more I've been saddled with *him*, that ungrateful and spoiled young cuckoo,' and he lunged at James and gave another conductor's wave before backing to the door. His body disappeared, then his briefcase, which had been dumped on the floor at the outbreak of hostilities, and with his head poking round the door he gave his final grimace. 'Spongers, the lot of you,' he said, '*parasites!*' and slammed the door.

A strange silence always falls after a bravura performance.

James packed a bag and set off for London. I retreated to the Manor with Netta.

ETTA HAD ARRIVED at Coniston just as Uncle Frank was arriving home from work. She had come to pass on the news that Birgit's boyfriend Martin, the Blacksmith, was in hospital, suffering from terminal cancer. She told me this as we walked down the lane to the Manor. We went in to find Birgit watching the news on television. Nicholas York was being interviewed outside the Houses of Parliament.

Naturally enough, Birgit was in a sombre mood, but she enjoyed our tale of family life at Coniston, and slapped her thighs several times during the narration, savouring the words *pervert* and *queer* and rolling them around her tongue. When I protested that none of it was true she shook her cropped head, heavy with its weight of experience, and held forth about fetishism, mother-fixations, and the infinite variety of human needs. She wanted me to know that if it *were* true it would make no difference. Not only Michelangelo but probably Jesus Christ himself was of the same persuasion. It was either a matter of one's genetic construction, or sometimes simply a question of taste: some people liked Brie while others preferred Stilton. She understood these things and I must learn to understand them. We could not all fit snugly into some pre-ordained bourgeois pattern. I was invited to stay the night.

Birgit and Netta went off to see Martin in hospital at Chichester, while I watched *Panorama* on television, since my erstwhile drinking companion, Nicholas York, was prominently billed. Then I wandered about the empty house as I waited for the two women to return. I went up to Netta's room. Her bed, of course, was still unmade, and I fancied I could detect the print of her body in the rather grubby sheets. This was the room where she undressed each night. Here was the pillow where she laid her head and where she dreamed her dreams. I looked in her drawers and cupboards and saw her clothes and shoes and bangles, and read the postcards which I had sent from Venice and Steinpass. These were the inconsequential things that helped to make up Netta's daily life – the Nefertiti bedcover, the blue-stained pine bed, the shelves with her books and potplants and invitations from people I did not know that stung me with jealousy, but mostly familiar things, clothes draped over the wooden chair, the black bikini she sometimes wore, her school books. Netta's presence was very strong. It was all around me. The sense of Netta's being. The sacred emptiness of her room.

I heard the door open and a familiar voice call out, 'Anyone at home?' It was the doctor. I didn't answer. I hoped he would go away but when I got downstairs I found him ensconced in the throne with a glass of wine in his hand. As Martin lay dying his old rival was preparing to ease himself into his place. It was his turn to enjoy the lap of comfort and to sup at the table of content. Martin had had his hour of splendour; he would never come back.

When I related the afternoon's events to the doctor he simply shrugged his shoulders, as if he'd known all along. 'Pretty girl, your mother. Always had a soft spot for her,' but he wouldn't be drawn further on family affairs. I accepted his offer of a glass of wine. We were now confederates. When our women returned they confirmed that Martin had about six weeks to go, or so they thought. Then Birgit knocked up one of her little dishes: grilled avocado on toast with Stilton and red peppers. Birgit preferred Stilton. The four of us then enjoyed several bottles of wine before retiring for the night. Since the doctor and Birgit went upstairs arm in arm, and Netta and I followed shortly after, perhaps the word *retiring* is more polite than apt. I leave you to judge. Birgit had made it clear that it was quite all right for me to share Netta's bed. We were all grown-ups together.

Netta and I were having a honeymoon breakfast in the morning when the telephone rang. It was James phoning from Father's flat. He had momentous news to relate. After we'd parted the previous day he had set off for London by train. There had been a scene at Victoria station; Uncle Frank had got there first and in the ensuing struggle had accidentally acquired a black eye. James had then announced that he was on his way to see British democracy in action, and that he planned to meet Uncle Toby and Nicholas York at Westminster which was generally thought to be a respectable place, and had bolted.

Later that night, when Father and James were watching from the Strangers' Gallery as Nicholas was speaking, Uncle Frank had appeared and had interrupted the proceedings by making a speech of his own in which the words *spongers* and *parasites* and the personages of Uncle Frank's grandfather and Lord Castledown had received a mention before a couple of attendants had grabbed him. As they were dragging him away he had shouted 'York's a queer' to the assembled gathering. However, Harold Wilson had come backstage after the show and smoothed everything over and Uncle Frank was quietly seen off the premises. Nicholas was his old masterful self, dismissing Uncle Frank as overwrought, which James considered to be an understatement. No, James would not be coming back to Uncle Frank's grandfather's house. He had a favour to ask of me. Would I be a sport and get his things together and take them to Netta's? He would be staying at Father's flat until he went up to Oxford and he and Father would be down in the next few days to collect them.

When I got back to Coniston later in the day, Aunt Mary and Mother were busy making blackberry jam. Life had to go on, they said, and listened to my story before telling me theirs. Frank had returned home at about two in the morning. There had been a lot of crashing and banging about before he had settled down. They had noticed the black eye at breakfast but had thought it better to say nothing, and after a hearty meal Frank had retired to the Holy of Holies, presumably to read Wordsworth or *Girls of the World*.

A week later I received a card from James which bore a Scottish postmark. The card was a picture from the Tate entitled *The Cholmondeley Sisters*, and depicts the two eponymous sixteenth-century sisters holding their identical babes. I detected Father's influence. It read: *Staying with paternal grandparents. Much to report. Collecting things Thursday en route Oxford. Will you be there?*

I was indeed there to see James off to Oxford. In fact I was in the garden of the Manor making love to Netta when he and Father arrived. We hurried our business and got to the front door to find Father standing on one leg, dressed in a blazer and wearing a Magdalen tie. He was leaning on his umbrella-stick holding forth to Birgit. James stood beside him in jacket and jeans looking for the first time like an outsider. 'No, alas, it's not my old college, but I suppose it's better than nothing, not that . . .' said Father, and here he mentioned the name of the middling institution to which Netta and I were bound, 'isn't perfectly acceptable, of course. I believe I know the Vice-Chancellor, Lady Eleanor Hopton. She's the cousin of a great friend of mine who disappeared, you know, the son of Lord Castledown.'

The Valkyrie stood before him with hands folded. 'Of course. James, it's so good to see you. Come, give me a kiss. You look so handsome,' and to Father, 'Would you like lunch?'

'No, I think we should be on our way, don't you, James?' At this point the doctor appeared. Netta, James and I just kicked our heels.

'Toby, it's been a long time. Still teaching?'

'Your things are inside,' said Birgit to James, 'you'd better get them.'

'Oh yes, one has to earn an honest penny.'

'Which school are you at now?'

'Ha-ha, yes, well, it's been a pleasure seeing you all again, come on my boy, we might get to Oxford in time for lunch at the Randolph unless you'd prefer the Turf. Henry used to whizz up to Oxford for lunch in his Aston. We might just make it.'

CHAPTER 12 · *Academic Cares*

LAH-BLAH. BLAH-BLAH. The last trump. Punctually at twelve-thirty Netta pulled into the drive at Coniston and announced her arrival in the hearse; Birgit had agreed to drive us in style to our university but since, as usual, she was running late, Netta had driven over alone. Within the space of two minutes my bicycle and bag had been put in the back with Netta's things and we were ready to depart.

'We *must* say goodbye,' she said. 'We can't just go like this. It's not right,' and contrary to the agreement forged between us over breakfast that very morning, she got out of the hearse, went to the back door by the wash-house and walked in. I followed.

'It's no good,' I said, 'there's no one at home.'

'The caravan,' she announced, after touring the house, and marched down the garden. 'Hmmm, it seems you're telling the truth for once,' and we got back into the car. She started the engine and off we jerked. How she passed her driving test I shall never know. 'We'll try the Red Lion,' she said, pulling into the car park and jamming on the handbrake before the beast had stopped. 'Come on. It's the least we can do,' and I followed her inside. 'Hello,' she said, seeing them sitting up at the bar drinking barley wine with the landlord. 'We're just off and wanted to say goodbye.'

'Netta,' they said in unison. 'Hello, haven't seen you for days.'

'So kind of you to drop by, Thomas,' said my mother.

'How very kind,' said Aunt Mary. 'Netta, would you like a drink?'

'I expect they're in a frightful rush, my dear. We don't want to hold them up. See you at Christmas, if you can spare the time.'

'If you've nothing better to do, of course. We wouldn't want to be a nuisance, would we, Mary?'

'Yes, do call in, we'd love to see you, if you're passing this way.'

'We just wanted to say goodbye,' said Netta.

'I'm sorry . . .' I ventured, 'but . . .'

'Tut tut,' they said in unison, arching their eyebrows and wagging their forefingers. 'Off you go then. Bye bye,' and out we went, for the present at least, out of their lives.

We returned to pick up our magnificent chauffeuse. Some hours later, when I was feeling weary from the terrors of the journey, the hearse pulled in at Netta's hall of residence which, as Father had forecast, was built of red brick. Here Birgit abandoned us as instructed. Before us was what looked like a Victorian villa, set in a small park. I thought it didn't look too bad, all things considered.

We went inside to a pleasant hall with runners on the floor, portraits of elders on the walls, and eagles on pediments at the foot of the stairs. Up we went, Netta and I, along to the very end of the corridor. There Netta knocked once and pushed open the door to find a homely northern girl clad in spectacles and decorative woolly bustling about. This was the girl with whom Netta was to share. 'You must be Annette. I'm Hilary,' she said. 'Would you like some tea?'

I left them in order to find my own lodgings, which were off campus, in a modern development of university flats which I didn't like. It was bleak, inhospitable and utilitarian. I sorted out my things – an advantage of being a caravan dweller is that you tend to have few possessions – and found my way back to Netta's where unofficial permission was granted for me to stay the night. I slept on the floor next to Netta's bed, and as I drifted off to sleep I held on to her hand as long as I could until the darkness claimed me and our fingers slipped apart.

There was some decent country near by, and within a few days of our arrival at the nameless university, Netta and I had explored the locality. The weather was fine during the early part of the term, and we had soon discovered an extensive area of woodland about three miles from the town. Here, one bright October day, we spent several hours naked, picnicking and making love. Around us chestnuts fell as if in benediction and the leaves beneath us rustled as they had rustled at the undoing of Tess and Emma. We believed ourselves to be invisible in our golden bower, a few yards from the track, but a pair of English setters sniffed us out. Their bearded keeper, a man of large frame and curling locks, was, however, engrossed in a cricket magazine and walked on for some time before realising that his charges had abandoned him. 'Rum, Christie.' Some introductions are best effected from far off. It took a good deal of shooing before the dogs, snuffling and licking us as we hurried into our clothes, heeded their master's voice. Night was drawing nigh and shadows of the evening were stealing across the sky. It had been a wonderful day and Netta and I headed back with our arms around each other's waists, and wheeled our bicycles to a pub we had passed on the outward journey.

The bearded man and his two setters were sitting at a table on the far side, where he was still engrossed in the cricket magazine, sucking at his thumb the while. Not so the dogs, which jumped down from the bench and rushed over to renew our acquaintance, slobbering over us as is the way of dogs. Their keeper took no notice.

A few evenings later, when Netta, Hilary and I were on our way to a party near the same pub, we stopped there first for a drink. Since Hilary was reading music I was holding forth in lofty manner on the subject. 'Good music ended in 1949 with the death of Richard Strauss.'

'Captain of the second eleven,' cut in the bearded fellow we had seen with the dogs. 'King of the second-raters.'

'I have no idea what a second eleven may be, but I can't agree that the composer of *Arabella*, *Till Eulenspiegel* and *Don Juan* was in any way second rate and what's more, Rum and Christie are drinking your beer,' I said.

'Rum, Christie, stop that will you. How do you know my dogs?'

'We met them the other day in the woods,' said Netta, introducing herself and us.

'Well, my name's Hugo Parry, but I'm known as Uggers. That's what my housemaster called me at school.'

'Why did he call you that?' said Netta, in all seriousness, frowning under her fringe, 'and those dogs are at it again.'

'Rum, Christie, do stop it ... Well, I am really, don't
you think? Ugly, I mean.'

'Nonsense,' she said, 'I think you're handsome in a rugged
sort of way, and very charming, don't you, Thomas?'

'If you want the truth, no, except in a second eleven,
second-rate kind of way.'

'This means war. Arm-wrestle, arm-wrestle,' he called out
and he had soon forced my arm to the table. 'That'll cost you
a pint and anyway what's so wrong with my looks? Elucidate,'
and he flung back his Rastafarian locks in a parody of nobility,
sucking in his lower lip with its pendulous counterpart.

'You really want me to tell you?' I said, and he nodded,
inclining his profile half an inch higher. 'Well, to start with,
you are of gross build.' This met with apparent satisfaction and
he proudly inflated his barrel chest another few inches. 'Your
eyes are furtive, like those of a sick lion.' He bared a ragged
set of teeth and grinned. 'Your hair is disgusting, like that of
an unwashed gypsy. Your skin's foxed like a bad painting.'
(Having a loathsome stamp on my own cheek enables me to
speak with authority on disorders of the complexion.) 'Your
head's the head of a hydrocephalic dwarf ... Netta!' She was
kissing him. Only in the most chaste fashion, you understand.

The next thing I knew was that I was being carried
over Uggers' shoulder out into the night air where I was
dumped in a trailer attached to a parked tractor. The trailer
was empty but there was evidence that it had recently been
used for the transportation of animal dung. And then the four
of us, accompanied by the setters, walked on in the direction
of a low throbbing and wailing that emanated from a dimly
lit house some two hundred yards off.

I took a last breath of air as we went in, to find an
almost impenetrable wall of gyrating bodies, writhing and
groping through the pages of the *Inferno*, immured in smoke.
Damned, no doubt, all of them, and under their feet snuffling
and baffled, the two dogs.

'This is home,' mimed Uggers. 'I live here.'

Home was a rambling Victorian house stuffed with students.
We stayed the night, Netta, Uggers, the dogs and I sleeping
together with various anonymous guests in what he maintained

was his bedroom. Sometime about midday we made our way downstairs. 'You have to look out for viscera,' he explained, 'the cats . . . and goat droppings. Algernon sometimes wanders in for titbits, don't you Algie, don't you?' and Uggers abased himself in front of a goat which was happily munching some leftovers, and advanced until their heads clashed. Both started to push until, after a while, Uggers declared the match a draw. 'That reminds me,' he said, 'you remember the seventeenth of August?' We both shook our heads. 'The day it rained in Kennington? The Oval? The *Test Match*? You do like cricket?' Again we shook our heads. Uggers shook his locks in disbelief. 'You *don't* like cricket? You don't like cricket? I suppose you don't like *music* unless it's by Richard Strauss.'

We threaded our way over still-recumbent lovers back to his room, where he kept a wind-up gramophone, and soon the strains of Gilbert and Sullivan were reverberating around us and drifting down the stairs.

> He sobbed and he sighed, and a gurgle he gave,
> Then he plunged himself into the billowy wave,
> And an echo arose from the suicide's grave –
> 'O willow, titwillow, titwillow!'

Guests were leaving. Uggers had been blind to their existence. 'Next week I'm having a party at Wychford, my parents' house. It's forty miles from here. Will you come?'

The following Saturday, crammed into Hilary's Mini – which contained Netta, Hilary attired in one of her many colourful sweaters, seventeen stone of Uggers, two English setters and me – I felt an authentic thrill when, careering up a badly maintained drive, we saw before us on the far side of an ornamental lake a grey stone house, with a pillared porch and, to one side, a wall enclosing a courtyard with stables and outbuildings. It seemed the perfect English country house, a Gainsborough.

Uggers hadn't told us anything about the place or what the 'party' was for. It was to be a work party. His parents filled us in with the details. The house had been completed by the family in 1725 when the Parrys were newly rich. Now they had fallen on hard times. They desperately wanted to stay but the upkeep was killing them, so they had decided to turn the outhouses into holiday cottages, and that is where we came in. They fed us, we slept on their floor, and we did some useful work.

'How are you with a sledgehammer?' Uggers asked me, conscious of the disparity in size between us. Spurred on by this challenge and the expression in Netta's eyes, I battered vainly at the unwanted wall until I could no longer stand, before handing the doughty tool to Uggers, who with the confidence of a seasoned strongman stripped before us, flexed his muscles, sucked in his lower lip and swung the sledgehammer with all his might. Ceilings shook, plaster crumbled, but the wall remained intact. Sweating and panting, with a slight sneer and the laugh of a fairy-tale ogre, he passed the sledgehammer to Netta at her request. There was a tradition of demolition in her family about which Uggers knew nothing, and within three minutes Netta had the wall tumbling about our ears. Our cheers rang loud and long.

Before we set off back to the university, Uggers asked me if I wanted to see the cellars, and down into the underworld we went. First I was introduced to Jacob, the cellar toad, who had lived in a particular corner as long as Uggers could remember. I was sure he felt an affinity with it, massively ugly as it was, and he told me of the hours he'd spent in his youth watching Jacob copulating with a series of lady toads and spoke with tenderness of their clammy embraces which, he assured me, could last for days and days. He then showed me the storeroom which was full of tinned food, of a type which might have been taken on expeditions at the beginning of the century.

'My mother was a General or whatever they have in the Wrens. She lives in constant anticipation of war. There's enough here to have withstood the siege of Troy.'

The tour continued to a smaller cellar lined with hundreds of bottles, all of them empty and made of thick dark-green glass, with necks of varying lengths, some short and stubby and others long and sticking out at angles. 'Eighteenth century,' said Uggers. 'Grab a few, will you? Put them under your coat.' He gave me a furtive glance and added, 'They won't know. I get two pounds each for them in the antique shops. They sell for twice that. I always take a few back with me. You can keep one if you like.'

I did as instructed and followed my brigandish friend out of the darkness into the light of common day.

When we arrived back at Netta's hall of residence there was a message for her on the noticeboard headed URGENT. She rang home. Martin, the blacksmith and lover of Birgit, was dead. The funeral had been arranged for the Friday, near Folkestone. She arranged to return home at once.

HAD GIVEN James a telephone number where I could be reached, and since Netta was otherwise engaged, I arranged to see him at the weekend, and on the Saturday following the blacksmith's immolation, I arrived at Oxford station with my weekend bag. James was there to meet me and was standing by the barrier beaming, hands folded, wearing an old flying-jacket and leather boots. It was a younger version of the photograph on the wall of Father's flat.

'They were my father's,' he said. 'Come on, I've got something to show you.'

Outside the station was a black Norton motorcycle. 'It's new,' he said. 'I collected it yesterday. It's an advance from my trust fund, for education and training. What do you think of it?'

He kick-started the thing and we roared off into Oxford, the city where my father had been born, but which I had never seen. As we hurtled through the streets, James gave an inaudible commentary over his shoulder, but he pulled up briefly on Magdalen Bridge. 'That's Magdalen where Uncle Toby went, and that's his old school over there,' and he pointed to the opposite side of the road. 'We'll go into Magdalen tomorrow. I'll show you what the bike can do now,' and we shot off at terrifying speed along the by-pass.

'What do you think?' he said, as we climbed off.

'Wonderful. Amazing.' I was shivering with cold and fright. My epithets applied both to city and machine.

I followed James up some stairs and into his room at Corpus, and yes, I did feel jealous. This was the world I wanted to belong to, a world older than red brick.

'I'm treating us to a meal at Woodstock, you know, at the Bear, the place Uncle Toby goes on about. My father, the honourable you-know-who, used to whizz up for lunch in his Aston. I can't afford one yet. I'll lend you some warmer clothes.'

I noticed that a number of James's clothes were new. I hadn't seen them before and I supposed the trust fund was responsible. I borrowed a sweater and a greatcoat, and off we roared once more, this time into the night. James led the way into a smart country hotel, we had a beer and were shown to our table; he had a natural confidence which I had always admired, and I felt a new kind of envy. It had seeped in with my other feelings for James. I loved him and I envied him. James was himself, no longer a schoolboy but a handsome, charming and capable young man, a young man devoid of the self-doubt and self-consciousness with which I was plagued. Young Lochinvar had come into his own and he wanted to tell me about it.

'It was a strange experience, meeting my grandfather for the first time. Uncle Toby was quite frightened of his wife – my step-grandmother. It was funny to see him scuttling off whenever she came on the scene. The castle is wonderful but it's falling down. They live in just a few rooms on one side. The others haven't been occupied for years. It's a bit like Blanc Hall in that respect, but smaller and made of granite. And it's older too. The family seat was in Ireland, but my great-grandfather had to sell it to pay off some gambling debts. He's supposed to have lost it in a wager at the local inn, where he bet that his fly would get to the top of the wall before another one did, and he lost. "There goes Ireland," he's supposed to have said, and the family retreated to more modest quarters in Scotland. It's pretty run down. Some of the stable roof has fallen in, but it's a marvellous place. There's masses of stuff just lying about, stags' heads, tennis rackets, portraits like old Clotworthy – my grandfather gave him to Uncle Toby, you know – and in the stables gigs and broughams. That's where I found the flying-jacket and the boots. I spent ages cleaning them up. They really are the ones my father was wearing when he had the accident, when he got that dent in his head. Yes, the ones he's wearing in the photograph. I think my grandfather was a bit taken aback when he saw me wearing them. He said they'd never been close. In fact he said, "Henry had none of the qualities I admire in a man," but he wouldn't tell me any more, except that Henry had always been extraordinarily vain.

Henry's mother had a house in Park Lane, and he was sent there for a bit as a baby. All the nannies loved Henry and his father didn't like him when they next met. He said Henry had been spoilt by all the attention.'

'Did you like him, though?'

'Oh, I found him all right in a gruff sort of way. He's got an ancient kind of face, the face of that Crusader in Chichester Cathedral, the one lying next to his wife. Yes, the Arundel tomb. But my step-grandmother's a dragon. I don't think she cared much for Uncle Toby. They knew Nicholas York. He'd been brought up to stay when Henry and he were at school. He told my grandfather that he was going to be Prime Minister. "When I go up to Oxford I'll be President of the Union, then I'll be called to the Bar, enter Parliament, marry Princess Margaret, and be PM before I'm forty," that's what he said.'

'He must be at least forty,' I said, 'and he's not married to Princess Margaret.'

'No, that's what my grandfather said, and he seemed rather pleased about it. I checked about the Blackshirts, and it's true that Mosley promised Scotland to the old boy if he'd support him, but he wouldn't. He said calling them BFs was a big mistake. I found out some more about the disappearance, too. My father hired a sailing boat called the *Imogen* from Chichester Harbour and was planning to sail round the world, or certainly to Australia. Then he disappeared. The boat was found drifting, and the dinghy was washed up on a beach a few months later. One reporter had thought he was living on the boat with a woman, but no bodies were found. And for some reason he was using Uncle Toby's name! My grandfather said he thought he just wanted to be difficult. He didn't think he was a spy or anything like that. Have some more wine. I'll order another bottle.

'And I found out from Uncle Toby that it was after he'd hired the boat that he sent him the watch and links and this ring, with a sort of final letter. Uncle Toby's funny about it, though. Sometimes he says "Henry is dead" and sometimes he says Henry wasn't the type to kill himself, and then when I said about the final letter and so on, he said that Henry was the sort to do things properly. And after the disappearance they set up a trust fund for my education. My grandfather knew all about me from the start: my mother made sure of that. They thought he should have married her, but for some reason, probably his natural contrariness, he didn't. Said he wouldn't be trapped, that sort of thing.'

Sunday. A bright November day. A golden day. November, the month when the world dies.

Morning service at Magdalen Chapel in memory of Father, 'and my grandfather too,' said James. 'He was up at Magdalen when Edward the Seventh was crowned. Imagine that. Think how different everything was then, though some things don't change, thank God,' he added as we came out of the chapel into the bright autumn light. 'That's New Building where Uncle Toby had rooms. We'll go up, just to have a look, and then I'll show you Oscar Wilde's old rooms. There's a Coca-Cola dispenser in them now, and we can take a punt out. How do you fancy that? We'll retrace my father's infamous voyage with the deer, when he nearly got Nicholas and Uncle Toby the sack, and then we'll get your things and whizz off to the Trout at Godstow and straight to the station from there. How does that sound? I'm reading Matthew Arnold at the moment, it's a sort of fad, and I'm going to find all the places mentioned in *The Scholar Gipsy* over the next few weeks, on the bike.'

Bagley Wood, the Hinkseys, Cumnor, Fyfield, Bablock Hythe, all helmetless by Norton. Lunch by the stripling Thames at Godstow where I thought I saw Netta for a moment, but of course it was another girl, and in the distance the dreaming spires.

And then you saw me off at the station. Your last wave. Yes, I remember that. Goodbye James. Goodbye for ever.

James was killed on his way back to College after seeing me off. In due course there was an inquest and I learned that a girl undergraduate had stepped into the road from behind a parked car, and that he had swerved to avoid her and had lost control. At the inquest a policeman said that James had been accelerating hard and estimated his speed at the time of the accident at forty miles an hour. According to one witness, who heard the accident but did not see it, James had taken his hands off the handlebars before he turned from the High into Merton Street. He had had the required driving licence for three weeks and had owned the machine for less than forty-eight hours. As he waited for the ambulance, which arrived in under eight minutes, James regained consciousness for a while and was heard to say 'Sorry'. The Coroner deplored the fact that a young man with everything to live for and a promising career ahead of him should have died so pointlessly. He was an inexperienced rider and the machine was a powerful one. Alas, this was not the first time that he had been obliged to listen to such tragic facts. It happened all too frequently.

Death is no lady. She waits for you on street corners, and when she steps from the shadows nothing can save you. Neither your youth nor all your strength can save you. Your father's flying-jacket cannot save you. There is no magic strong enough to save you.

James, James, James. I call your name. Nothing. There can be no reply. Only the emptiness between the stars.

Let your soul be carried on the wind's back. Accept him, stars: a brave, true spirit.

CHAPTER 14 · *The Chase*

S LIFE ABOUT the harm, the loss, the damage we suffer? Do we start off whole and get whittled away? *There was a time when meadow, grove and stream . . .*

As I walked down the lane to the church, I tolled the names of the trees as James and I had been taught by Uncle Frank: sycamore, hornbeam, ash, elm, oak, elm, elm, yew, that's how they went, and I recognised a few of the cars, of course, notably Father's two-tone Humber. There he was, ahead of me, complete with umbrella-stick, limping his way to the funeral. And there was the hearse, not Birgit's hearse, but a hired one that had carried James back from Oxford, Father's natal city, here to this quiet Sussex parish where nothing ever happened to shake the world. So James was dead. It seemed impossible.

Uncle Frank was wearing his blue Crombie and from beneath his trilby hat his breath steamed heavenward. As the putative father he was one of the principal mourners, and I made my way through the crowd without speaking to anyone to take my place in the queue with Mother and Aunt Mary. I could see the undertakers hauling the coffin out of the hearse in jerks and watched them steady themselves to take the weight. In we filed for the service; Uncle Frank sat at the organ, and the Rector, Mr Travis-Blean, officiated. I was sitting some twelve feet from James. James, still James, but soon, in a week, a month, a year . . . James's golden locks that time would never turn to silver . . . And the eyes, the lips? Don't think. Don't think.

The hymns were the best part. James had always enjoyed belting out a good hymn and he went out to *Brightest and Best*, one of his favourites. Aunt Mary stood there like rock, pale as limestone, with Mother at her side. They looked elegant and old-fashioned in black and I later found out that they had raided their mad mother's trunk for their outfits, which must have dated from the twenties. What a scene that would have been, when they tried on the clothes for this occasion. I kept my eyes on the ground as much as I could.

The Lord giveth and the Lord taketh away: cursed be the name of the Lord. God, they'd put some grass cloth, the stuff they have on fruit stalls, over the earth. *Man that is born of woman hath but a short time to live and is full of misery*. No, James was never full of misery. *He cometh up, and is cut down like a flower; he fleeth as it were a shadow*: the men were letting out the ropes, in fumbling, amateurish fashion. It must be a performance for them; you could see them exchanging knowing looks as if to say here we go again, as the coffin jerked its uneven way into the hole, a very neat hole: the hole old Mr Knight had been digging all morning. *Thou knowest, Lord, the secrets of our hearts*. Dost thou? I hope not, I hope not. Mine is full of hate. *For as much as it hath pleased Almighty God of his great mercy* – add that one up if you can – *to take unto himself the soul of our dear brother*. My dear brother. No, think of something else. *In sure and certain hope of the resurrection to eternal life* . . . Crap. When you die you're on your own.

Quoth the Rector: *Nevermore*.

Around the grave Netta, Birgit, Uncle Frank who is crying. Father ashen and drawn, complete with umbrella-stick and Magdalen scarf. He doesn't look at me once; he won't look at me. Aunt Mary and Mother, pale, but controlled. The doctor and his wife, the latter giving her fur coat an airing, I thought. Seven of James's grand friends from school and Oxford. The usual crew of neighbours and busybodies, out for the show. Mr Knight, our bellringer and sexton, stands cap in hand, at a respectful distance. A good sort, Mr Knight. No Scotch laird, what would be the point? It's too late now. An awkward pause before we begin to edge away from the grave when talk sounds false. Lifts are offered and accepted. Father tosses back his scarf and shuffles off to the Humber.

I've always thought it a strange custom that in England we turn our backs on the grave before the hole's been filled in. It's like leaving the theatre before the curtain comes down. Netta takes my arm but I shake her off. She understands. Mr Knight seems to understand too. Well, sort of. When they've all gone he lets me take his spade and shovel in the earth. The last service I can pay to my brother, my friend. I leave Mr Knight to tidy up, and walk slowly back along the damp November lane, my arms aching, my boots heavy with mud. Back to the house. The ordeal of going in. No James to help me now. Not ever.

I don't remember much more, except that Father didn't come back to Coniston. Aunt Mary gave me a set of keys to Father's flat which James had had, and asked me to return them to Father when I next saw him. What impressed me about Aunt Mary was her self-control as she handed round the sandwiches and chatted with her guests as if nothing had happened.

Next day Netta and I went back to our university by train and somehow I got through the rest of the term. Those days are a complete blank to me. In due course term ended and I retired to the caravan. I could be alone there. Oh the sound of the rain peppering the tin roof.

On Christmas Eve I was already at Birgit's when Mother and Aunt Mary arrived. There is always something peculiarly ghastly about a jolly occasion after a tragedy, and I believe I must have shown less than common courtesy to my family. I think it was over the advertisement placed by Uncle Frank in the local paper . . . *in a tragic accident, only son of Frank and Mary* . . . I thought he was doing it simply for the sake of form, and I disapproved. With hindsight I can see that he too had loved James in his difficult way and had been proud of him and he wanted people to think James was his son. This wasn't good enough, as far as I was concerned. I was going through a period when I hated everything and Uncle Frank was fairly high on the list.

Birgit got me alone for a talk in the library. She was kind and understanding and wanted me to talk. I didn't want to talk. I didn't want to get things out of my system. I wanted them to stay there and fester. Birgit gave me a lecture on good manners. I could accept it from her. She also told me that I should try to see life as a circle rather than a straight line, so that the past and the future are always with us, and I remember her telling me that if I was really an atheist I would not have been so angry, and that I shouldn't be so hard on people for uttering clichés, since even clichés can be comforting, like old clothes. Birgit knew a little of suffering. She had just lost Martin, of course, and this in my eyes put her in the league of those whom God had offended. Somehow my mother was too close to be considered.

Netta drove me to Chichester Cathedral for the midnight service. We had made it a ritual over the last few years. Really we, and James who had been with us then, had been asserting our independence from the old order. Carols around the piano with Birgit was corny, Turkish delight that left white dust on your lips had lost its sweetness and we no longer enjoyed charades. After Birgit's fish supper, a legacy from her Nordic ancestors, we took ourselves off. It was a cold raw night and the Cathedral was crowded; perhaps, though, even then, I was beginning to find comfort in ritual, in seeing the turn of the year under that familiar roof.

Boxing Day was bloody cold, but I wanted to get out. I needed to make myself physically tired. It was all I could do, the only help I could offer myself. Oh yes, it was nice to make love to Netta, comforting too, but I needed to be out. Out hating, I think it was, hating God. If you can stand up to God and defy him, in a way you become his equal. Do your worst, God, I'm going out.

I took James's bicycle out of the garage and cycled off towards the downs. It was early in the morning, and very cold, but so what, I had the day to kill. At Slindon I turned off into the woods by the gatehouse and cycled along the footpath through the beech wood, every tree a pillar of the temple. Back on the main road and right to Rackham. Arundel Castle in the distance beyond clouds of woodland, and all under a huge Sussex sky. Then down a steep hill and over the bridge at Amberley, a good mile without pedalling, and past the ruins of Amberley Castle.

Bright sunlight, so bright on the wet road that I had to shield my eyes. An untidy line of horses clattering along the road, their nostrils steaming. Land Rovers and horse boxes everywhere. A sign, CARE PLEASE HOUNDS. I'd seen huntsmen before, and plenty of foxes, but I'd never followed a hunt. (Clotworthy would never have *followed* one.) A trail of riders bobbed up and down, and amongst them, an ancient lady dressed in black was riding side-saddle, incongruous among the Land Rovers and Minis.

An unexpected entertainment was being laid on, something to help fill the gap between sleep and sleep. Why not? I propped the bike against a tree and followed the riders into a stretch of sandy heathland, all gorse and birch.

There was plenty of noise; voices, the thud of hooves, the barking of dogs. Horses snorted as they trotted past. After a few minutes I walked on alone, dodging the yellow puddles. On one side a fence some three or four feet high enclosed a plantation of young pines, and as I went further in I noticed that they had been planted in squares, with straight firebreaks or rides dissecting the plantation so that the landscape resembled a giant chessboard. A nice conceit for a hunt, I thought.

It was a strange business. You know how you expect a foxhunt to be. The fox streaks ahead, with the baying hounds following, and behind them the scarlet huntsmen, all like a set of toys. But this wasn't like that at all. Most of the time nothing happened. Now and then a hound smashed through the bracken, lifting its ugly jaws (and they are ugly close up) to sniff the air, and all went quiet again. At one point I know I had been alone for some minutes when a pair of riders trotted by, and a third cut across their path at a right-angle. I heard the shrill note of the horn from another direction, turned towards it, a rider spattered from head to foot with yellow mud cantered by, and I was alone again. Through an avenue of blue pines I saw a pale moon shining. How beautiful, how strange. It just wasn't happening. It just wasn't real.

I waited for a while before turning away from the moon, and realised I was lost. At the next crossroads I came to a gathering of riders sitting still on their horses, and stopped again a few yards from the first of them, a boy who was eating a sandwich. Beyond him a woman, filthy with mud, was climbing down from her horse. She pulled some chocolate from her pocket. There were voices in the wood, and a man with four or five terriers headed for them and soon disappeared from view. Horses stretched their necks in an attempt to crop the grass. I could smell horse, frost and leather.

'Gypsy . . . Hero.' Voices came like shots from the wood.

'He's out,' snapped a man's voice. The horn blared. Everyone began to move at once. A man bolted a sandwich and struggled back into the saddle.

Suddenly the undergrowth in front of me crackled like a bush fire. Out darted the fox, crossing my path within a few feet. On its tail was a huge brute of a hound and then another. They vanished into the bracken, and a moment later I could see the steam rising from the fox's body. A man dismounted and waded towards the struggling hounds, shouting at them to keep off. He picked up the dead fox (yes, it was a quick death) to get it clear of the hounds, and then put it on the ground again. He took out a pocket-knife, cut off the brush, lifted the body into the air once more and held it at arm's length like a sacrifice. The hounds ran about, flailing and scything the air with their tails. Then he tossed it back into the bracken. My, my, foxhounds, what lolling tongues you have.

Figures hurried past. I was cold. Suddenly I found I was being violently sick into the bracken.

And this event, which you may think is of little significance and possibly irrelevant, has haunted me ever since. It gave me material for a thousand dreams. I'm usually in pursuit. Sometimes we catch it and its brush flicks across my eyes, leaving me blinded with blood. Sometimes I'm on foot and I try to save the fox by picking it up and putting it over a wall or by closing a door just in time. I'm not against hunting; I've seen a fox caught in a wire snare with its neck half severed. Why am I telling you this? I choose to set it down as it happened because I want to. Because it has become an image of my life.

CHAPTER 15 · *Observations*

HAD IN my possession James's keys to Father's flat, and I planned to return them to Father before the end of the Christmas vacation. I made several attempts to speak to him on the telephone, but could get no answer. This suited me well, since there were a lot of things I wasn't clear about where my father was concerned, and I welcomed the chance to have a look around. In fact, the idea had grown almost into an obsession within a matter of days. I had to get into the flat. I had to find out. But what would I be looking for? I had no idea.

Netta agreed to drive me up to Brixton so that I could hand them to him. I did not tell her about my proposal to search the place or that Father, as I had established by several clandestine telephone calls, had been away for days.

In due course Netta manoeuvred the hearse into the turning by the block of flats I had last visited with James. With my girl at my side, and a few backward glances, I quickly made my way into the entrance. Once inside, we hurried past the lift to the stairs and ran up the four flights to the landing. There was no one about. I rang the doorbell. No reply. I struggled with the three keys, as I had seen Father struggling with them, and after half a minute of anxious fumbling the door opened. The same smell of coffee, Brasso and bleach. 'Are you sure this is all right?' said Netta. 'I don't like snooping.'

'Of course it's all right. Father said I could drop in any time. Come in.'

'But they're not your keys. I don't like it.'

'Look,' I said, 'that's a picture of James's real father, Henry Usher, and that's Clotworthy, one of his ancestors, and that knife was taken from a Dacoit who was trying to murder Father. He was killed by Henry.' We went back into the hall and I opened the second drawer of the chest. 'This is the pistol I told you about. Father took it from a Japanese soldier he killed.' I took it out of the holster and handed it to her. 'Yes, it works, and this is the original belt. Can you see the bullet holes?'

'Are those bloodstains? How horrid.'

'And here's the photograph album. Somewhere there's a photo of the previous owner. Look, here he is.'

'God, how morbid. Come on, let's get out of here,' said Netta. 'This isn't right. I'm not going to be a party to this, Thomas . . . I'm going outside, all right,' and out she went, leaving me alone in Father's flat. For fear of the supernatural I turned the key in one of the locks and put the bunch in my pocket.

I did a quick tour of inspection. A postcard embossed with a maroon portcullis read *Venice for Christmas? Ring. N.* So that's where he was. He and Nicholas York were living it up in the Maiden City.

Father's bedroom contained a single bed, a desk filled with clutter, a chair and an enormous mahogany wardrobe with sliding doors. I looked in the desk first. Keys, string, Lion Gum, and what was this? French letters! And all marked *Wien* like the ones he had given me. What could Father's woman be like? It was difficult to imagine old people doing that sort of thing, but with Father the idea seemed absurd. But the evidence was there. The other drawers were full of clothes, maps and general bachelor junk. I tried the wardrobe. One end contained all his jackets and suits, and his academic get-up. More shirts and mortar-board on top, and on the floor countless bandages and dressings. I shut the door and opened the one at the other end. On the floor beneath a row of hanging shirts was one of those nasty executive briefcases with a combination lock. Really, Father, I'm surprised at you. I tried it. Locked. Good. This looks promising. Three numbers each side. No problem. It'll either be his telephone number or his birthday, and I sat down on the bed and tried the first three digits of his telephone number . . . no luck. His birthday . . . one side snapped open, then the other. I looked inside and saw a sealed envelope containing, so it declared in Father's handwriting, his will. Both ends of the envelope were sealed with Sellotape under which he had signed his name. Who did he think was going to pry into his affairs?

Building Society passbook, Premium Bonds. What was this? Yellow newspaper cuttings held together with a rusty paperclip, and a few old letters:

Campbell and Rosyth Banking

Major T Lamb, M.C.,
.......................School   July 1956

Dear Major Lamb,
                    Re: The Hon. Henry Usher

I thank you for your letter of the 26th Ultimo and am pleased to note that the sale of the Aston Martin has been effected and that we may anticipate receiving a substantial payment in the near future. As you will realise, nothing will give me greater pleasure than to clear this unfortunate transaction from our books.

  I would take this opportunity of thanking you for your kind help and assistance in this matter and if you do manage to obtain Mr. Usher's present address, I would be greatly obliged if you could advise me of same so that I may correspond with this gentleman direct.

                    Yours sincerely,
                    Robert M. Fraser
                    Director

I just can't tear myself away! There are *thousands* here in L.A. and I am busily working my way through them. So far I have made a good start!
                    Nicholas

DINGHY FOUND
Hunt for Missing
Heir Continues

The dinghy from the 36 foot ketch Imogen has been found near Wittering off the Sussex coast, according to Sussex police. The Hon. Henry Usher, heir to Viscount Castledown, is missing from the luxury yacht which he hired from a local boatyard on March 1st.

Although signs of occupation were found on board there is no trace of the missing heir who was last seen on Monday morning when he left the Seaview Hotel for the boatyard. He had been staying at the hotel for two weeks. He had booked the room under the name of Toby Lamb and had told the proprietor that he was planning to circumnavigate the globe.

Local police suspect that the yacht may have gone aground on a notorious sandbank outside Chichester Harbour and that the missing man may have taken to the dinghy in order to summon help.

May 1954

The Hon. Henry Usher

To one shooting-stick Umbrella

£10-10-0d

ACCOUNT OVERDUE

MISSING HEIR; GIRL SOUGHT

A young brunette may help to solve the mystery of the vanished playboy, the Hon. Henry Usher, the handsome son and heir of Viscount Castledown, who vanished last week.

The girl was seen visiting the 39-year-old six footer shortly before he disappeared from his luxury yacht. At first, police suspected that Mr Usher had drowned, but although there were indications that he had recently been on board, his passport and other personal effects were missing.

Police sources have confirmed that they believe the missing man to be in Paris. Interpol has been alerted.

A soldier was found dead outside the entrance to Piccadilly underground station late last night. His identity is not being revealed until next of kin have been informed. He is thought to have been battered to death.

MISSING YACHT; PEER'S HEIR SOUGHT

Police and Coastguards are still searching off the coast of Sussex for the 39 year old heir to a Scottish title who disappeared from the luxury yacht *Imogen* which was found adrift last week.

The Honourable Henry Richard Walter Levinge Fitzpatrick Usher is still untraced. The playboy son of Viscount Castledown, who was six feet-four, raced motorbikes and drove an Aston Martin, had been using the name of a friend, Toby Lamb, who was not available for comment yesterday.

The missing heir's father, speaking from his family seat, Keep Castle, in the Scottish Highlands, said yesterday "I have been told by the police that my son is missing and that he was using an assumed name but apart from that I know nothing. I have no idea who the crew were or whether he was planning to sail round the world with a girl."

BODY FOUND

A **headless** corpse was washed up off the Sussex Coast at West Wittering yesterday. It is thought that the badly decayed remains may be those of the Hon. Henry Usher who was believed lost at sea last year. The body has been taken to Portsmouth for a post-mortem examination.

copy   Sheet 2

try to obtain a little more than Rupees twelve thousand only for the Aston, and I can expect at least four thousand for the Norton and the Vincent. As soon as I receive his reply I shall at once accept even if he persists in the offer at that price and that will be that. Please be reassured that I shall, of course, settle the account in full the moment funds are received.

May I ask you to be kind enough to keep my passport safely so that it may be returned to Nicholas York as soon as the final cheque has been cleared, and to extend to me just a little more of your kind indulgence which I have much appreciated. Actually, your money is perfectly safe.

Yours sincerely,

(Henry Usher)

My dear Toby,

Thank you so very much for your letter and for the £1 you enclosed with it. I shall at last be able to have my shoes re-soled. Your extraordinary generosity has saved me from the humiliation of having to line them with newspaper.

Toby, I am sending this by express delivery in order to impress on you the urgency of getting at the very least £100 into my account. Will you please go straight to Coutts and transfer the money immediately on receipt of this letter. By doing so you will not only be storing up treasure for yourself in heaven but will have the honour of serving

Your devoted friend
Henry

TELEGRAM
MAJOR LAMB
ARE YOU ALL RIGHT PLEASE TELEPHONE EARLIEST
CONVENIENCE=H+++

TELEGRAM
MAJOR LAMB
REQUIRE IMMEDIATE ASSISTANCE=H+++

Toby, my old and respected friend what shall I say
to you at the last, what shall I say? So sorry, dear
old man. I know I've failed you but if I can wait
for you I will, or if I can help in any way, I will.
Am sending you my signet ring. Wear it with my
crest always in memory of one who always loved
you, honoured you and respected you. Please get
my Rolex out of pawn – Only £10 – and wear it.

H

THIS IS THE LAST WILL of me HENRY RICHARD
WALTER LEVINGE FITZPATRICK USHER made
the 4th day of May one thousand nine hundred and
fifty four
1. I hereby revoke all former wills and testament-
ary dispositions heretofore made by me especially
one drawn in favour of Nicholas York since I consider
his friendship of late to have been rather limited and
that he has been amply rewarded for his services by
the provision of a first class ticket to Bombay . . .

The sound of keys jangling outside a door can have an
arresting effect. 'Ha-ha.' Voices. Oh my God, Father was back.

I slipped into the wardrobe with the briefcase. It wasn't
Netta's voice. The stranger was a man. Should I have brazened
it out? After all, I had an excuse, I was there to return the keys
he had given to James.

I tried to quieten my panic-stricken breathing. The wardrobe
door was not quite closed. As if by design the tiniest crack
remained. Just enough for me to see out. Scared as I was,
my thoughts were racing. Did Henry, too, have a shooting-
stick umbrella, or had he given it to Father as a present? A
trivial point, but what about those newspaper cuttings? They

dated from the time when Father had appeared after the daffodil-picking to announce his imminent departure; Henry had disappeared at the same time as Father, having hired a boat in Father's name. And what about the brunette?

'Help yourself to a lager, Kevin. There's a glass in the kitchen on the shelf. I'll just change my dressing.'

Oh God, Father was opening the wardrobe, but at the other end. Now he was shutting it again. He hobbled off and I could hear him in the bathroom. Sound of running water, coughing, spitting, gargling, flushing water. Kevin was now in the bedroom sipping lager from a can a few feet from me. He was sitting on the end of the bed: a stocky fellow, scruffily dressed and with a tattooed forearm which he kept raising as he drank. Who was Kevin? What was he doing on Father's bed?

He put down the empty glass and started to take off his shirt which he dropped on the chair at the side. The fellow was getting undressed! Sounds of hobbling offstage. Father was on his way. Now a zip was being undone and a pair of trousers followed the shirt, and then some Y-fronts.

'Ha-ha, I hope you're good and ready. You seem to be all right! Mmmm! Arrgh!' and they disappeared into the bed. As the bed was at right-angles to my end of the wardrobe I could still see what was going on. Father's hairy chest was visible under his blue vest and he was reaching over to the drawer of his desk, fumbling with a tube of something and a French letter.

Oh God, Father was climbing aboard.

'Ooo yes, mmm, you are a bad boy. What's this, mmm, all ready for action. I've found what I wanted,' and a minute of frantic heaving and groaning followed. 'Mmm, yes, yes, YES, I like that I like thaaaaooOOOAAAAAAAAA!' So it wasn't just when he sneezed that Father turned the volume up to max. He swung out of bed and I caught a glimpse of bandaged leg and, for a moment, of the organ that had generated me, wrapped as it was in its plastic sheath. 'ARRRGH! Well, that was pretty successful. I'll just go and mop up. I haven't had so much as a wank for a fortnight.' He hobbled away.

Kevin swung out of bed and reached for his clothes.

Offstage: running water, coughing, spluttering, gargling and now, as he hobbled back, the smell of Dettol. 'Want another beer before you go?'

'No, thanks, Toby. I've got another job lined up. Shaftesbury Avenue.'

Father was scrabbling in his wallet as they made their way out of the room. 'Seven and six for the taxi, and I'll make it ten shillings for the extra this time. Is that all right?'

'Yeah, Toby, thanks a lot. When d'you want me to come over again? I got nothing on Tuesday.'

'Give me a ring. Not this week. I'll need some time to recover, ha-ha. Yes, next week sometime, before I go away. Wednesday afternoon. The flight leaves at five, I think it is. You can take me to the airport afterwards. How about that?'

'Okay, done. I'll book you in for the afternoon. See ya, then, Toby. Thanks.'

'Bye . . .'

I had seen some strange sights that day, but what seemed to me to be the oddest thing was still to come. While I pondered my fate in the wardrobe and reflected dully on what had happened and what it signified, I could hear Father making tea in the kitchen. At some point I would have to make a break for it. But not yet. Father was bound to take his tea into the sitting room, and, with luck, I could then slip away.

Yes, he was limping along the corridor rattling a tray. So far, so good. 'ARRGH!' He was settling down in his armchair. 'James, James, James,' he said, and then it began, the strangest thing of all, the unmistakable sound of sobbing. Father was weeping, howling rather, over his tea.

'Drive,' I said to Netta a few minutes later. 'Just drive.'

CHAPTER 16 · *Visions*

A DAY OR TWO later I was lying on my bed in the caravan trying not to think when I heard Mother's booted footsteps slopping on the grass outside. She announced her presence with the usual 'Are you there?' and opened the door. She had a letter in her hand, and panic set in. 'From your father. For God's sake don't leave it lying about. God knows, Frank's difficult enough at the moment. Are you planning to lie there for ever?'

'How's Aunt Mary?' I said.

'Bad,' she said as she tossed the letter on to my bed. She shut the door and I heard the sound of her wellingtons retreating over the wet December grass. A letter from Father. Christ! He'd found out about my snooping! *The letter killeth.* Before opening it I put on the kettle for my morning tea. I needed to steady my nerves.

> Dear Thomas,
>
> I am planning to leave England next week and would like to see you before I go. I suggest we meet for a sandwich at the Salisbury in St Martin's Lane at half past one. St Martin's Lane runs north from Trafalgar Square, and the pub is a quarter of a mile up on the left. I enclose £1 to cover expenses. If you don't telephone I will assume you are coming.
>
> As ever,
> Father

What on earth did this portend? What evidence had I left behind? Wednesday, the day Father had told his tattooed friend to drive him to the airport, presumably after various preliminaries had taken place. Where did I fit in?

'I think you need a holiday,' said Father who was perched

on a high stool at the bar. He had draped the umbrella-stick over the brass rail and knocked it so that it swung every time he moved his elbow, 'and I propose to make you a small allowance. I'm going away this afternoon . . . Oh, a little trip. Didn't your mother teach you not to be inquisitive? And I thought you might like to have the use of the Humber . . . At least a year . . . I may pop back of course, in which case I might ask you to bring it up to Brixton. It's in the garage. Here's the key. I disconnected the battery in case you didn't turn up. You didn't reply to my letter. Netta can give you lessons. You can pass your test in a few weeks. I've arranged for your name to go on the insurance. The allowance should cover tax and maintenance costs. Have you got a bank account? I've signed the form. All you have to do is fill in the details and send it off. If it breaks down seriously you'll just have to do the best you can or else dump it. These old things keep going surprisingly well. Twenty pounds a month. You get the maximum grant, don't you, because you haven't got a father, that's right, isn't it? And the holiday, yes, I thought you and Netta might like to get away for a week before you go back to your studies, on what do they call them? A package tour. Madeira or the Costa Brava or somewhere like that, so here's a hundred pounds cash, strictly on that understanding. Agreed?'

Blood money. Father had never shown any inclination to shell out on my behalf before, except on the holiday with James, and, mercenary child that I was, I thanked him and held my peace.

Half an hour later a stocky fellow with a tattoo hidden beneath one arm of his scruffy pullover put his head into the pub, and in response to Father's nod and the slightest wave of the finger of command came forward and permitted himself to be introduced.

'Hi, Toby.'

'Kevin, this is Thomas.'

I didn't say that I'd seen him before.

'Hi, I'm Kevin. Taxi's outside, Toby.'

'Just coming. Oh, while I remember it, do you know what happened to Henry's signet ring? Would you mention it to Mary? I'd like it back some time. Must be off. I hope the car won't let you down. Don't go killing yourself in it, will you?'

'Goodbye, Father.'

'You're sure you know the way, Kevin?'

Netta and I went to Chichester next day and booked a week's skiing in Bernwald, a resort in the Tyrol some five miles or so from Steinpass. A special offer was advertised in the agent's window at £40 a head, departing Saturday. I had, of course, telephoned the hotel at Steinpass and had learned that it was shut for the winter because there were no facilities for skiing. I desperately wanted to go back. It was nothing to do with my mistress of the campsite. She belonged to a different past from the one I wanted to explore. This time it was James I wanted to see.

I had mentioned to Netta that Bernwald was close to Steinpass, where I had stayed in the summer with Father and James, but I hadn't told her how excited I felt about being within striking range of the place.

I had to try hard not to like skiing. For the first time since James's death I was enjoying myself and I felt guilty about it. I didn't want to enjoy myself. I didn't know, at that time, that you should fend off grief as long as you can; it'll get you in the end of course, when you least expect it, but you can often give it the slip for a while, and if you can, you should. But I felt it my duty to grieve. I was a man with a mission.

After a day on the slopes when I pushed myself so hard that the instructor shook his head and asked what I had done that I wanted such punishment, Netta and I dragged ourselves back to the hotel, where we compared bruises, made love and slept. I dreamed of snow; whiteness, covering, forgetting, obliterating, blanking out, and awoke to remember that James was dead, and to think of him rotting in the earth. Death's black wings had closed over him and he was falling further, ever further from me, and even as death corrrodes the flesh the knowledge of death corrodes the souls of those left behind. James was in his grave. I was on a skiing holiday with Netta staying a few miles from Steinpass, where James and I had been so happy a few months before. Could the world change so dramatically? Was it possible?

And on the second day, after lunch in a mountain café, which was crowded because so much snow was falling, I made an excuse and abandoned Netta to the afternoon class. I packed a small bag with spare socks, boots and a quarter-bottle of duty-free whisky and set off to catch the afternoon bus to Steinpass. I had done my homework. It was easy.

Half an hour later, I stepped out into the snow and listened to the bus chugging away. As the smell of the exhaust faded, I found myself alone, overlooking a flat, snow-covered plain; the lake had vanished, and all the familiar features, the hotel, the castle, the church and the bridge, had been scaled down by the thick layer of snow which covered them. Everything seemed much smaller, everything except the mountains. There were no colours. This was a white landscape etched here and there with black and I was seeing it through a snow-filled sky, through the heavy snowflakes which fell on my lips and eyes. ˗

A sign in Gothic script on the door of the hotel proclaiming it shut came as no surprise. I knew the hotel was shut until March. I set off down the track past the church. There were no footprints. The past was obliterated. I was the first man. Adam in Eden could not have felt more alone when he saw his footsteps imprinted in the dew.

The wooden bridge we had clattered over in the Humber was now a white ramp over a snow-filled gulley. All was quiet as death. There was no sound of rushing water from the stream and waterfall. There was no sound at all save my creaking footsteps and the whirr of snowflakes. There was only silence, the peculiar dead silence of snow.

The Villa Maria, where I had spent so much time with Trudi, was shuttered and locked. Somewhere over there our tents had been pitched. Now blanked out, vanished. Six months ago I hadn't heard of Steinpass. How different the world had been then. How different from when I had first stood here with James.

The snow was so thick that my tracks were ankle deep, and if I stood still for a minute they vanished before my eyes. The present was being erased second by second. I turned up the path that led to the castle. It was hard going in the deep snow and I reflected that for Father, walking must always be like this. That he had kept going so long seemed amazing, and yet he always made light of it, allowing himself to be treated as a comic turn. I stopped on the Roman bridge and looked down across the valley. The snow was beginning to ease up. A few big flakes drifted to the ground. The air became less suffocating. Behind me was no sign of the waterfall which James and I had climbed in the summer – only a white depression in the jagged wall of mountain marked its course and on the other side was the castle to which the mad king had repaired on days like this.

When I had stood on this bridge for the first time with James and Father, James and I had been ignorant of the truth. We had mistakenly believed that Father had been the parent of us both and had been none the worse for it. Father had been a man I admired, worshipped even. Now I knew him for what he was. And James? He lay rotting in a Sussex churchyard. It did not seem possible. Of course at that time I hadn't even had a girl. Was the state of manhood a blessing or a curse? Was the price of understanding too high? If I looked at the snow-covered lake I could see James and myself in our little boat, just as we had been. I could see him laughing as he related his adventures in Vienna. James, James, James. Had I uttered his name aloud? When I reflected afterwards on the events of the day I could not be sure.

Some snow slipped from the roof of the castle with a thud. I looked up. It was then that I saw him. In the window of the projecting turret above the wall painting, I saw a face. High cheek-bones, square jaw, fair receding hair. An older version of James. *It was Henry Usher.* Perhaps the vision lasted two seconds before it vanished. Nothing. An empty window in a deserted castle. I struggled on through the snow to the big archway leading beneath the castle and tried the heavy door.

It was locked. I banged hard. No reply. I banged again and again. Silence.

Had I imagined it? Had I created a vision out of my own despair? I ran back on to the Roman bridge and looked back at the castle. There was no one there. It was beginning to get dark, as dark as it ever gets when the whole world is covered in snow. The bus home was due in ten minutes. I took a swig of whisky and hurried back the way I had come. After a hundred yards I could no longer see my tracks. The wind-blown snow had covered them.

'Where the hell have you been?' said Netta. A fair enough question. 'If I hadn't thought to check that your skis were in the cellar I would have called out the mountain rescue. You are so bloody inconsiderate. Okay, you've been to Steinpass, why shouldn't you? But don't you think you could have said? And you're drunk. You really will go to pieces if you don't watch out.'

I told her what had happened. Previously, I had mentioned nothing of what I had discovered at Father's flat, but now I told her of the newspaper cuttings, and what they had revealed of Henry's disappearance. I could not convince her that I had really seen James's father at the window. She told me that I had imagined the face and that I was overwrought. Was she right? Had I imagined it? I couldn't be sure.

She agreed to go to Steinpass with me in the morning.

We caught the early bus. It had stopped snowing, and by the time we got off at Steinpass the sun was shining from a clear blue sky. The GESCHLOSSEN sign hung on the front door of the hotel. We walked up to the castle. There was no one there. Netta listened quietly to my rantings as we walked back down the track. She was curious and wanted to see more. We walked around the Villa Maria. Under the snow-covered eaves the message read the same:

Zur Herberge hier für kurze Zeit,
Die Heimat ist die Ewigkeit.

'This is your hostel for a short time, the home is eternity,' translated Netta in her prosaic way. 'I suppose this is the place where you screwed that woman. Well, why not? You had to start somewhere and without that you wouldn't have had the courage to try anything with me. So I suppose I should be grateful.'

I took her down to the lake and we did something I had not done before. We walked across it. Here the snow was pure white and untouched and so deep that our dragging boots left four straggling lines. From the other side we looked back for what seemed a very long time, at the castle, the Roman bridge, and the fantastic backcloth of snow-covered mountains. This was surely the landscape of dreams. When I had seen enough and felt sufficiently chastened and subdued we walked slowly back the way we had come.

I returned to the castle once more, on the last day, alone. Getting off the bus outside the hotel I caught sight of Erhard. He was surprised to see me, although he remembered who I was. We sat by the tiled stove together and I told him about James and about my visit to the castle and about the face at the window. Erhard made me some hot chocolate and a ham and gherkin sandwich. No one had lived there since the war, he said. He knew nothing of Henry Usher. Sometimes there were workmen ... the snow got in ... Then we walked up to the castle together, and stood looking over the white and desolate landscape, before he drove me back to Bernwald in his Mercedes.

CHAPTER 17 · *Academic Cares* (*Continued*)

HERE ISN'T MUCH more to say about the past that is relevant to my story. Just a bit of tidying up. Father went away, and I only saw him once in the next ten years and I know little of what he was doing in that time. He told me on one occasion that he had been working for the British Council and on another that he had been teaching at a minor public school. I made no further discoveries about Henry or Father and found out no more secrets. Looking back, I am surprised I didn't at least try to get more information from Mother and Aunt Mary, or even from Uncle Frank, who might have had a greater need to confide in someone. Perhaps I didn't want to know more. Perhaps I had already found out too much.

And Netta? What went wrong? How did I come to be relegated to the world of the outcasts?

We went back to college in the Humber. It had a certain beat-up style and we felt rather grand. Netta had arranged to move from her room in Hall into a house she was to share with four other girls, three of whom she had known at school. The Manse, as this house was called, was one of the houses to get hold of, if you were a student, and it had been carefully passed on from generation to generation. It was not as big as the house Uggers shared which was on the other side of the village, but it had certain attractive features, such as an orangery, a yew hedge and neighbours with peacocks. The Manse was built of mellow brick stained with patches of lichen and was set in half an acre of abandoned garden. The hedges sprouted roses and brambles in wild disarray. The principal indoor feature was a huge Aga which formed the centrepiece of the living room.

There always seemed to be a girl leaning against the Aga, and sometimes there would be a whole row of them. They were long-legged beauties, girls with moneyed-sounding names – Sophie, Pippa, Georgiana, Lucinda. I was overwhelmed.

Sometimes, even now, I ring their names like bells. Where are they now? Middle-aged housewives, no doubt, living fat and prosperous lives. One of them was to be an instrument of my downfall.

I was still grieving bitterly for James. Because of his death there was no longer any right and wrong. Ordinary rules no longer applied; his death tainted all that was good and confirmed the rottenness at the heart of things. I was lost. Even Netta's love could not redeem me. Netta was kind to me, even maternal. She humoured my evil moods and offered comfort when it was needed. I didn't reciprocate. James's death was my loss. No one else was entitled to a look in. I became a Young Werther and stormed in and out at will. Acting is a tiring business and I needed the solitude of my room in the faceless block to rest between performances.

Netta taught me to drive, or rather she accompanied me while I was learning, giving advice now and then like the infamous 'Accelerate round corners. Go on. *Go on,*' and the thrilling 'Zig-Zag, *Zig-Zag,*' whenever the new level-crossing was about to close. Even before I passed the test I used to drive alone whenever I felt so inclined. If I was defying God, lesser authorities didn't count for much.

I saw a lot of Uggers, whose idiosyncrasies struck me as extraordinary for a young person. It usually takes fifty years to develop them, but Uggers appeared to have been born eccentric. The key to his personality appeared to be a complete lack of self-consciousness. How many times I arrived to find him clutching a doorhandle which had become detached from a door and staring at it in amazement, or explaining that the shelf in the kitchen had fallen down when he had reached up for a tin. All the furniture in the house he shared was broken. He was unable to sit still in a chair without rocking forward and from side to side at the same time. Furniture wasn't constructed for people like Uggers.

I was out bicycling one Sunday afternoon when I saw a harassed-looking Uggers scrambling down a bank followed by his two setters. He was clutching a large canvas bag and having difficulty with brambles and mud and he was eating a sandwich. 'Uggers! What the hell?'

'I had to pull the communication cord and jump out a mile from the station. There were inspectors on the train. *Inspectors.* The first one I pulled didn't work so I tried another, just like that, and we had to scramble out – didn't we, Rum, didn't we, Christie? These old bottles are damned heavy. I've got a bumper selection this time.' He slid down to the lane, sweating profusely and covered in dead leaves, sticks and mud. 'The guard and one of the inspectors chased me. Actually *chased* me,' he continued as he took the last bite of sandwich. 'I had to run like crazy and lift the dogs over a fence into the Rector's garden. I couldn't get them over the wall into the lane. I had to open the back door to let him know I was there. He was rather uncivil as a matter of fact. Told me to get the dogs off his leeks, didn't he, Rum, didn't he, Christie? He was having some kind of reception. This sandwich is very good, I must say. I wish I'd taken more.' A car screeched to a halt. 'Rum, you naughty girl, Christie . . . You're not going over to the Manse by any chance? No . . . why not come back with me?'

Uggers always seemed to be at the Manse when I called in. I didn't notice at first and when I did I took no notice. I couldn't take this amiable and bearded circus strongman as a threat. He organised more work parties at Wychford and asked me along. I didn't go. Neither did Netta, the first time.

Netta became less available. When I arrived at the Manse having been out all day blessing the woods with my grief, I sometimes found that she was not there. She went to Uggers' for tea and she spent hours listening to his old gramophone. They went to parties together. I wasn't cross with her. Not really.

The Manse was never locked. When I turned up one evening I wandered in and found that the Aga was bare. No one was riding the range and I thought the girls were all out until I heard a voice from upstairs. It was Sophie. I pushed open the door of her room and sat down on the edge of her bed. The others had gone to a party, she said; she hadn't felt like going herself. I slipped my hand under the covers, more to see what would happen than anything else. She was wearing only a man's collarless shirt, and as I ran my hand along her thigh she made no attempt to stop me. We continued to talk as if nothing was going on. I eased off the covers and as I looked down I could see the sweet dark mound of hair parting under the pressure of my fingers. You can guess what happened next.

Sophie said there was no chance of Netta coming back early and hinted that Netta was carrying on in a similar fashion with Uggers. I didn't believe her and I didn't want to stay. Having committed the act of darkness I wanted to get out.

The girls took it in turn to prepare Sunday lunch in the Aga, usually roast chicken or a casserole, and I rarely missed this. After one of Netta's bourguignons, cooked to Birgit's recipe, I slipped upstairs to find Sophie. The thought of Netta being only yards away added spice to my crime.

Similar activities continued for several weeks. I didn't tell anyone and I assumed Sophie would also hold her peace, but alas, she didn't. After a while Netta became distant and I grew alarmed. So alarmed that I suffered the humiliation of impotence with Sophie. It's an embarrassing business being in bed with an eighteen-year-old beauty who wants you to make full use of her body when you can't oblige. Yet in a way I was pleased, because I felt my fate as far as Netta was concerned was sealed by my failure with Sophie. I thought I knew the next step.

A couple of days later I woke up in Netta's bed and asked her to marry me. I was both shocked and relieved when she said no, but I wanted a reason. By way of an answer she told me that she wanted to sleep with Uggers. Not that she *had* slept with Uggers but that she wanted to. I was stunned. Uggers of all people. Uggers, the performing bear, the bottle pilferer. I stormed out. How could she behave like this when I was prepared to make the supreme sacrifice?

I went straight to Uggers' place and let myself in. He was still in bed, lying in sepulchral gloom complaining of a headache. I flung back the curtains and spat out my accusations. I accused

him of betraying my friendship and my trust. I threatened to
kill him, and I succeeded in making him blanch. Uggers was
impressed with my anger, just for a while, and when he had
stopped saying 'I see, I see,' and stroking his beard in sage-like
fashion, he got out of bed and stretched his Sumo-like frame
before me, clad as he was in his underpants. He then patted
my shoulder in paternalistic fashion, looked at his watch and
suggested a trip to the pub. He was calm and full of understanding and let me buy the beer.

She spends every day with Uggers. She's there the whole
time. Why doesn't he fuck her and get it over with?

All is dross, including Helena. Had a session of *haut-chagrin*
for ten minutes but recovered in time for dinner with Sophie.
No sex. Her lap is a sea where other boats than mine will
founder. I just await the death stroke now. When it comes
it is expected and will give no cause for outward display or
over-indulgence. Cold, cold, my boy.

The fatal call: 'I have slept with Uggers, but I'm ready
to come back to you for good.' I hung up.

> There are some things Netta which cannot be forgiven.
> I know this doesn't sound fair or logical but emotions
> are not fair or logical. They exist on a different plane. I
> concede that I expect higher standards from you than I
> have been prepared to consider for myself, but this does
> not affect the present position. Uggers is no better than
> an animal and how you could demean yourself in this
> bestial fashion is beyond my comprehension.
>
> Whatever the arguments, the outcome must remain
> the same. You have betrayed me and must be excised
> from my life. This is the price we both have to pay.
> The operation must be carried out as swiftly and as
> painlessly as possible.
>
> You may think that without you the foundation of
> my life will crumble and that this towering mansion
> must totter and fall . . .

As swiftly and as painlessly as possible. Ha-ha, as Father would say. Brave words. Reckless words ... You could say that twenty-four years later one of the patients has not fully recovered from the operation referred to.

Of course I took the letter back a few weeks later. I found it in her handbag when I was going through her things and pitched it into the Aga. Even though I felt it to be a masterpiece I didn't want anyone to see it ... Not then.

At first I didn't appreciate how far it all went, or how much I loved her. It was as if my feelings had been underground, percolating in undefined channels, as the law of Tort defines the risk involved in keeping dangerous substances on your property. My feelings for Netta had seeped inside over all the years I had known her and had crystallised in some secret part of my body. I thought I could cope, but suddenly the pain started, the terrible ache of absence.

I was in the faceless block tidying up my room at the time. It was as if I had been struck with an axe, it came so suddenly, the realisation that things could never be the same. You may have felt a similar sense of despair at some stage but, when you weigh the accounts, please remember that I had known Netta all my life. I could not remember having existed without her. I could not imagine not having her in my life. I had not always been aware of my love for her. I had taken her for granted, but only in the same way that I took my own limbs and organs for granted. I *was* Netta and Netta *was* me. I can see myself pacing up and down inside my little white cell, the hot tears starting to my eyes. Oh, the interminable length of a single minute ...

I hated her of course. She had been so intolerably arrogant. In order to teach me a lesson she had gone ahead with cold-blooded murder, a crime for which there was no forgiveness. The fatal knife had been plunged. There was no going back.

I'm not saying I didn't sleep with her again. I did, but I did it out of hate. A couple of weeks later, for instance, I forced her, ripping her blouse and leaving money for her on the table as compensation. *Here's money for your pains.*

No doubt I wasn't in my right mind. I hadn't slept for days. I kept going over the whole business in my head. Her with Uggers, inch by inch, *the slime that sticks on filthy deeds.* I felt a sense of limitless despair, of despair without hope of end. I'm told it's a common enough phenomenon.

Later in the day I sent a telegram. The Browning Version. Can you imagine the telegram boy's red BSA ticking over outside as he opens the gate and knocks on the door, and Netta's face as she reads it in the girl-lined room?

JUST THIS OR THAT IN YOU DISGUSTS ME HERE YOU MISS OR THERE EXCEED THE MARK

After sending the telegram I felt pleased with myself, like a child who packs his bags having told his parents that he's leaving home. *Home.* And I've never been able to get back. I still dream of it, of course, but even if the door is open, the room, or the garden, is empty.

I'd been back in the faceless block for an hour when she charged in. 'You think you can do just what you like, don't you? You think you can get away with murder, and all because of James. You think you're the only one who's suffered, that you've been singled out by fate ... it hasn't even crossed your mind that other people might have cared about him too. I loved James, do you hear me? *I loved James.* Yes. You were second best. He even tried to make love to me, oh yes, and I wanted him to, but he couldn't – he was too knotted up about your bloody father. Yes, that's it. *I would have had James if I could.* You were second best, second bloody best. And how you had the nerve to send that *foul* telegram when you've been screwing that cow I live with . . .'

I sat down on the bed. Netta went to my cupboard and pulled out the silk shirt Father had bought James in Venice and ripped it in half. I turned towards the wall. 'Carry on. Smash the place up if you want to. It won't change anything. You're no better than a whore.'

'If I'm a whore, you're a male whore. What's the difference? At least I *like* him. No sane person could like *her.* Oh, what's the use?' and out she went, slamming the door. After a minute's indecision I picked up my jacket, and followed. I was too excited to hang around and calculated that I could easily get over to the Manse in the car before she got back and if Sophie was around I could take her to the pub. Netta wouldn't take that lying down.

I looked around for the Humber for a few minutes before realising it had disappeared. Stolen. I got to a telephone and rang the police. Would I go round to the station and give details?

I was halfway to the police station before I noticed that my keys were not in my pocket. Back in the block I re-ransacked my room. No sign of the keys. Netta had pinched the Humber. I went down to the phone, rang the police once more, and told them I'd found it.

I cycled over to the Manse. There was no sign of the Humber or Netta, but three of the girls were riding the range, as usual. 'Was she mad,' said Pippa. A statement, not a question.

'I've had enough,' said Sophie. 'I'm moving out at the end of the month. Netta's been foul. She came roaring through the gate in your car, banged her way into her room and banged out again. She didn't say a word. Then she roared off. I reckon you're in big trouble.'

'So you don't know where she's gone?'

'Haven't got a clue, but I hope it's a long way away. Honestly, I reckon she's mad enough to kill someone ... That telegram you sent! We all thought it was ... well, you know, a kind of corny marriage proposal ... She went kind of bright red and tearful and screwed it up. We got it out of the bin later, didn't we, Luce? That telegram was a *big* mistake on your part.'

I cycled off to Uggers' place. I don't know what exactly I had in mind if the car had been there, but it wasn't. I went to the pub and strode in like the hero of a Western. There he was, leaning against the bar. 'Mon cher ami, not going to assassinate me I trust? You look dreadful. Please let's not have any violence. You nearly got me a few minutes ago.' I noticed his coat was covered in bracken, rather as it had been when he had escaped from the ticket inspectors on the train.

'What do you mean,' I said, 'I nearly got you?'

'You came at me in that car of yours. I had to dive into the hedge. I could have been killed. I've been feeling rather fragile lately anyway. My central nervous system's shot to pieces. Allow me to buy you a beer. A pint for my murderous friend,' he called to the landlady.

'Problems? Women?' she said to me as she pulled. 'Don't worry, dear. You're young. Things'll sort themselves out. That's three and six.' I looked round for Uggers. 'Gone to the Gents, love,' she said, holding out her hand for the money.

I paid and Uggers re-appeared. The door opened and the dogs went to meet a new arrival, someone who shared with Uggers. 'Ah, Charles. Tom here tried to kill me tonight. Do get him a beer, Tom, there's a good chap. Truth is I'm a bit strapped for cash. There's no market for bottles at the moment. The bottom's fallen out of it.'

'I expect you've glutted the market,' said Charles. 'Have you known each other long?' he said to me.

'Too damn long. Somehow your friend has managed to smash up my entire life, or what was left of it.'

'I heard about your brother. I'm very sorry.'

'My cousin . . . Thanks.'

'Thanks for the beer. Uggers, do try and keep these dogs under control.'

'Rum, Christie, don't be such naughty girls. Charles, this is Tom who tried to murder me just now. Tom, this is Charles, my oldest and richest friend. Last time we dined together he offered me strawberries. *Strawberries*. Don't you remember, Charles? I'm allergic to them. I was in the san three times at school with swiss roll.'

'We were at prep school together,' said Charles. 'He was always a hypochondriac. But we felt he made up for it in other ways. Before going to bed he used to put his chamber-pot on his head, like a helmet, didn't you, Uggers? Until Broad pissed in it first. Don't you remember?'

'Rum, Christie, come here . . .'

It gave me a measure of consolation to think of my rival clad in pyjamas with a piss-pot on his head. Charles got a round. I liked him. 'Don't remind me about Broad, for God's sake,' said Uggers. 'At least it was bath night and I was able to go to matron for another hair wash and a clean pair of pyjamas. Okay, one friend tries to kill me, another reminds me of Broad ... Rum, stop doing that, will you? But you did. I saw the car. I know the number ... What? Netta's pinched it? Why would she do that? Why should she be upset? We're civilised people. And what's wrong with you? Why are you shaking? Look, I'm very fond of her. She's a dear girl, a dear girl. I'm not saying you can't see her. Not *share* exactly. It's just that we don't own each other. You're awfully old-fashioned. Come on, let's arm-wrestle ... No? Come to think of it, I've got a frightful headache,' and he shook his Rastafarian locks as if to test the veracity of his contention.

'Yes, he was always a hypochondriac,' said Charles. 'You can't leave any kind of tablet or medicine about when he's around. He helps himself ...'

'No, Charles, for God's sake ... Oh, very well. Yes, I did help myself to Jonathan's tablets and, yes, he did swap them with Lula's pills, and I swallowed a couple. But it's not true that I started to grow breasts. It's a gross calumny. Okay. It makes a good story. Go ahead and laugh. It might have done me serious harm. Tom ... could you possibly lend me ten bob? It's my round.'

At about three in the morning Netta burst into my room and put on the light. 'I hope we're not going to have a repeat of the earlier performance,' I said. I had been shielding my eyes from the bright light, but I now saw her standing before me brandishing a pistol. A not unremembered pistol. Father's pistol. I sat up.

'It's loaded.'

I was rather enjoying myself. 'Go on,' I said, 'pull the trigger. You'll be doing us both a favour.'

'I never understood what you saw in that film,' she said and thrust the gun a little closer to my head. She was frowning in a most unpleasant fashion and I thought, perhaps this is it, perhaps my number's up. Her face had an expression of cold concentration. She looked desperately unhappy.

'You drove up to Father's flat, in the Humber?'

'Full marks for observation.'

'If I'd returned James's keys when we collected the car I might have lived longer?'

'Don't be funny. This is it. I'm sick of being treated like this. You say you're finished with me, that I'm a whore . . .'

There was an awkward pause. I realised I was scared. These things do happen, after all, especially in novels. 'You must be tired. Why don't you put the kettle on and we'll have some coffee?'

She made a sort of growling noise, jabbed the pistol at me a few times, turned the barrel towards the ceiling and fired two shots. I looked up. Two very small black holes had appeared in the polystyrene above my head.

'You're lucky it's such a long drive,' she said. 'My anger kind of dissipated.' She put the pistol down on the table. There was a knock at the door and my neighbour's head appeared. 'I thought I heard shots,' he said.

'Sorry,' I said. 'We blew up a couple of French letters and popped them. The bang was bigger than we expected.' Netta's head was in her hands. He left us to our fate and went back to bed.

I suppose those two bullets still lodge in the ceiling of my old room in that faceless block. Two Japanese bullets intended for an Englishman . . . intended for Father.

I played with the gun for a while. I might have shot Uggers. I might have shot myself. I did neither. In due course, when I happened to be passing and after making the usual phone calls, I replaced Father's war-time trophy in the drawer in the hall of his Brixton flat amongst his underpants. This time I didn't stay. There was a pile of correspondence on the mat, and another on the table. Someone else must have had a key.

And so I lost Netta. Whether it was because of Uggers or because Netta had undergone some kind of catharsis of the soul, I'm not sure. Maybe she had simply outgrown me and the little incident with the gun was merely the parting shot. For me, though, it was a catastrophe.

PART THREE

The Philosophic Mind

CHAPTER 18 · *Earthly Freight*

———

I T'S HARD TO believe that Netta and I have known one another for forty years. We grew up together, studied together, went to bed together. I have always known what was going on in her life. There have been errors and omissions, of course. For instance, twenty years ago, she married someone else. No, not Uggers, but a poncey art dealer introduced by Birgit. She was naïve enough to tell him about us and as a result her doors were closed on me for some years. It was, in many ways, the most difficult time for me – my Blue Period, I call it. As I had forecast at the outset of her foolish venture, however, it didn't last, and after ten years they split up. Netta, who is a partner in a London firm of solicitors, did the divorce herself. It was a simple case; no children and a fifty-fifty carve-up. After that we saw rather more of one another. We became lovers again but somehow we could never be happy for long. She told me that I tried too hard, that I was too intense. I confess I found making love a disturbing and upsetting experience. Nonetheless I still believed and hoped that things would work out. The crisis occurred shortly after last Christmas when I behaved in the most corny fashion. Dining at Rules after the Opera, where we had champagne during both intervals, I asked her to marry me over the trifle. *We can't live together*, that's what she said. And she was right; we can't. The trouble is that although we love one another, whatever that may mean, we have completely different temperaments. In simple terms she has the rational approach and I have the imaginative approach. She thinks illusions are bad for you. I think you have to have them to keep on living. When we get cross she calls me unreasonable and sentimental. I call her soulless and a barbarian. On the morning after that fateful night I told her that the modern woman has abolished the concept of love and replaced it with friendship-and-sex. 'What you want', she said, 'is a bloody goddess.'

What does Netta mean to me now? The truth is that I'm no longer sure. I used to call those painful spasms, when you feel the knife plunging into your heart, moments of *haut-chagrin*. I don't have them now. Little waves of sadness sometimes lap at my toes and from time to time lick even further up my etiolated and scraggy frame. There are times when I long for her, knowing that I cannot have her, knowing that she doesn't exist. Such moments are wind-borne, wine born, and sometimes even contrived; given the mood I can resuscitate them and savour them as a kind of pleasure. I remain faithful to her in my fashion. Perhaps it's the only fashion for people like me who can't accept the real world. I want Netta to be as she once was, the Netta of a quarter of a century ago, the Netta of those pre-university days, of Halnaker Mill. How long ago it seems that we climbed that golden path and lay together in the grass looking down at the distant spire of the Cathedral. We still had James then. Chance is such a powerful god. Incidentally, I didn't believe that business about Netta and James. They may have had a harmless flirtation – after all, youth is a series of flirtations – but I am sure there was no question of *love* other than the love between siblings or their equivalent. I would have known, and, besides, James's sense of honour was too strong. Netta was simply trying to cause me pain by implying otherwise; after all, she was thinking of shooting me at the time. James's character is unimpeachable. He is without stain.

But I know in my heart that if she had married me instead of the poncey art dealer there would be little left by now. To feel intensely for any length of time you have to be alone. You need to suffer. That intensity would surely have seeped away with the dishwater long ago if she had married me. Ours would have become a meat-and-two-veg affair like all the rest; for every moment of heightened sensation there would have been a million ordinary ones when I would have seen her through ordinary eyes. The irony is that she would always have wanted me to see her through ordinary eyes. The Netta I loved was never real.

Steinpass, 20th September 1993. I am sitting on the balcony of my room at the Villa Maria, where, in obedience to Father's instructions, I went to register that afternoon a quarter of a century ago. I don't get tired of the place. It still amazes. There's more traffic, of course, and the hotel would be almost unrecognisable except that I've watched it grow through the years – a huge extension, a gigantic terrace, another floor on top, and even at this time of year there's plenty of trade. Coaches disgorge parties of Hausfrauen in the car park on the other side of the new bridge, and they waddle across to stuff themselves with apfelstrudel and chocolate cake. And the shop by the car park. What tat it sells! This morning I could hear the piped Tyrolean music while I was rowing on the lake. I must speak to Erhard about that. The lake is still impossibly green and as clear as glass. You can see every stick and stone from a rowing boat, and the trout oblige by jumping for flies with a little splash. The colour of the water is constantly changing. Green of course, but every imaginable shade of green, right down to black. It's the same delicious lake all right.

Here at the annexe, a mere quarter of a mile from the hotel, away from the traffic, it is truly quiet. My room is made of wide pine boards stained with a matt grey dye which allows the grain to show through. The roof slopes down to give a large balcony under the eaves where I am sitting now. As soon as I awake in the morning I force myself to step out here in order to see the effects of weather, and in particular, of mist. This morning was fairly typical, for instance, with mist curling up the flanks of the mountain like smoke. In front is a stretch of meadow, then the track, then the campsite.

There is no one about except for a party of gypsies picnicking fifty yards off. Their clothes are those beautiful shades of subdued bright blue and orange, with a washed-out brightness that I like. I suppose they remind me of Mother and Aunt Mary as they used to be. A little girl with long hair and black eyes is playing by the stream. I know her eyes are black because I've just come back from a walk, and passed close by. The old man greeted me in a strange tongue. The women are lolling on the grass with a surly confidence and the men sitting very upright with the natural dignity of outdoor types. Perhaps they work in the forest, and their wives in the hotel. Behind, the mountain rises steep as a cliff and is covered with pine trees, except near the top where a gash of yellow rock streaked with black stands out stark and bare. I say the yellow gash is near the top of the mountain, but from the lake half a mile away it is apparent that this is an optical illusion. From close up, the steepness of the lower section obscures the fact that the mountain goes on rising and rising to a peak that was this morning covered with snow. I can't see the waterfall from here, but I can hear the blast of the water. If you like silence you can find it at Steinpass, but you have to come in winter when the streams are frozen and the lake lies beneath a flat crust of ice and snow. I love the sound of rushing water probably more than any other sound, but writing this makes me realise that I like silence more. The castle is strangely impressive when no one is there. Best of all, I like to think of it in winter, when packed snow glistens white under the stars, and nothing disturbs the ice cold silence.

The sense of calm, of peace, of being at one with nature has been shattered. A few moments ago there was a knock at the door and I opened it to find Erhard standing outside with his huge Alsatian. He had come down specially to hand me a letter and to impart some news by word of mouth. I could see from the handwriting that the letter was from Netta. As you would expect, however, the other news reached me first. *Father is coming.* He had telephoned to announce his impending arrival and I have been ordered to collect him at Munich tomorrow morning. Erhard, like me, is both pleased and dismayed. Dismayed because Father is such a demanding patron and pleased that he is only staying for one night, although, to be fair, I know that, like me, he has a sneaking affection for the old man. His eyes rolled heavenward, and he raised his hands in a gesture which included horror, amazement and surrender. Erhard would have made a good martyr. His expression is just right. Acceptance of what must be endured. Despair through which a heavenly light can be seen shining. I asked him if he wanted a walk, but alas, he explained, his mother was waiting for him. *She says I always leave her*, he said, and we both laughed heartily.

Reeling from the news he had imparted I fell back into my room clutching Netta's letter. I had written to her a few times – well, four times to be exact. I have been lonely here. The letter in my hand was her second reply. Fair enough, you may think. I have time on my hands. If Erhard had been free to come for a walk I could have saved the letter for later. How I would have enjoyed that! As it happened I tore open the envelope like a madman.

> Dear Thomas,
>   Thank you for your letters. It was good to hear from you. I was down in Sussex last weekend and I saw your mother at Birgit's. She says that Frank is in a bad way. He sits in a chair all day and seems to have lost interest in just about everything, even music. Getting old is such a horrid business. She'd been down to Blanc Hall to check your flat, and said it was okay.
>   I suppose I should get to the point I wanted to mention, which is about me and Hector. We've decided to get married. It's fixed for — October at the Registry Office in Chichester. I am sorry that you will have to cut short your holiday but I do hope you will be able to come. I am writing to Uggers to invite him. We both want to keep it small. Hector will be asking a couple of friends at most. Please write and let me know that you can make it, or better still, give me a ring.
>   Lots of love from,
>   Netta

I reached for the whisky. Then I reached for it again. Later, I went for a day-long walk into the mountains. I enjoyed a splendid meal at the hotel before returning to my room. I drank a lot more whisky. I cursed a little. I wept a little. And then I slept the sleep of the damned.

I awoke at about eight and went on to the balcony. It was cold and misty and beautiful. *Nature never did betray the heart that loved her.* I got dressed and walked along the path by the stream to the hotel. The gypsy woman was picking elderberries and putting them in a laundry-basket. After a breakfast of boiled eggs, rolls, ham and cheese I set off in the car through the mountains to collect Father at Munich.

Since Father's return to England, four years ago, I've seen more of him than in all the preceding twenty years. He likes to get up to town when he can, using his free bus pass, and, although I hesitate to admit it, I've really rather enjoyed our weekly lunches in the restaurants in and around St Martin's Lane; I could walk over from the Temple. I tried to get down to Brixton too, at least one night a month, when I would purchase some fillet steak, and cook it for us on arrival. Father would provide the wine, and with luck a bottle of port, and I'd stay the night on the couch. Now that I've packed up working as a barrister and sold my London flat, I don't know how things will work out. We'll see. He's a difficult old man, as you can guess, but at least we did manage to establish some kind of *modus vivendi*.

The train arrived on time and I ran down the platform looking into the windows of the carriages for Father. I couldn't find him. I turned and ran back along the length of the train, worried that I might have missed him. Beyond the platform was a forlorn-looking figure in a wheelchair, surrounded by bags, covered in a rug and sporting what looked like a Bofors gun on his lap. It was a zimmerframe, a replacement for the umbrella-stick of old.

'Thom–as, did you get lost? You never had much sense of direction. I borrowed the chair from the Social Security. What do you think? Now where are we? I think a beer and a sandwich would be appropriate and then I want you to wheel me into the town. I want to pay my respects to some old friends.'

It was a waste of time to suggest leaving things to me. Off came the tartan rug and he hobbled away on the zimmerframe at alarming speed. 'You can put my case in the wheelchair.' I felt like a porter in a Victorian expedition.

'Your hair's looking good, Father.'

'Yes, it's a new one. I think it's better than the others. Just a touch of grey. It's important to look your best when you're my age, don't you think? We'll have a beer over there.'

He waited while I removed his battered leather case and sat down. I wheeled him with one hand and carried the case with the other until we had reached a bar on the far side of the station.

The beer was certainly good. It was a pity I couldn't have drunk more but the authorities are reputed to be a bit hot on drink-driving. Patrons stand outside the bar beside tables. They don't have seats. I suppose it's to encourage them to drink and be off, or to drink and drink. Father was quite happy of course; he was the only customer with a seat.

Time for the off. Kerbs are a problem – how not to tip the old thing out. Also you tend to feel a bit of a villain whenever there's a shout or scream from the passenger. I can still blush (boyishly I like to think). You have to keep your eyes open for the ramps, and plot the next move in advance. Father seemed to take more of an interest in the shops than anything else. If you're shut indoors on your own most of the time it's a treat just being out amongst people doing ordinary things, I suppose.

We came to a busy junction. On the far side was a pedestrian precinct which could only be reached by going down an escalator. How was I supposed to negotiate that with a wheelchair? I stopped.

'Why are we stopping?'

'I've got to see how we get across, Father. It looks a bit tricky. Hold on, and I'll nip downstairs. I expect there's an information office,' and I ran down the escalator to Information, where a pleasant young lady informed me that in Munich there were special lifts for invalids. It was no trouble.

Running back up the escalator, overtaking housewives, babies, rucksacked trippers, I emerged once more on to the street. Father, wheelchair and zimmerframe had vanished.

Beside me was a glass tube with a picture of a wheel-chair embossed on it. Perhaps he'd gone down there. Not daring to follow I retraced my steps and leaped down the escalator, losing myself in a complex of shops until suddenly I was arrested by an announcement over the public address system. *Mr Thomas Lamb.* It was the voice of the young lady at the information desk. Worse was to follow. In the air all around me I could hear a ghostly *Thom–as Thom–as* uttered in Father's querulous tones. *If you're looking for me I'm here.*

When I got to him he was holding forth to the young lady and the Bofors gun was vibrating with the force of imaginary bullets. She seemed as amused as Father. This one always got them going.

'Ah, there you are. Would you like a map? May I present Fräulein Danbauer from Munich.' He affected an apologetic air. 'This is my son Thomas. He doesn't have a sense of direction. None of us is perfect. I can't ski.'

Off we went again. Up in the lift this time and out into the pedestrianised high street. 'Stop here,' said my passenger, 'I want to go into the church.'

Mass was in progress and I wheeled him in as quietly as I could. He did not want to sit at the back. He wanted a Cook's tour in the rattletrap. When I protested he looked over his shoulder, threw off his rug, leapt up with the zimmerframe and clip-clopped towards the altar. At the far end of the church, beyond the altar, was a flight of steps leading to the crypt. 'Ah, here it is,' he called. 'Some old friends. The Wittelsbachs,' and down he hobbled. 'Here we are. ARRGHH. This one's Ludwig, the mad king. I always like to pay my respects.'

All around the crypt were lead coffins, some plain, some fancy. Not to be buried like Wordsworth or burned like Shelley, but to be placed on permanent exhibition, seemed a strange way to end up. I didn't care for the idea, but I could see it appealed to Father.

Back in the precinct he indicated that he wanted to change his dressing and I urged the mobile throne in the direction of the invalid WC. The signs ended with a huge metal door which looked like one of those airlocks you see in films about sinking ships. There was no obvious way in except by means of the buttons at the side. Next to the buttons were some baffling instructions. I pressed: one, two, three. Nothing. I pressed all the buttons at once, and at random. The door swished open and as if by a miracle a young mother clutching her baby emerged from within. To the right of this aluminium cave was the nursing mothers' section. Invalids were straight ahead. Father went inside and shut the door, leaving me in no man's land encased in metal.

Father was taking his time and when a nursing mother appeared and opened the door I rushed out into the subterranean air.

After a few minutes I began to worry that Father was stuck inside and unable to escape. Once more I hurled myself against the buttons and tried the steel wheel and levers. If this had been the *Titanic* I would certainly have gone down with it.

An angry electronic voice began an attempt at interrogation. I tracked it down. By the buttons on the side of the door was a small loudspeaker. I couldn't understand it and it couldn't understand me. In my despair I prayed aloud to the unseen god of technology to get my father out. While this one-sided discussion was going on the door whistled open and out rolled Father as if leading a military procession. I fell in behind.

'Can't you push any faster,' he said. 'I want a sleep before supper.'

Eventually we reached the car. 'The chair folds up, very simply,' said Father. 'It's designed for defectives and helpless cripples.' At that moment, the projecting leg support, which had been swinging wildly about, fell off and clattered to the ground. 'No, you can't tighten it up. I took the bolt out before I left home. To make it easier to manoeuvre.'

CHAPTER 19 · *Intimations*

'M GOING TO have my nap,' Father announced when we arrived at the hotel. 'You can call for me at seven. Not before.'

At three minutes past seven I knocked at his door.

'Come in.'

I obeyed the frail command. Mozart on the radio, the usual clutter of bandages, tubes and jars, *The Golden Treasury* and a P.D. James, but no Father.

'I'm in the bathroom. My toes are quite dreadful. Come and look.'

'I could do with a drink. Shall I see you in the bar?'

'Just look at those feet.'

A somewhat premature butterfly had emerged and was clinging to the bathroom door. Father was dressed in a navy-blue vest half covered with an unbuttoned shirt, gold boxer shorts and a thick knee-length bandage on one thigh. The other leg looked pitifully thin. He began to expound on his more recent operations. 'That bolt's gone and the big toe's doubled back on itself. And that little toe . . . just look at it . . . AARGH . . . that's the arthritic hip; I've tried everything. Brufen, anti-inflammatories . . . you must see the view from my balcony.'

He staggered round the bed, holding on to the furniture like a toddler, until he reached the balcony door which he flung open with all the pride of a Landgraf.

'Better than the campsite, don't you think?'

A lorry thudded by, followed by a procession of cars.

'Better than Brixton, Father.'

'Come up for a bath if you like. I'm sure you'll soon get tired of being down there. It's so primitive. You're such a barbarian. You were always such an awkward boy, not at all like James. How long is it since he died?' Father shrugged his shoulders and looked desperately sad, a familiar expression these days.

'On with the motley . . .'

'Don't rush me. You don't realise I'm not as young as I was. Is that a spot? Ugh, I'd rather have both legs gone than any facial disfigurement.'

'For a man of your age you look pretty good. Hardly a grey hair.'

'Yes, it's like finely spun silk, don't you think? You're beginning to grow grey at the temples. I didn't like to say anything, but when I saw you at the Hauptbahnhof I couldn't help thinking how *old* you look. I expect you think it looks distinguished. Ha-ha. Do you like this tie? I bought it in Venice last year. Do you think it goes with the shirt?' I nodded. Henry's gold Rolex was clipped into place and he began to fiddle with the cufflinks. 'Would you like to help a poor cripple? My fingers are so bent I can hardly use them. Henry left me these links in his will, and the watch, or rather I should say that he sent me the pawn tickets. Henry was never able to manage money. He took the view that it was there to be spent, even if it wasn't.'

'Do you think he faked his own death to claim on the insurance?' I said.

'He had plenty of money from a family trust,' said Father. 'Enough of this nonsense. It's time we were going down for supper.'

'And I suppose it doesn't really matter either way since, as you're always saying, *Henry is dead*.'

'You're so pedantic,' said Father, 'and almost always wrong. You have a touching faith in everything I've ever said. Henry had two passports. He might well have gone to South America. They found a body, you know, a headless corpse, but it wasn't Henry. I didn't tell the coroner about the tattoo. Sometimes one has to edit ... Yes, didn't you know that Henry had a ducal coronet tattooed on his left buttock? He had it done in Bombay. He always had questionable taste. I always thought I should have had a title. I would have carried it so well.' He made a few last-minute adjustments to his hair. 'There,' he added, 'ready,' and lurched forward on the zimmerframe. I followed like an old retainer while he fumbled with the key and locked the door.

Guests staying at the hotel are expected to sit down to

dinner by seven-thirty. We had been lingering in the bar and the waitress had come to give us a tactful reminder, handing Father the à la carte menu which he waved aside, saying, 'Comme d'habitude je mange en pension.' The waitress, a simple girl from Bernwald, looked confused. He waved her away and we stayed firmly in our places until a lost tribe of Americans appeared in search of the dining room. This was Father's cue, and grabbing the zimmerframe he flung himself between them and the corridor, looked back over his shoulder, let out a few gasps and slowed right down. As we processed along the corridor to the slow tap of the zimmerframe and the shuffle of his specially built-up brothel creepers, he looked round and said, 'I hope I'm not holding anyone up,' and stopped for a moment to tidy his hair.

'That's an excellent peruke, Father,' I ventured.

'What is?' he said and lifted the finger of command. 'Honour thy father. Assuming I am your father, of course.'

This was the first time the issue of my parentage had arisen. 'Are you denying paternity, Father?'

'I've given you my name. Isn't that enough? I shouldn't worry. We're all high-nosed Romans.'

We made our way in stately fashion into the dining room and sat down. The waitress brought the soup. The paternity issue had been one of Father's throw-away lines, but I was not going to let the matter drop. 'Do you think James and I were more than cousins, Father?' He gave me one of his ingenuous looks. 'Do you think we may have had the same father?'

'Did I say anything about Henry? ... Well, if you really want to know, it is a possibility, although I wouldn't wish to disown you. Not entirely anyway. Your mother was a very pretty girl in her day and she may not have been as virtuous as you think. She certainly carried on with that doctor fellow.'

'You mean Netta's stepfather?'

'Yes, that's the chap. I caught them at it one day in the raspberry canes. Don't look so shocked. And what about her and your Uncle Frank? It's my guess she didn't wait long after her sister's death to take over her duties. If you don't believe me why do you think she stopped asking me for money after Mary died? Your mother has a sense of right and wrong. Now

when was it that Mary died, four or five years after James? I
was very fond of her, you know.'

'Fond enough to swap partners with Henry when you
were in Venice together?'

'Ah, here is Erhard with some champagne.'

'Mister Lamb ... How are you?' Erhard gave me a
sympathetic roll of the eyes.

'Thomas's mother always had a sense of right and wrong,
Erhard. The thing about Thomas's generation is that they
seem to think they were the first to discover sex.'

Erhard turned his eyes towards heaven.

'My father has suggested that I might not be his son after
all. He says I might have had the same father as James.'

Erhard looked embarrassed then gave his melodramatic
look. 'I must leave you to enjoy your meal.'

We dined in relative silence. The atmosphere was almost
strained. This was unusual since, as a rule, Father was not
aware of other people's feelings. I knew I had scored a hit.

When the last plates had been cleared Erhard reappeared
and looked over to our table.

'Do join us, Erhard,' said Father. 'Thomas's powers of
conversation are limited.'

Erhard obeyed. He looked far from relaxed. A host should
always be put at his ease, so I spoke. 'I shall have time on
my hands again when Father leaves us tomorrow,' I said.
'You know you said you would show me inside the castle
one day, Erhard? How about it? I know you're busy with the
hotel, but if you could find the time? I've been coming here
for over twenty years. I think I deserve it.'

'Of course I must show you. I will take you when your
Father has gone. You will be lonely again then, yes? You
are going to Venice tomorrow, Mister Lamb, and Thomas
will drive you to Innsbruck for the train? And Thomas also
will be leaving soon for the wedding.'

'Wedding?' said Father. 'Who's getting married?'

'Just an old friend,' I said.

'It's not Netta, is it?' asked Father with his usual perspica-
city. 'Netta', said Father to Erhard, 'was far too intelligent for
Thomas, I always thought. And she knew her own worth. She

used to measure it in raisins if I remember correctly. A woman always knows her price. They make Tokay from raisins, don't they, Erhard? Ha-ha, a fine drink.' Erhard squirmed. 'Do you still go to Garmisch, Erhard?'

Erhard made one of his distinctive sounds, halfway between a tut and a shh, and shook his head. 'No,' he said and snapped his fingers at the waitress. Another bottle was needed.

'Why not?'

'No, no, I don't go there since last winter ... tssch ...' and he looked sheepishly round the table. 'It's my mother. She waits for me ... tssch ... She *knows*. Last time when I come home from Garmisch I have a mark on my neck *here*,' and he indicated the spot, with some pride. 'It was late ... about half past two or three ... so I take off my shoes and I go upstairs on my toes ... and then I look up and my mother is at the top of the stairs with her arms folded like this going *tut tut tut*. So I have to stop.'

'Poor Erhard,' said Father.

'When did you first meet Mr Usher?' I asked Erhard. He looked alarmed.

'Mister Usher? ... I was only a boy when he was first here. He was very tall with the blond hair and was very important,' and he nodded in order to lend gravity to his recollection. 'Of course, he was an English Lord.'

'Irish, actually, from Scotland,' added Father, and began to recite:

> Years have roll'd on, Loch na Garr, since I left you,
> Years must elapse ere I tread thee again;
> Nature of verdure and flowers has bereft you,
> Yet still are you dearer than Albion's plain.
> England! thy beauties are tame and domestic
> To one who has roved o'er the mountains afar;
> Oh for the crags that are wild and majestic,
> The steep frowning glories of dark Loch na Garr!

'That was Henry's favourite poem.' Father bowed.

'I sometimes think you must be an actor,' said Erhard.

'James and I thought they were spies,' I said.

'How quaint,' said Father, 'although someone did once ask Henry and me if we were spies. We were driving down to Canterbury in the Aston one day to a cottage we'd rented and we picked up a young soldier hitch-hiking. He was awfully good-looking. After a while he said, "Are you sure this is the way to Folkestone?" "Don't worry, I know the way," said Henry. Eventually we got to the cottage and asked him in for tea, and he stayed the night of course.'

'Tscch.'

'He had to since he would have missed the last boat. In the morning, before he left, he said, "I hope you don't mind me asking, but are you Burgess and Maclean?" Ha-ha.'

'Was Henry a spy, Father? Is that why he disappeared?'

'Henry was far too conspicuous to be a spy. Couldn't blend in.'

'And how's Nicholas? You still see him, don't you?'

'From time to time. He and his wife live off Belgrave Square. I went there for dinner last year.'

'Nicky . . . tschh,' said Erhard, with a wide grin.

'I saw in the paper that he's had a stroke,' I said.

'Did you? How clever of you. That was some time ago. He's quite lively again now. We both are. Did I ever tell you that Nicholas, Henry and I nearly bought a gunboat? Henry's father was in charge of disposing of them after the war. He sold a lot to the Dutch, if I remember; they were fighting a colonial war. Henry thought we should get one and sail round the world in it, calling in at exotic ports for crew who could be dumped at the next port if they weren't up to scratch, ha-ha. "Man, woman or beast, fling it on the bed." He had a romantic streak. Nicholas said it would have given a whole new meaning to the term gunboat diplomacy: "Send out fifteen of your finest youths or we'll blow the place up." Lord Castledown was, alas, not happy with the scheme. He'd never liked Henry. Nicholas was insatiable in those days. One young man reported that he'd arrive from the House of Commons, throw down his *Times* and umbrella, toss his hat into a chair and then . . . ha-ha . . . "Mr York was just like an animal," that's what the young man said.'

'Tschh . . .' said Erhard, gaping with delighted horror.

'Nicholas may have tried it on with Henry once or twice but Henry wasn't having any of that. You know Henry actually paid for him to travel to Bombay first class, of course, but something happened. Mind you, Henry expected one hundred per cent loyalty and two hundred per cent attention. Henry cut him out of his will after that. He was not a man to cross.' Father reached across for the last of the champagne. 'ARRGHH. The leg's been quite good, really.'

In spite of this declaration, I could see that Father was looking far from comfortable. The evening was coming to an end. He turned his head to check that the zimmerframe was in position. 'I miss the umbrella-stick, you know. It's got quite a history, but I won't tell you about it tonight. I have to use this thing now,' and he tapped the barrel of the zimmerframe before adding, 'I wonder if I'll get here next year?'

'I'll miss you when you die, Father,' I said.

'I'll miss you when you die,' he said, and clattered out of the dining room.

A bright warm morning. I had arranged to meet Father at ten to take him out in a rowing boat, and I set off up the track to keep the appointment. Grey bell-hung cows grazed in the lush meadow in front of the Villa Maria. The leaves of the birches had turned gold. The apple and elder trees were heavy with fruit, and wild mushrooms were growing by the path. Men were hard at work in the timberyard and I observed one with an axe stripping the bark of a felled tree while his companion followed up with a hoe-like tool. Wordsworth would not have felt out of place here.

Father was at the breakfast table surrounded by all the paraphernalia of war: dressings, bandages, wheelchair, zimmerframe. He saw me looking. 'No woman's ever loved you enough to shoot you,' he said. 'Do you know a good lawyer? I'm thinking of suing the Japanese government ... for bad marksmanship. They were rotten shots. Will you have coffee?'

I nodded. Father continued his morning monologue. 'What do you think of this shirt? I see you're wearing green. I can't abide green, can you? I'll order another pot.'

'But Father, it's gone ten. Erhard said the weather was going to change for the worse.'

Erhard appeared and confirmed this was indeed so. 'The weather yes, it will be sunny early on and then much rain,' and he put out his hands and rolled his eyes heavenwards.

'We're taking a boat out, Erhard,' I said, looking at my watch. 'Don't you think we'd better get started, Father?'

'I must have my coffee in peace,' he snapped.

'I think I'll go for a walk,' I said.

I walked up the path by the waterfall, as I had done with James twenty-four years before. I was feeling gloomy as any deep wood. Netta was getting married again. Father was as difficult as ever. I forced myself to calm down. Some years ago I acquired the habit of reciting aloud when on solitary walks. It's a sort of exhibitionism which involves me and an imaginary audience; usually God or Netta, or perhaps both. If only Netta knew how much I suffer. And how interesting I am.

> and again I hear
> These waters rolling from their mountain springs
> With a soft inland murmur. – Once again
> Do I behold these steep and lofty cliffs,
> That on a wild secluded scene impress
> Thoughts of more deep seclusion; and connect
> The landscape with the quiet of the sky.

Just before the Roman bridge you can scramble down one side and get to the river bed. From there it's not too difficult picking your way up the mountain. At this time of year the flow of water is relatively light, and you can jump from side to side, criss-crossing the water and climbing up the rocks. By the first turn I stopped and looked back at the bridge – so far, so good – and decided to press on. I suppose I wanted to prove that body and nerve were just as sound as they used to be.

After about half an hour's climb I got as far as I was going, sat on a rock the size of a small room, and looked down at the wild and unfamiliar landscape. The view wasn't as beautiful as you might expect; it was too desolate, too wild, and since the path of the waterfall twists and turns I could only see a few hundred yards. There was no sign of the castle or bridge nor of any other familiar landmark. It was a savage landscape, littered with boulders, stones and broken tree trunks, perhaps more of a floodscape – a scene that might exist at the bottom of a lake.

I looked up at the pines, and the lively sky above them, and I thought of Father. What was I going to do with him? That man had got so much strength in his body, and the spirit to match it. Even with the leg, a murmuring heart and arthritis in all his joints he'll still go on, creaking and groaning, for ever. I got out the notebook I keep in my jacket pocket.

> Father halted by the Roman bridge panting from the effort of the climb, and supported himself on the granite stonework. He didn't look down, but gazed up, up at the face of the mountain with its tiers of trees which stand row after row right up to the summit. In his mind he saw his old friend, the great friend of his life, Henry Usher, beside him. This is the exact spot where they had parted so many years before. Not a day had passed since then but he had thought of him. Tiers of black pines, row behind row behind row, gazed down upon the stage. Orchestra stalls, dress circle, amphitheatre (a place he'd never been). What would it be tonight when they drew back the curtain? He breathed deeply into the cool air, and with his white hand reached into the army bag. He heard the thunder of the waterfall (I hear, I hear) and tasted the sourness of steel as he put the muzzle to his mouth. And then the movement of one small finger brought to a shuddering halt the life of that curious engine, my father.

But where would I be without Father? What would be the most appropriate finale for such a man? Perhaps he might fall into the Grand Canal and drown, while trying to retrieve his umbrella-stick . . .

Preoccupied, I hadn't noticed that the 'lively sky' was now full of black clouds racing along at an alarming speed.

Lightning. Suddenly, up there in my eagle's nest, far above the castle, I felt scared. What if there was a terrific rainstorm? The waterfall and the gods of destruction would go mad for joy. All the rain falling on the mountain would in no time be channelled into this gorge, and what of me? I had no James to help me. No longer could I say that *honest James was with me, my encourager and guide*. I was on my own. Would I perish on the big mountain? It grew suddenly dark. Then a regular polka of thunder and lightning. Take it slowly, that's the thing. Steady . . . steady. The first spot of rain. Christ, it seems a long way down. Where do I go from here?

I jumped to the rock opposite and landed on a massive slab of granite, winding myself. I felt like Isaac waiting for the knife. But I was all right, only a grazed hand.

I didn't get very wet, apart from my feet. Only a few drops of rain fell, as it turned out. The hurler of thunderbolts had wandered off to have words with the blameless Ethiopians. I made my way down with all the caution that befits a man of mature age and yet when I had reached the safety of the path by the castle I felt myself swagger just a bit. I had survived. With a lighter step I continued to the new bridge and down to the lake. A rowing boat was making steady progress in my direction. I heard Father laugh above the splash of the oars. 'Enjoy your walk?' he said and his laughter echoed across the water.

Father's train was due to leave Innsbruck at about four in the afternoon but he wanted to arrive in good time in order to have a beer at a beergarden behind the hotel in which we had stayed with James so many years before. I was to drop him off before parking the car. It took me a good half hour to find somewhere to park and to make my way back to the beergarden. When I saw him next he was ensconced at a distant table eating a Wiener schnitzel and holding forth to a young man.

'Did you get lost? This is my son Thomas,' said Father. 'May I present Friedrich, a soldier from Bregenz.'

'Hello,' I said, and ordered myself a beer.

'Friedrich and I are just going inside for a few minutes if you don't mind waiting here. Don't go wandering off. I don't want you making me late for the train.'

Twenty minutes later, Father clattered up to me on his zimmerframe. 'How was it?' I asked.

'Very successful. I don't know which of us enjoyed it more. Are you going to fetch the car?'

We got to the station just in time for Father to buy a one-way ticket to Venice.

CHAPTER 20 · A Consecrated Pile

AT ELEVEN NEXT morning I met Erhard at reception. He was clutching a ring of enormous keys and his Alsatian was snuffling around his legs in anticipation of an outing. We set off up the steep steps to the sound of panting, padding and jangling. To me, the castle has always been an illusion, an illusion built of stone, perched on a crag, its turrets and crenellations a landmark for eagles and the weather. I expected to be disappointed.

Erhard unlocked the iron grille inside the wooden door at the foot of the tower. The Alsatian bounded up the steps in front of us and I followed Erhard inside. We were at the bottom of a steep flight of spiral steps which were flanked on one side by the bare rock of the mountain, black and wet. The door at the top led into a large empty hall. The walls were covered with antlers and framed sepia photographs of hunting parties. I crossed to the windows, and looked down over the pass to the green waters of the lake and the mountains beyond.

We passed through some smaller rooms to another staircase. Upstairs were a number of rooms of different sizes, full of old-fashioned iron beds, deal chairs and tables and a kitchen stacked with utilitarian white crockery. Erhard explained that during the war this had been used as a kind of youth hostel. He was always reluctant to talk about the war but it was easy enough to imagine a group of brown-shirted lads in lederhosen in residence.

A corridor led us into the older part of the castle. 'This is the State Room,' said Erhard, throwing open the door. 'King Ludwig stayed here when he came to Steinpass. You know the picture in the hotel?' I nodded, looking around me as I did so in an effort to take it all in. Solid Victorian furniture, faded tapestry hangings and rugs, a heavily carved four-poster bed, a long wooden table and throne-like chairs. It was as good as the set from *Don Giovanni*. Paintings of saints and portraits of Tyrolean gentlefolk adorned the walls, and overhead was a magnificent painted ceiling, depicting this, the older part of the castle, with black, cloud-like wings in Baroque style as a surround. Here and there blisters of damp showed through like cold sores.

'We have much trouble with the snow,' said Erhard. 'The roof is flat here and it is not always possible to keep it dry. It is a pity . . .' and he glanced at me for approval, 'because it is such a fine room.'

I could hear the waterfall as it battered down the mountainside into the lake. The window-ledges were covered with dead flies. I looked out of the window at the Roman bridge and the fantastic view beyond. What would I not give to live in such a place! 'Did your family live here?' I asked.

'No one lives here since the war.'

'Why don't you do something with it? It's wonderful . . . amazing.'

He pointed at the huge tiled stove in the corner. 'It is much work to be able to live here. It is too much work . . . There is no heat, no light, no bath, no shower . . . and it is difficult for the guests to get here . . . The steps are . . . so steep . . . No, I think it is not possible . . . You would have to make so many changes, and it is beautiful. Yes. Perhaps for me I will make an apartment one day.'

'Yes. You'd be just like King Ludwig.' He looked hurt. An unintended arrow.

'That's what they call me . . . Ludwig . . . It's not funny,' he said and shook his head sadly. 'You like it here? Yes, it is very fine. Sometimes I come up here when I wish to be alone . . . You know . . . When I want to escape from the hotel and the guests. I have a . . . er . . . in the kitchen . . . a little cooker that works with the gas and I even make a meal for myself. You would like for me to cook you something? It will be very simple and there is no light. I can bring some wood for the stove? You would like that? It will give me much pleasure. I am not working this afternoon so you will come at seven o'clock, yes? But it will be simple. I hope this will be all right . . .'

*

When I set off along the track to the castle night had already fallen. There was no moon and the darkness was pierced only by my friends the stars. I reflected, not for the first time, on the fact that black is not an absolute. There are shades of black. The looming mountain seems black against the lighter sky, but then you round a corner to find a deeper black in which surely nothing can be seen. But soon you find that you can distinguish something even there.

I stopped by the Roman bridge to gaze up at the white streak of the waterfall. It was even light enough for me to see the time: seven o'clock. The castle looked wonderful by starlight. In one window was a trace of a flickering light and, sure enough, I could see the silhouette of a man's head where I had once conjured up the image of Henry Usher's face. Erhard waved and indicated that he would be down to let me in.

He was carrying a candelabrum containing three guttering candles as I followed him up to the State Room. The autumn evenings are cold here in the mountains and I was glad to find that Erhard had lit the stove. He had also tidied up. The dead flies had gone from the window-ledge and the huge table had been laid for two. 'You want to help me with the cooking?' said my host, and led me through an ante-room to a modest kitchen, where there was a cold tap and a simple Calor gas cooker. Erhard opened the oven door and pulled out a casserole dish and stirred the contents. 'It is *hirsch*. What do you call it . . . venison? I shoot it myself in the mountains. It has been in the freezer at the hotel,' and he set to work to sauté some potatoes. He let me cut up a red cabbage and uncork a bottle of wine. In the candlelight our shadows looked splendid against the wall.

'Tschh,' he said. 'It is so nice to have someone to do something for. You remember last year when you were at Steinpass and we walked around the lake together? It was very beautiful, yes? You wanted to see the moon in the water and you said how the moon is the same size in the water as in the sky unless the water is . . . is . . .'

'Rippling.'

'Yes. Unless it is rippling and then the light spreads out

all over the lake. And you said some lines from a poem . . .'

'Small circles glittering idly in the moon,
Until they melted all into one track
Of sparkling light.'

'Yes. I remember. Who writes this poem? It is very romantic. It is like you.'

'Have you been to Garmisch lately?' I said. That old joke.

'Tschh . . . You always tease me.'

Erhard led me back into the State Room and lit the candles in a second candelabrum on the table, the twin of the one he had been carrying. The surroundings suited me very well. I don't know if I should tell you this, but I am still capable, at my age, of being thrilled by certain inconsequential things. This was Gothic-Baroque. Dining in the castle was like taking part in an opera. It was splendid. He served the casserole which was, as I had anticipated, excellent, and the wine, too, was good, chosen from a cupboard full of bottles. I wondered how often he dined here and imagined it was where he brought his special guests for romantic evenings. I knew he was lonely, but there could surely be little danger of him harbouring thoughts of that nature towards me after so many years. Still, I confess I felt a little uneasy. It would have been horribly embarrassing.

Netta had never entirely convinced me that I had imagined seeing Henry's face in the turret window. Sometimes I thought she was right and sometimes I thought I was right. I had been planning to tackle Erhard about it but was nervous of grating the gears when I brought up the subject. Here goes. 'Do you remember', I said, 'when I came here in the snow that time and told you I'd seen a man's face in the window?'

Erhard rolled his eyes in melodramatic fashion. 'Yes, I remember.'

'And you told me no one had lived here since the war?'

'Yes, I remember.' He looked nervous.

'I had imagined it. I was in a pretty worked up state.'

'A worked up state? You mean confused? . . . Yes. You have much to suffer at that time. It was terrible about James.' There was a pause as he lowered his eyes. When he lifted them again to look me in the face I knew he was going to say something

important. 'You know . . . I have to tell you this. Before I have
not told you the truth.' I steadied my gaze and waited. 'He
was here when you came. It *was* him that you saw. He stayed
here in the castle. I am so sorry I did not speak before, but
then we did not know each other as now . . . and when you
came in the snow and told me, I was afraid. I did not know
what was happening. Herr Usher was very frightening when
he was angry and he had made me swear on my mother's life
to keep it secret . . . That time I had been away to my sister's
house with my parents for some days . . . When I came back
I went straightaway here to the castle to see him, but he was
not here. He was gone and his things are also gone . . . There
was nothing . . . so for me too he vanishes and from then I
have never seen him,' and once more he looked down at the
table, shaking his head sadly.

'Did my father know he stayed here?'

Erhard nodded. 'Your father should not bring you here that
time when you came with James. He should never bring you
here. But he can't help it. It is like him to do this. He likes
it here and must show off . . . When I saw James that time
I could not believe my eyes. He was so like his father . . .'
and he shook his head once more. I felt a wave of resentment
for Father who was, no doubt, holding forth to a Venetian
audience. He was always a couple of steps ahead of me. 'Yes,
your father stays here many times . . . I ask you not to tell
him. He will be angry with me. Tommy, I am sorry, believe
me please.' Erhard had never called me Tommy before, but I
let it pass. 'It is all so long ago now. How long is it since you
were first coming here?'

'I was seventeen . . . but tell me about Henry.'

'He came with your father the first time. It must be
after the war . . . my parents tell me since then . . . I
don't remember, I was a little boy . . . about four years
old . . . tschh. The first time I remember him I was about
thirteen when they stayed here, and then they arrange to rent
the apartment at the castle, and then they go on to Venice I
think, and Herr Usher comes back without your father and
he stay two, three months, and after that he comes back in
the winter and he stay here perhaps half the year. Not all at

once. He comes and he goes. It's his own private apartment
and he has one in Venice, in a palace . . . yes, and I know he
also stays for a time in India.' And he opened his eyes wide
and nodded his head slowly. 'He uses a different name always
from Henry Usher . . . his passport says Henry *Unstead*, not
Usher. Sometimes he has a friend to stay, and once a lady, very
elegante, very fine clothes, and every year your father comes to
stay here some days. When I was twenty years, in the summer
your father comes with the friend . . . Nicky. He was very nice
to me, Nicky . . . tschh.'

'Nicholas York? You met him here?'

'Yes, that was his name. You know him?'

'We have met,' I said, 'but I haven't seen him since the
scandal.' He looked shocked. I continued, 'You mean you don't
know about it, about the scandal?'

'Scandal . . . no . . . what scandal? . . . I know we have
a time together, and he is very charming . . . tschh . . . very
gemütlich.'

And I told Erhard what had become of Nicholas York.
How he was a member of Parliament and had been very
much in the public eye, and how at the height of his fame,
when he had achieved high office (I can say no more) he
had fallen from grace in the most spectacular fashion and
how there had been a major scandal almost in the Oscar
Wilde league. But Erhard had not heard of Wilde and knew
nothing of this either. Scandals by and large are only scandals
in their own country, and Nicholas York was not a king or a
prime minister or even a viscount.

'Oh,' he said, shaking his head. 'I did not know he was
so important. Tschh . . . And now we must have some Tokay,'
and he got up to fetch the bottle. 'Your father and his friends
used to drink that together when they stayed here. Herr
Usher had plenty of money. He had an apartment in Venice.
He show me photographs,' and Erhard's eyes were wide with
astonishment at his own tale. 'He has a balcony over the water
. . . It is very fine . . .' I thought of the time when James and I
had been taken by gondola to the mysterious palace. Could the
giant in the mask and black *tricorno* have been Henry? 'When
he stayed in the castle I know he sometimes is lonely, and

one summer when I was fourteen or fifteen years he ask me
to walk with him and we walk many times across the pass to
Bernwald. We ski together also. He was a fine skier and very
strong. I never know him to be tired. And then after you came
here in the snow and I drive you back to Bernwald in the car
he is gone when I return . . . and from that time I have seen
him never,' and Erhard shook his head. 'It is sad for me and
my mother and father because we have no goodbye, nothing.
Your father when he comes pays the bill and has a story why
this has happened, but I do not believe it. It is all so strange.
To me as to you Herr Usher has disappeared. It is . . . how
do you say . . . a mystery. There is one other thing. I said to
you just now that when Herr Usher disappears from here he
leaves nothing behind. It is not quite true. He was writing his
memoirs. It seems he only just has started. I think that he was
planning to write this book during the winter. You came and
disturb him and he leaves here. He puts the book in a hiding
place under the window where he does the writing. He leaves
the book behind, in this cupboard, where it is hidden at the
back, behind a piece of wood. I will let you take it to read.
It is not long. It is the writing . . . of a . . . It is . . . *ausser-
gewöhnlich.* . . He was not like other men. And he *hated* his
father.' He shook his head. 'No, Herr Usher was not ordinary.
But then he was a Lord of Ireland and Scotland. It is all very
strange.'

Before I left the castle, Erhard pressed a school exercise book
into my hand. I could hardly wait to get it back to my room.
I turned on the overhead light and took the book, a blanket,
a glass and a bottle of whisky on to my balcony. Without the
curtains drawn it was light enough for me to read. Swathed
in the blanket, with trembling hand, I opened the cover. The
writing was familiar. It was a hand I had seen before, a firm
hand, written in blue-black ink. I took a large swig of whisky,
looked up at the stars and back at the book.

1.

I was born without an anus, a distinction given to few.
The physicians, in their wisdom, call the abnormality from
which I suffered an *imperforate anus*. If you doubt the existence of such a fundamental problem I suggest you look it up
in any medical dictionary. The condition with which I was
born is commonly found in pigs. I can assure you that if I
had been sired by a Saddleback or a Gloucester Old Spot,
rather than the ninth Viscount Castledown, I would be a
happier man. Ah, my father, in what cold furnace was your
heart forged?

As I was not a normal child my parents would have
left me to die, and had it not been for the ministrations of
Mrs Logan, the local wet-nurse, and her husband, I would
no doubt have suffered a swift and painful exit from the
world.

Logan had come from a family of pig farmers, and was
blessed with a strong stomach. Once it had been made clear
that no medical help was to be sought and that I had been
abandoned to their care, I was placed belly-down on the
table in their cottage kitchen and while Mrs Logan held my
cheeks apart her husband lanced the obstruction with a red
hot implement, the offending membrane was pierced, and
thus I was parted from my virginity. For this relief, Logan,
much thanks.

Eventually, be it in a month, a year or a decade, I would
have been entitled to call myself Viscount Castledown. Had
I not been officially declared dead in 1963, I would have
acquired the title as a matter of course on the death of my
father, but, for reasons which I may or may not choose to
relate in these confessions, I disappeared in 1956. Being possessed of a degree of intelligence, in spite of my immediate
ancestry, I fooled the authorities, and since my 'death' have

lived variously in a Rajah's palace in India, in an unassuming palazzo in Venice, and here, in a castle deep in the Austrian Tyrol. I am, by nature, a pilgrim, a wanderer. I shall never return to the family seat. The day will come when I will read my father's obituary in *The Times* and on that happy day I will be able to declare that mine is the family seat. It was in order to assert my claim that after a night of drunken revelry in Bombay I foolishly had my left buttock tattooed with the family crest: on a tower a war-horse, passant, bridled, saddled and accoutred. If anyone cares to examine my nether region they will find it stamped with the hallmark of a gentleman.

I see myself as a late Romantic, a Romantic of the second wave, of the school of Byron. I appreciate the wonders of nature and the beauty of life, but at the same time, unlike Wordsworth, I am aware of the futility, the vulgarity, the ridiculousness of it all. Wordsworth suffered not only from smugness and pomposity but from a conspicuous lack of a sense of humour. He was always trying to uplift. He was a slave to duty. He was old-fashioned; he failed to acknowledge that man is half angel and half devil. That is why he is a bore; he turns his back on the truth. Byron was only too aware of the diabolical side of his nature. Whilst greeting the light he acknowledged the dark. He distrusted himself; that is why he is more real. When he made love to a beautiful girl or boy there was a black detachment about him. Even when happy he wore melancholy about him like a cloak.

Allow me to quote from the great Lord Macaulay. Byron

> had naturally a generous and feeling heart: but his temper was wayward and irritable. He had a head which statuaries loved to copy, and a foot the deformity of which the beggars in the street mimicked. Distinguished at once by the strength and by the weakness of his intellect, affectionate yet perverse, a poor lord and a handsome cripple, he required, if ever man required, the firmest and most judicious training.

Where was my father when I needed him? I pray that his hell will be a frozen and lonely waste, a desert of ice. May he weep perpetually and may his tears freeze as they fall so that he will spend eternity amongst the evidence of his own misery.

I was always a greedy person. There was nothing I did not wish to try. And I was born an actor: to create thunder simply by being there, to be admired, to be loved, this is what I craved. Was this because my father had rejected me at birth, and for the simple reason that I was born imperfect? Was Byron culpable because his foot was twisted? Was I to be condemned for a morsel of skin?

2.

My early years were spent in the care of Mrs Logan, who acted as my nanny, although never officially given such a title. She was fond of me and I was happy, a combination which did not please my father. Accordingly, at the age of three I was dispatched to my grandmother's house in Park Lane.

I was a pretty child and the favourite of the nannies in Hyde Park. I had a mop of golden curls and I liked attention. These faults in my character brought about the event which forms my first memory. My father happened to be in London and it came to his notice that I was the darling of the park because I came home crying, since I wished to stay amongst my circle of admirers. He did not want his son to turn into a milksop and made a rush at me. I was dragged screaming into the kitchen, hoisted into the high chair and fastened in. He then proceeded to shear off my golden locks. He did not have a delicate touch and his experience in hairdressing was limited. Some years later I was not surprised to hear him cite this incident as evidence to support his contention that I had none of the qualities he admired in a man. When I grew up I was too powerfully built to be a milksop. If this had not been the case I would have tried my best to be one simply to annoy him.

Do you consider he carried out this action with character-building in mind, or do you think perhaps that it was an act of gratuitous sadism? It was for neither of these reasons. He did it simply because he didn't like me.

I am pleased to relate that my father's appearances at this stage in my life were rare. I regarded them in the way that primitive peoples may have thought of the weather. He seemed like an unpleasant phenomenon of nature that had to be endured. If he left havoc in his wake at least his visits were brief. Soon the birds would dare to sing once more and the flowers to show their heads.

It was unfortunate for me that my grandmother died when I was five. She had been fond of me and I was not unhappy under her roof. She was an interesting woman, a repository of family history and an accomplished storyteller. I have always found it difficult to distinguish fact from fiction and I attribute this to her influence. My grandmother was frequently otherwise engaged, but I know she, as well as I, enjoyed our bedtime stories. I would drink hot chocolate in bed as she read to me, or told me a story of her own invention, or better still, related my favourite piece of family history, the tale of the Burnt Lady, whose portrait hung in the hall of Keep Castle.

The Burnt Lady had been a Miss Usher born in the early part of the seventeenth century at Castle Usher at a time when Ireland was wild and lawless. At nineteen she had married a dissolute and reckless man by the name of Wills. Our family was English in origin and the Ushers had been Protestants since the Reformation. Wills was a Catholic and felt that his wife too should be of that faith. She steadfastly refused to be converted. This provoked many quarrels and the Burnt Lady had a great deal to put up with. In spite of this she did not complain to her family and kept her own counsel.

In due course, after a particularly violent quarrel, the evil Mr Wills took action. He locked his wife in an upstairs room, took the key and went down to the cellar below where he had previously ordered a large pile of firewood to be placed. He set fire to this and retired to the garden to watch the flames and to listen to the screams of his wife. One of her servants hurried to the stable and mounted his master's fastest horse. He rode hard to Castle Usher and related the events of the night to her brother Henry. A force of retainers was hastily assembled. Alas, they arrived too late. Wills Castle had been burned to the ground and the lady had perished.

A battle ensued during which the Ushers feigned a
retreat; Wills rushed on, since this wicked man was
no coward, but Henry Usher was lying in wait for him
in the churchyard where he ran him through . . .

My Grandmother's house boasted a considerable library of
which I now possess one volume borrowed on a permanent
basis from my father into whose custodianship it passed on
her death. That volume is a poorly bound one entitled *The
Annual Biography and Obituary for the year 1825* and it
happens to contain the obituary of my hero, Lord Byron, and
some information about his antecedents. My grandmother
must have read this to me before I was five years old and
it left a lasting impression. What it demonstrates to me is
that there were fantastic people who lived in the past,
people who nowadays would be declared impossible by
virtue of popular taste. Listen:

William, Lord Byron acquired considerable influence
at court, so much so, as to procure the office of Master
of the Stag Hounds, in 1763. Being, however, a man
of ungovernable passions, he was, in 1765, sent to the
Tower, on a charge of having killed his relation, Mr.
Chaworth, in a duel. This duel took place, under very
peculiar circumstances, at the Star and Garter Tavern,
in Pall Mall. It originated in a dispute at table; and was
fought, in the evening, in a small room, with the light
which one glimmering candle afforded. Being the more
expert swordsman of the two, Lord Byron inflicted on
Mr. Chaworth a mortal wound; although he lived long
enough to settle his affairs, and supply such information, as led the coroner's jury to return a verdict of
'wilful murder' against his lordship. The trial, which
excited intense public interest, came on at Westminster
Hall, before the House of Lords. It lasted two days, and
ended by an unanimous conviction of manslaughter,
pronounced by upwards of two hundred and fifty
members of the upper house. Upon being brought up
for judgment, Lord Byron pleaded his privilege as a
peer, and was, in consequence, discharged. After this
affair, he was shunned by his relations, and retired to
Newstead; where, though he lived in a state of perfect

exile from persons of his own rank, his unhappy temper found abundant exercise in continual war with his neighbours and tenants, and sufficient punishment in their hatred. One of his amusements was feeding crickets, which were his only companions. He made them so tame, as to crawl over him; and used to whip them with a wisp of straw, if too familiar.

It does not strike me as too great an absurdity to think that such 'early reading' may have had its influence on a receptive infant.

3.

To say that as a child I had no home would not be an exaggeration. I was sent to boarding school at the age of six. Windy Ridge was an Edwardian house just outside York with accommodation for eighty boys. It lived up to its name. I remember little about the place except that it was cold. We were taught by three ladies: the headmaster's wife, who had white hair, Miss Parker who was kind and liked us, and Miss Williams who had a squint and did not like us. She once smacked me for an offence I had not committed. I never forgave her.

The great event of my time at Windy Ridge was my mother's first visit. She wafted into the cold and gloomy corridors one dark winter's day bringing with her the scent of roses and musk. She seemed like a goddess, glamorous and beautiful, almost unbelievable. She drove me into York.

My mother had a green Bentley sports car. She had always liked fast cars. To sit beside her and shiver with cold and terror as she drove this fearsome machine through the lanes at breakneck speed was the greatest thrill imaginable, and it was not for some years that I discovered a thrill I liked better. Being deprived of her presence when she dropped me back at school was compensated for to some degree by my elevation in the sight of my contemporaries; my mother had made no small impression on them and I basked in the glow of her personality. In her absence her scent lingered on both in the air which she had breathed and on my flesh.

I don't know how long she stayed or how often she

made the journey to Windy Ridge during those two years. Perhaps she came four or five times in all. Looking back, I should hate her rather than worship her. She visited me as a charitable lady might have visited a caged dog in Battersea.

By the time I arrived at my preparatory school, at the age of eight, I was an old hand and this gave me a great advantage over many of my peers. While they wept I gloated. While they were homesick I was unmoved for I had no home. I was used to living in a loveless world.

I won't bore you with an account of my time at this school. I just want to mention the swimming lessons which were conducted with style by Mr Glyn whose soubriquet was Fingers. Whether this name derived from his habit of massaging the shoulders of favoured boys as they conjugated their Latin verbs or from his activities as master in charge of swimming had been lost in the mists of time. He used to throw the boys into the river at the end of a rope and not let them out until they could swim. It was most effective and rather enjoyable if you happened to be a swimmer, as I was. When the poor creatures came spluttering, half drowned, to the surface and reached for the wooden stage in desperation, Fingers would stamp on their hands until they let go. Much importance was attached to swimming because the river ran along the bottom of the school grounds. It was for their own good that they suffered. I am sorry to admit that I felt pleasure at seeing my fellow pupils struggling for their lives, and there must have been something of the bully about me then, a quality which I do not admire in myself and have tried to suppress.

4.

I enjoyed Eton. I saw it as a haven, a place of refuge.

I was encouraged to stay with friends during the school holidays but, of course, this was not always possible and I was sometimes obliged to return to Keep Castle. I have always been proud of my lineage, with the notable exception of my father, and I liked the place in spite of the fact that no one, apart from Mrs Logan, had ever tried to make me happy there. I read Stendhal at school, and I gloried in the name of Usher every bit as much as the hero of *The*

Charterhouse of Parma gloried in the name of del Dongo, and naturally identified with Fabrizio, who, like me, had not enjoyed good relations with his father.

I wanted to think my father was thoroughly evil and no doubt I exaggerated his failings. He was a man of the world, like Fabrizio's father. At that time Sir Oswald Mosley was a frequent visitor to the house and I understand he offered my father Scotland in exchange for his support. My father lacked the vision to accept. Had I been the ninth Viscount I would have clasped such a gift without the slightest hesitation. My father had no flair. At heart he was a coward.

During my first summer holiday from Eton I had a revelation. I realised that my parents hated each other. Two people could live adequately without meeting in such a big house and I soon observed that they met simply to wage war. Their bedrooms were in separate wings. Their quarrels were bitter and sometimes violent. I thought of the Burnt Lady. Perhaps I should have intervened on my mother's behalf? Nothing would have given me more pleasure than to have run my father through with one of the swords that hung in the hall. Although I worshipped my mother and would gladly have killed for her I saw that I was out of my depth and let them get on with it. I spent most of my time out of doors.

During that summer I saw a lot of my old friends Mrs Logan and her husband. I often called in for lunch or tea, or to dry off before their fire in wet weather. Friends sometimes express surprise when I take them to a greasy spoon café and the proprietress rushes to embrace me. The truth is that I have never lost the common touch. And I have always wanted to be liked.

In my opinion the worst quality of the English as a race is their passion for the suburban. I have been insulted a number of times in my life but at least I have never been called that. I can't help thinking that people are influenced by their surroundings. The landscape in the neighbourhood of Keep is anything but suburban. It is dramatic, colourful, harsh, excessive. It suits me admirably. I am only sorry that I cannot climb those paths again. On any day the mountains can appear black and threatening at one moment and then without warning the clouds disperse and the scene can burn with a brilliant light. I spent my days walking in the mountains. I thought them as wild and remote as any in Afghanistan.

My parents decided to live apart shortly after that summer and at the same time began to take more of an interest in me. I was a weapon of war and they competed with each other for my company. And thus I went to Paris with my father during the following Christmas holiday. I was allowed to explore the city whilst he pursued his own interests. We met at breakfast and dinner and took these meals in silence; he had never pretended to like me.

At the end of the holiday my father dropped me outside my mother's house in Lennox Gardens. That January day will remain etched on my mind for ever. I took my case from the boot of the car and he drove off leaving me to go in alone. I let myself in and called my mother's name. She did not respond and it was several minutes before I thought of looking in her room. I saw that she was lying in her bed. She did not speak. I should have realised that she was dead but I wanted to be sure. I took a needle from the silver box she kept on the dressing table and pushed it into her hand. There was no blood. There was no response of any kind. I went downstairs and telephoned the police. When the sergeant arrived I did not like him. He treated me like a suspected murderer; my mother was lying dead upstairs. She had been dead for three days. She had taken an overdose of tablets on the day when I had visited Père Lachaise in order to see the tomb of Oscar Wilde.

5.

Sexual pleasure and the idea of love can be quite distinct. It is possible to love someone with whom sex is unsatisfactory or unthinkable and it is possible to have the most thrilling sex with a person one has picked up in the bazaar for a few rupees and whom one has no wish to see ever again.

I did not fall in love until I was fourteen, if indeed love is the right word for what I felt. Fane was three years older than me. He was handsome, strong, clever and a first-rate athlete, in fact everything I wanted to be. We never had sex, or at least Fane did not have it with me; at Eton I regained my virginity several times. I had to go to great lengths to attract him. In the end I was forced to turn to crime; I left him with no alternative but to beat me. I cannot tell you how eagerly I awaited punishment. Before he had administered the first stroke I had an erection and before he had administered the last I had enjoyed my first non-manual ejaculation. I determined to repeat the experience.

It was not long before the power to beat was vested in me. I had discovered my vocation.

6.

Nicholas, who was my great friend at Eton, invited me to spend the summer holidays in Venice after our last term. His parents habitually rented a palazzo near the Madonna dell'Orto during July and August. It was not a grand palazzo like the one my dear Contessa inhabits, but a seventeenth-century merchant's house of no particular distinction, and I realised that at the time when anybody had enough money to build a passable house in Venice it would be called a palazzo, just as in Ireland and Scotland any partially fortified dwelling would be called a castle. I have always liked anything that smacks of privilege.

Beneath the palazzo was a cellar that fronted a small canal and here we found an ancient but watertight gondola. I had soon become a competent gondolier and we spent the summer exploring every canal and backwater in the Venetian lagoon. Sometimes we would arrive home late at night when all was black as pitch. Venice is the most romantic city in the world. If I ever die, which seems most unlikely, I propose to die in Venice. I like the thought of having my last resting place on the island of San Michele. Toby will see to it if he survives me. He has always claimed to be immortal.

I was fond of Nicholas and we had engaged in some experimental sex at school. We saw no reason to abandon our old ways during that long holiday. We spent some nights together, although sex between us had never been entirely satisfactory, and we also shared a servant girl called Gina; it was in Venice I discovered women. Whatever you queers may have to say, no number of choirboys can match a young woman at her peak. The trouble is that beauty vanishes and as a rule a beautiful woman doesn't like being sent back to the bazaar. Nicholas had been enjoying sex with Gina since he was fifteen and he continued to do so; we had got into the habit of sharing at Eton. Gina must have been three or four years older than us. She was dark and pretty and had a passionate nature. When I think of her now I think of Byron's mistress, the baker's wife, who, when confronted by her aristocratic rival the Contessa, proclaimed: 'You may be a lady but I am a Venetian.' I learned from Gina that I could never be completely satisfied by boys. I also discovered that my sadistic nerve is not engaged where women are concerned. With them the element of worship prevails.

Venice was wonderful. I was not to return there until after the war, when Nicholas, Toby and I had such a riotous time and I fell in love with the Phelips twins. They were marvellous girls. If I could have had them and half a dozen Anglo-Indian boys at the same time, I really think that I might have settled down.

My father decreed that I should not go up to the university on leaving Eton. In his view it was full of degenerates, aesthetes, pansies and revolutionaries. I was not regarded as fit material for the church, which I have always regretted bitterly; to have been an archbishop would have suited my vanity and drawn out my religious nature. To have worn the purple and to have been the familiar of cardinals and monarchs, to have lived in palaces and mixed with kings, would have pleased me. Alas, it was decided that I had to go into the army instead, and the Indian army at that, since my father and I had no wish to inhabit the same continent. After Sandhurst, which I hated, I went straight out to India.

Within a short time of my arrival in the sub-continent I was appointed ADC to General Beynon-Pritchett, the father of one of my school friends. I suppose my reputation must have gone before me since the old boy was a notorious queer and enjoyed nothing more than a good whipping. I quickly tired of my duties and as soon as I decently could I found a substitute to take on the onerous task of keeping the General sweet. Then the war came.

7.

I declare that we are born innocent and our time is short. We owe it to the gods to be happy if we can. We must disappoint the devils who try to bring us down. The world is a fascinating and a beautiful place. We must abjure mediocrity and seek out the lovely and the strange. I believe identity to be as much a question of will and temperament as it is of breeding. Each of us has the power to re-make himself if he so wishes.

Every son of man must contend with his own nature. I have a violent streak. My dear friend Toby pretends to disapprove of my continued interest in the lash. Only the other day he called me a worshipper of the Divine Marquis. Toby, I ask you this. Should the eagle's wings be clipped? Should the lion lie down with the lamb?

The last sentence, about the lion and the lamb, had been crossed out. A little joke about my patronym. At that point the script came to an end. Was it possible that its author had looked up just at that moment and seen a lambkin standing in the snow down below? I refilled my glass. How the waters roared outside, like so many lions, even as they would have roared for him.

Henry Usher! I was on his trail.

I made up my mind that, before returning home to England, I would follow Father to Venice. And, drunk as I was, I vowed that I would run Henry Usher to earth, in the grave or out of it. Now that Netta was marrying again the pursuit of Father and his mysterious friend was the only pursuit left to me. And I made that vow by the light of Father's old enemy, the moon.

CHAPTER 22 · *Tribute*

of Regret

I FELT UNREAL as I crossed the bridge linking the industrial mainland with its gasometers and chimneys to the old city, crowded as it was with gorgeous palaces and crumbling towers. I was happy to visit Venice on the slightest excuse; this time I had a mission. If only I could track down Father, how surprised he'd be! Even though the odds were that I should find out nothing, I wanted to confront him, to let him know that he was being pursued, hounded even, that I knew more than he wanted me to know. Was this how the gods of old were overthrown, I wondered, because their children knew too much? And perhaps the chase would lead me to Henry Usher, the tenth Viscount Castledown.

My little game was also intended to have some therapeutic effect. I needed something to do to take my mind off the painful subject of Netta.

I parked in the multi-storey and ten minutes later, bearing the smallest of overnight bags, I boarded a vaporetto and headed for the Rialto. My first shock was that the Ca' d'Oro had disappeared. The most beautiful building in Venice was entirely covered by wooden hoardings, no doubt for the best of reasons. It had gone. Venice was fading like a lover one had enjoyed years before. She had lost one of her front teeth.

I walked through the markets of the Rialto to the foul-smelling alley that led to the seedy *pensione* in which James and I had been conceived. I pressed the buzzer and the door opened in that quietly sinister way that I knew so well. The smell inside was not much better than that outside. It was different; danker, perhaps: the smell of rotting fabric, rotting wood, rotting stone, the smell of the dying city itself.

I took the key to my usual room and flung open the shutters. Instead of the Ca' d'Oro I could see hoardings on the far side of the canal.

Whither is fled the visionary gleam?
Where is it now, the glory and the dream?

I gazed out at Venice, the metaphysical city, the place where
the tourist is of no more substance than his shadow thrown into
relief on a crumbling wall. Generations of visitors had come and
gone. They had left no trace. No doubt their footsteps had worn
away the flagstones, that was all. How real had they been? How
real was Father? How real was Henry Usher?

Out I went into the alleys and squares of Venice. I had
lost Netta. I was full of gloom. I was a ruin amongst ruins. I
ate a solitary meal in a dull restaurant near the Arsenal and
walked on through the twilight towards St Mark's, sparing
a thought outside his church for Vivaldi and a sigh for the
view by the Bridge of Sighs. The Piazza was cold and windy
and a lone pianist played for the fluttering pigeons. The foot
of the Campanile and part of the front of the Basilica were
boarded up for repairs. Like me, Venice wasn't at its best.
No one was sitting outside Florian's. There was no sign of
Father.

In the morning I shuffled off to San Zanipolo, thinking
that I might perhaps take a vaporetto to one of the islands.
As I walked along by I Gesuiti with its wedding-cake angels
I saw a No. 5 pulling in from the direction of the Madonna
dell'Orto and ran to catch it. I got off at the first stop, San
Michele, the cemetery island, which was one of the few places
in Venice I had not visited before. It was possible, I supposed,
that the vanished viscount might be dead. In his confessions
he had expressed a wish to be buried here. Perhaps that wish
had been fulfilled. I had time on my hands. I could ask. And
as a bonus, I knew that Baron Corvo was lying in state
there. If I could not pay my respects to Father, perhaps
I could pay them to the infamous author of *Hadrian the
Seventh*.

'Baron Corvo?' said the attendant, 'Yes,' and produced a map
of the cemetery, tracing out a line in blue of the track I had to
follow. Tucked away in the poorest part of the cemetery, in a
gravel-filled alley, I found what I was looking for stacked high
up in a wall of tombs. He may have died in poverty, but the

master of vituperation had his last resting place at the top of the heap.

The outing was turning out to be quite enjoyable and I realised that I had almost forgotten the true object of my quest. I went back to the helpful official and got him to search the records for a dead Henry Usher or a dead Henry Unstead or a dead Castledown. For half an hour he pored over his papers but he could only find a record of a Jane Louise Unstead who had died in 1992. There was nothing else. I was not really disappointed; it had been a very long shot. As I had nothing better to do I found the lady's grave back in the foreigners' corner amongst the travellers and exiles. The stone proclaimed that she was the former Contessa di Ritaldi, an actress. Someone had placed an offering of flowers on the earth.

I also stood on the grave of Ezra Pound, which was marked by a flat stone bearing only his name. I found it by chance, in a scruffy shrubbery under a hairy tree, guarded by a lizard. So this is where the demented author of the *Pisan Cantos* had ended up. I then stumbled on Diaghilev and Stravinsky, and a bronze effigy of a beautiful Russian princess. Who now remembered her?

On my way out I gave the official a well-earned tip and left the sepulchral darkness for the dazzling light of the quay. Fifty yards off a water-taxi was cutting its way through the water. Seated at the open section at the back was the unmistakable form of Father who was paying some attention to his headpiece. At the front, by the driver, who was standing at the wheel, was Father's familiar battered suitcase. He was on his way to the airport.

I cursed, caught the next vaporetto, returned to the seedy *pensione*, paid my bill and set off back to Steinpass.

Steinpass, 2nd October 1993. I have been away from England for more than three months. It has been a strange time for me. I am in a state of shock and not only because Netta has chosen to desert me. The closet has been revealing its skeletons. I have found things out that I only half knew were true. Henry Usher didn't sink beneath the waves back in the fifties. He lived here, at least part of the time, and Father helped in the vanishing act. Father has enjoyed my discomfiture and making a fool of me. I thought that looking back would help me to set my thoughts, and more importantly, my feelings, in order, but in some respects I feel more confused than ever. I still don't know why Henry had to disappear.

I have heard things about my mother that I didn't want brought into the light. Mother and the doctor. Mother and Uncle Frank. Mother and Henry Usher? Could he have been my father as well as James's?

Netta? Damn her for marrying him. Only James will never let me down. But, as Netta would have pointed out, James is dead.

In a few days I set off for home. I shall be returning to the place where I was brought up. To Sussex. To my flat in Blanc Hall itself, which is a twenty-minute stroll from Coniston, where a mossy and decaying caravan that I once called home still stands. Until then I shall wander the tracks of my youth. I like to indulge my emotions. There is something about them, something more than wistfulness, that I don't want to end. And this place has a way of enabling me to distil the essence of them so sweetly, so sharply. When I first came here I was young . . .

> I cannot paint
> What then I was. The sounding cataract
> Haunted me like a passion: the tall rock,
> The mountain, and the deep and gloomy wood,
> Their colours and their forms, were then to me
> An appetite; a feeling and a love,
> That had no need of a remoter charm,
> By thought supplied, nor any interest
> Unborrowed from the eye. − That time is past,
> And all its aching joys are now no more,
> And all its dizzy raptures.

CHAPTER 23 · *Home*

HE JOURNEY HOME took three days, one day longer than I had planned. I got lost after making a detour in an attempt to find Phalsbourg, where I had once stayed with Father and James. In the end I was successful in my quest. It is an attractive place and the detour was worthwhile. I am always pleased to find my youthful tastes vindicated. It is the same with books or music. Henry's Confessions had prompted me to buy *The Charterhouse of Parma*, which I was fortunate to find in an English translation in Venice, and I think I enjoyed it on re-reading even more than the first time around. I have a weakness for the operatic.

The crossing from Dieppe was not unpleasant. I thought of Oscar trolling along the front as the boat pulled out of the harbour. Six hours later I was home.

I can't expect you to remember but at the end of the lane where stand the Manor, Ninny's Tomb, the church and the Rectory there is a track leading to Blanc Hall, seat of the ancient family of Blanc. When I was young – *ah, woful When!* – the eccentric old squire, Sir Richard Blanc, lived there like a hermit. When the last squire died the house was eventually sold to developers who converted it into flats. Now Sir Richard's remains lie in the churchyard not far from those of James and Aunt Mary, who died about five years after James.

I turned the Renault into the lane marked NORMAN CHURCH and was soon looking over to Birgit's for signs of life. I even allowed myself the luxury of imagining that Netta might have been there since she was getting married in Chichester in a couple of days, but I could see no one. I passed the pub and the church and slowed right down for the bumpy track leading to Blanc Hall. How quiet it seemed.

My flat is on the second floor and was once the nursery. It is one of the humbler flats in the building but it's still quite grand. A fire escape leads from the garden up to a little balcony, and

I can sit up there and look over the lawn to the walled garden and the woods beyond. I can also sneak in and out by means of the fire escape when I want to. Sometimes I even climb up to the roof. The view is remarkable in an understated English way.

I opened my front door. Before me stood Uggers, wearing only a dressing gown, a complacent and priapic leer lurking in the undergrowth of his beard. 'Dear boy! Your mother gave me the key. I'm here for the wedding and I'm not going back. News of the wedding came at just the right time. I was thinking of leaving Turin anyway . . .'

'Who've you got . . . Who's in the bedroom?'

'Someone I met on the train. She's from New Zealand.' No wonder he was hovering outside my bedroom door like some overblown Noël Coward. He opened the door and ushered me in.

'Hi, I'm Deirdre. I'm from New Zealand. I hope you don't mind us taking over. I've brought a bottle of bubbly.' The room was stuffed with luggage, his and hers.

Pop!

'Champagne, my dear friend, thou more than a brother. I hope you don't mind us using the bed, but I'm not getting any slimmer! I see you're going thin on top. I've got a cure for that. Olive oil. Just rub it in once a day.'

There was a funny smell . . . So that was it. Olive oil. Come to think of it, Uggers did look marginally less bald than when I had last seen him.

His friend, who resembled a small blond choirboy and was, I estimated, about twenty-two, was clutching modestly at the sheet, successfully covering her minuscule charms. She spoke in hectic antipodean tones. 'This is a great place. Have you lived here long? My ancestors lived in places like this. I've got my family tree in my rucksack. Would you like to see it some time? I'm closer to royalty than Princess Di. I hope you don't mind about me and Hugo. He says you're best friends from varsity. Hey you guys, I'll put some clothes on if . . .'

While the modest young thing was covering her shame, Uggers followed me into the kitchen, clutching the bottle and adjusting the belt of my dressing gown. 'I hope I haven't come

at an inconvenient time,' I said. 'How long are you staying?'
'Oh, just a few days, till after the wedding. I might have
landed a job in Oslo, or I may go to Athens.'
I thought of my telephone bill. He had the habit of
ringing distant places at length at other people's expense. 'It's
good to see you,' I said. It was. 'I was a bit surprised, that's
all.'
'I hope you're not upset about Netta's wedding.'
'Of course I'm not. Have you got any grub? No? I'd better
drive to the shops. It's Sunday tomorrow and I see there's no
milk . . . no bread . . . nothing.'
On my way out I heard a cry from the bedroom. 'Coo-ee!
There's a funny old guy with a wig out here. Come and look.'
By this time, Uggers and I had joined her at the open
window. She was stark naked. Down below, Father was
making slow progress across the cobbled courtyard behind
Blanc Hall, virgin territory for him. Over the zimmerframe
he had somehow hooked the portrait of Clotworthy which
had hung in his flat since time immemorial. It is not a small
picture. A jowly soldier in full armour sporting a long curly
wig gazed contemptuously from a large oval frame of gilt scrolls
and curlicues. An ancient warrior with an extraordinary shield
before his chariot was heading our way. 'Is that your dad?' asked
Deirdre. 'I'm sorry, Uncle, I didn't mean to be rude.' We ran
downstairs – the bearded Noël Coward, a choirboy clad in a
white bathtowel and the party she had just christened Uncle.
Me.
'I thought Clotworthy might fit in comfortably here. I
know you've always liked him. I won't come up . . . All
those stairs . . . I'm on my way to pay my respects to your
mother.'
'Have you hurt your leg?' said Deirdre.
'I had a bullet in it,' said Father.
'Who did that?' said Deirdre. Father went on to explain.
During the interval she turned to me and asked, 'Is Clotworthy
one of your ancestors?'
'I'm not quite sure,' I said.
Father was basking in the afterglow of his revelations. To
my knowledge he had not seen Mother for years. I had to say

something. 'Why are you visiting Mother? Uncle Frank's not dead yet.'

'Surely a man can visit an ex-wife when he wants to. Frank's got no rights over her. She's only his sister-in-law. I think I'm entitled to see who I like, come to that, without asking your permission. I see you got home safely. I'm surprised you found your way. Thomas has absolutely no sense of direction.'

'Erhard showed me inside the castle before I left.' I raised an eyebrow in a manner that was meant to convey more than I said.

'Oh, yes? What did you think? It's years since I was there with Henry.'

'How long would it be?'

'Oh, a long time. I must dash, I don't like to keep a lady waiting.' He clattered back to his car and with much aarghing and puffing sat down and tossed his college scarf over his shoulder. 'Well, goodbye all,' he said through the open window and drove off looking demure and harmless.

'I think he's great,' said Deirdre. 'He's a character.'

'What do you mean exactly?' I said.

'He's not at all like you, Uncle. He's a real laugh.'

'What's he doing visiting your mother?' said Uggers. What *was* he doing visiting my mother? And why had he given me the picture? I went back upstairs with Clotworthy and my near naked companions and amid much excitement from Deirdre and quizzical looks from Uggers hung the picture at the far end of the drawing room. It looked splendid.

After several minutes of listening to a history of Deirdre's ancestors I remembered the shopping, and left the lovers and Clotworthy alone.

When I opened the front door half an hour later, there was no sign of life. I took a quick look at Clotworthy before putting on the kettle for tea. Home! It really was rather pleasant. I wasn't going to let the fact that Netta was getting married and the fact that I had got home to find my best friend in bed with an antipodean dwarf and the fact that Father was for some unknown reason visiting Mother unsettle me. I put an ear to my bedroom door. Not a squeak. No doubt the young things would surface in their own time. I reflected that it was a sunny afternoon in my favourite month, October, and opened the door on to the fire escape. No one was about and I climbed the final stage to the roof.

As I clambered around the parapets and projections, past stacks of enormous chimneys and over the projections of battlements and the outside of domes I had the sensation of being on the deck of an enormous cruise-liner voyaging in stately fashion over the fields and pastures of Sussex. Down below, in their cabins, generations of Blancs and their retainers had lived their lives, set off for war or on dangerous expeditions, loved, hated, been born and been carried out to their graves. Nearly forty years had passed since I had first been inside Blanc Hall. Nearly forty years had gone by since the last squire had sat beneath its roof compiling his lists of one-eyed men, composers who died in Venice, and men who had died at the age of sixty. Those years had gone by so fast, and yet old Sir Richard, my childhood friend, and James too, and Aunt Mary, people whom I had known and loved, were all as dead as Ezra Pound, as dead as Stravinsky, as dead as that beautiful Russian princess.

From the western side of the roof I could see the spire of Chichester Cathedral above its green copper roof and to the north Halnaker Mill, the place to which Netta and I had climbed when I had returned from my first trip to Steinpass so many heavy years ago. Halnaker Mill had been a landmark in my soul's history. Between me and it lay miles of fields interspersed with copses and larger patches of woodland. Some fields were newly ploughed, some were scratched and scraped, and some striped black where the stubble had been burned. Autumn rain had washed it clean and left it shining in the bright sunlight. And behind the fields and woods, like an immense green wave rolling in from the sea, stretched the line of the Sussex Downs, leaving everything in its wake wave-washed and translucent, and all under a sky of towering Sussex clouds. No doubt there were prettier landscapes; no doubt there were more dramatic landscapes; but this was the landscape of my heart.

CHAPTER 24 · *Despondency*

N THE MORNING I wandered around the grounds, kicking up piles of leaves, for half an hour or so. I thought of walking over to see Mother and decided against it. I couldn't face talking to her just now, with the wedding looming. And what if Father had been smuggled in to stay the night, perhaps in my old caravan? I went back to the flat. Still no sign of life from within. I had breakfast like a condemned man. I decided I would go to Matins.

Lin Lan Lin Lan went the old bells as I hurried towards the church. I lifted the familiar latch and pushed open the door. Someone I vaguely recognised put a hymn book and a prayer book into my hand. 'Sorry your Uncle's so unwell.' I hadn't given Uncle Frank a thought. I felt guilty.

The smell of apples. Harvest Festival. At the back, behind the pew I was heading for, I could see old Travis-Blean, our elderly vicar, getting into his finery. I sat down with my back to a pillar. Above my head was a singed flag that I knew of old. Standing opposite me, pulling gently at two ropes, was Gordon Jones, the white-haired pilot and vintage Romeo of Blanc Hall. He nodded affably before taking his seat at the front amongst the marrows, eggs and Bramleys. The congregation rose and the vicar shuffled forward and announced, 'Hymn number two hundred and eighty-nine: "Come ye thankful people, come".'

With a wheeze from the organ the singing began. By the second verse I had noticed that there were two opposing factions; the bulk of the congregation, shall we call them the Royalists, followed the organ, but an old girl with a large chest sitting with a rival band of followers led the Parliament at a slightly slower pace.

> For the Lord our God shall come,
> And shall take his harvest home;
> From his field shall purge away
> All that doth offend that day;

> Give his angels charge at last
> In the fire the tares to cast,
> But the fruitful wheat to store
> In his barn for evermore.

I hadn't been to our church for years, except at Christmas when I came home to visit Mother. Nothing much had changed, other than the numbers. The conversion of Blanc Hall had doubled the size of the congregation. I moved along my pew. The singed flag had been tickling dreadfully.

Prayers. I sat and fumbled for an extra hassock, getting a handful of cobwebs as I did so, before kneeling like a choirboy with my hands before me, as taught by Uncle Frank so long ago. The prayerbook. Those comfortable words. The General Confession, the Absolution. The wheezing organ and the Civil War continued with the Venite. The vicar turned once more to consult the organist and announced in faltering tones: 'We will now sing Psalm sixty-five.'

> Thou crownest the year with thy goodness: and thy
>   clouds drop fatness.
> They shall drop upon the dwellings of the wilderness:
>   and the little hills shall rejoice on every side.
> The folds shall be full of sheep: the valleys also
>   shall stand so thick with corn, that they shall
>   laugh and sing.

I had thought it was only old Wordsworth who could almost (well, who can, as a matter of fact) bring tears to my eyes. Perhaps it's the associations, the memories. I don't know. Perhaps it's the language. Perhaps it's the fact that Netta is getting married tomorrow.

The first lesson. Most of the congregation dozed. Battle recommenced for the Te Deum and after that Mr Knight took the lectern and read the parable of the sower. I remembered James reading that same lesson at that lectern.

'I'm sorry you've only got me,' began old Mr Travis-Blean, who had officially retired some years ago but had been resurrected on the death of his successor, 'and not someone more important, on this very important day, and I'm sorry too that I can no longer get up the steps of the pulpit. Before I begin my sermon, I have a couple of notices for you. The summer fête raised three hundred and twenty-seven pounds . . .'

I climbed the stairs to my flat to be greeted by Uggers wearing only a white towel around his middle. He was clutching the handle that had been above the bath, complete with tiles and masonry. 'It just came away in my hand,' explained my seventeen-stone friend. 'Don't worry, I'll fix it,' he said and grinned. Some hope! His face reminded me of those battered stone lions you see in Venice. He pointed the bathhandle at me like a revolver and added, 'Oh, I nearly forgot. Your mother rang. Uncle Frank's on the blink. He's had a stroke.'

I hurried over to Coniston. The ambulance was in the drive and the ambulance men were half carrying and half dragging Uncle Frank towards it. Mother was holding his hand and I kissed her on the cheek before she climbed in beside him. 'You can follow in the car if you like,' she said.

I found my way through the overheated hospital to where Mother was sitting. Uncle Frank was being wired up and just stared straight ahead. Mother seemed more flustered than upset. She was anxious to get away. I went to the bedside. 'Is there anything you want, anything I can do?'

'Your father . . . Your father . . .'

'Come on, dear. He's rambling. Goodbye, Frank, I'll be in to see you in the morning.'

We walked to the car in silence and got in. I started the engine. 'What was that about Father?' I asked her. 'He called on me yesterday. He said he was going to see you.'

'It just happened that he decided to call in. That's all. Frank's been ill for months . . . Toby called in last week as well, actually. Why shouldn't he? It's just an unhappy coincidence that Frank should decide to have a stroke when he was here.'

'You mean Father was still here? He stayed the night?'

'In the caravan. He's not very well, as you know. He may have to have the leg off. He'd drunk rather a lot. I couldn't let him drive all the way back to Brixton. He said he'd seen you in Austria. He took me out to dinner as a matter of fact. Oh, Frank didn't know anything about it. He sleeps like a baby.' She looked at me rather sheepishly, I thought. Now was the time for a counter-attack.

'Did you know that, while we were away, Father suggested to me once that there was a possibility that he wasn't my real father?'

'Did he, dear?'

'And that Henry Usher could have been. He was joking, of course.'

'Henry was certainly more interested in women than Toby and so, come to that, was Nicholas York.'

'You didn't . . .'

'Haven't I told you before that inquisitive children have lying parents?'

'For God's sake, Mother! But . . . Henry Usher wasn't my father?'

'I don't think so, dear, do you?'

'But there is a possibility?' She said nothing. An old legal maxim came into my head. She who keeps silent agrees. 'And what do you think happened to him?'

'Oh, I expect he's around somewhere.'

'You don't think he committed suicide?'

'He wasn't the type.'

'So why . . . why the disappearance?'

'Oh . . . money troubles . . . James . . . women . . . any number of reasons. Did you know, Nicholas York's mother rang me once and instructed me to tell Toby to leave Henry alone? *These queers are always pinching each other's boyfriends,* she said. I don't know if I laughed or not.'

'But was Henry . . .?'

'Well, he wasn't as bad as your father. Of course, later she blamed Nicholas's fall entirely on Henry's influence. Your father worshipped him . . . followed him about like a puppy . . . perhaps that's why he disappeared. But no . . . I don't *think* Henry was your father, do you?'

'Father gave me the picture of Clotworthy,' I said.

'That dreadful old thing!'

'Yes, I wondered if there was any significance.'

'You've always liked it, haven't you? You never had any taste in pictures.'

'You don't think Clotworthy is one of my ancestors?'

'I suppose you'd like to think you were a viscount's son. Well, perhaps you are.'

'And perhaps I'm not? Is that what you're saying?'

'Does it matter whose son you are? For God's sake shut up.'

CHAPTER 25 · A Wedding
or a Festival

EVIL DAY. Today Netta will marry her squat, whey-faced American professor of physics and nothing short of a bullet can stop it. The poncey art-dealer was bad enough. Sometimes I wonder if Netta isn't unbalanced. The wedding is fixed for three o'clock, an evil hour if ever there was one. Anyhow, the die is cast, and here we are trailing into an adequate though far from ostentatious restaurant as guests of the happy couple.

Picture the gathering. Birgit: time has worked at her face with his engraver's tool, yet she is still a handsome woman, although somewhat larger than when you last saw her. She is resplendent in a voluminous purple kaftan and attended by her husband, the village doctor. In her wake are a couple of Netta's female solicitor friends from the city in their fem-dom gear, a friend of the prof from the scrublands of Academe in tasteless brown, Uggers, in baggy cords and enormous rug-like sweater, and me, tastefully attired in the same grey pin-striped three-piece that I had worn when I saw her in London last year. Not that she'd remember it even if she did remember something of what followed. She let me make love to her after I had been rejected. I suppose that is some kind of consolation. He doesn't know *that*, I'm sure. Making love to Netta is like being out on the windy plains of Troy where skirmishes and full-scale battles are constantly raging. She'll be dragging his shapeless carcase around the city walls tonight.

Alas, Mother is unable to come. The deathbed vigil.

Birgit's laugh hasn't got any quieter with the passing years, and as for the groom, well, if he had any dress-sense he'd be dangling his bonnet and plume all right. Poor Netta. The man of her choice chooses mineral water. Saving himself for the rigours of the night no doubt. It does little for his conversation. I am pleased to relate that his university is what

Father likes to call *red brick*. It would have been too much to bear if he'd been a lecturer at Oxford or Cambridge. He may have a silent face but he certainly lacks Newton's dignity. In fact he looks a complete nonentity. Uggers catches me peering at the fellow and gives me one of his ragged smiles. I suppose he thinks I need sympathy. He rocks dangerously on his chair smoking a foul-smelling French cigarette and attempts to look sympathetic, worldly and undrunk at the same time. How little the years have changed him, apart from his baldness; in the sphere of good looks he had little to lose.

It is half an hour to blast-off and the groom tries to attract Netta's attention by jabbing at his watch but she is too busy haranguing her stepfather on important feminist issues. Birgit is roaring with laughter and roaring at the universe in general. Well, just roaring really. She is drunk enough to take on the cosmos at large and certainly more than a match for anything physics can throw at her. Why should I suffer my genial spirits to decay? 'Thank you, Netta, I will have some more.'

'It's two-thirty, honey . . . It's two-thirty, honey.'

Netta gives the fellow a contemptuous wave of the hand and pours me another glass. He throws up his hands in despair. For a moment I almost feel sorry for him, marrying Birgit's daughter. He doesn't stand a chance.

'I don't think your Uncle Frank's got long to go,' says the doctor, addressing himself to me, prompted no doubt by the groom's insistence over the question of time.

'Is it true you had it off with my mother in the raspberry canes?' I ask.

'I had a weakness for soft fruit. Always liked your mother, and Mary too. They were a smashing pair of girls. Always envied your Uncle Frank. Lucky chap. Here, have another glass.'

At ten to three Netta wags a finger at the paleface prof as a sign that it is time to depart. He has already handed over a credit card and what looked to me like an over-extravagant tip. Everyone gets up from the table except for Uggers and Birgit, and I see my bearded friend tap the mini-skirted waitress's bottom and make signs at her to indicate that a further bottle is required. The groom has long since given up the struggle and hands over a banknote. Uggers gives me a familiar sideways look and Netta says, 'Five minutes', in stentorian tones as the lesser members set off, leaving the bulk of the party behind.

The Register Office, a not unattractive Georgian building. We are instantly ushered through to the portentously named Marriage Room, possibly because we look like potential rioters. Let's have a wedding! The lady Registrar rattles through the pre-nuptial paperwork in double-quick time.

'Now we come to the ceremony itself,' she says. We are all (except for Uggers and the bride's mother, that is) sitting comfortably, listening to the beautiful words, when the sound of a struggle is heard outside. The door bursts open and in wafts the bearded pard, floating on Birgit's purple kaftan. The Registrar gives an official cough, Netta responds with a nervous laugh, the groom blanches to a whiter shade of pale and the proceedings continue to the bitter end.

There isn't a wet eye in the house. Looking about me I observe, and duly admire, two plaster busts, one of Chopin and one of Schubert, which stand at either end of the Adam chimney-piece. They are bigger versions of the ones of Bach and Beethoven which Uncle Frank keeps in the music room at Coniston. Like Marcel's madeleine, they take me back, and I think of Uncle Frank lying in a hospital bed, only ten minutes away from the scene of Netta's crime, afraid no doubt, in spite of the ministrations of his sister-in-law.

The deed is done. I shuffle out with the others as the usual hand shaking, cheek kissing etcetera burst like flak all around me. Professor and Mrs J. Hector Smith. Now there's class.

Outside into the dry October air. Not even the heavens weep. So much for the pathetic fallacy. Those with cameras advance, those without retreat. At the first flash, Uggers produces from the folds of his capacious designer-jersey a sizeable bust of Schubert. 'A wedding present,' he says, with something of a flourish. *Flash*. Netta, who doesn't want to appear too much of a harridan on this happy day, smiles graciously, and passes it to me. *Flash*. Naturally, as a barrister of the Middle Temple, albeit retired, I know my duty. You can't be too careful in your profession, as Father used to say when I had one. I duly return Schubert to his rightful home. Chopin looks pleased. The happy couple have chosen Venice for their honeymoon. *Venice!* Before they leave for the airport I point out to the groom that George Eliot's husband threw himself into the Grand Canal from the window of their honeymoon hotel and had to be fished out and forcibly returned to the matrimonial bed. I like to be helpful. Netta gives me one of her frowns and then smiles sadly and shakes her head. 'We're old friends,' she explains, but the groom continues to look confused. No doubt he thinks George Eliot is a man.

A little confetti, and off they go. I would like to report that the happy couple travelled to the airport in the hearse; it would have been a fitting end for such a day. Alas, Birgit was drunk and incapable. She couldn't have driven to the end of the road. Both she and her husband and Netta and hers went their separate ways by taxi. Good luck, Netta . . . Good luck, Hector . . . I hope the plane crashes . . .

Uggers and I walk from the Register Office over to the hospital. We trail in noisy fashion along the arteries and entrails of the building until we find Mother and Uncle Frank. 'Thank God,' she says, 'I can get a cup of tea. I don't suppose I can get anything stronger in here, although I should think I could get drunk by breathing in your fumes.'

'I'm not drunk, Mrs Lamb,' says Uggers. For a moment I think he is going to challenge her to an arm-wrestle.

'The prognosis is poor,' says Mother, 'though I wouldn't be surprised if he lasted for years. His appetite has always been good. He was eating like a horse only yesterday.'

'I suppose Father's visit had nothing to do with the latest attack?' I say.

'You think he tried to bump him off?' says Mother with a chuckle.

'I wouldn't put anything past Father.'

'Tom!' says Uggers, by way of reproof. 'I'll come with you

if you're having tea, Mrs Lamb,' and they set off down the corridor. At least Uncle Frank has a room to himself. I think he knows me. His stares are alternately blank and comprehending, almost as if a light in his head is being switched on and off. 'Dorothy?' and he turns restlessly in the bed. 'Mary?' He isn't the first to have confused them.

I don't know quite what to do or how I should behave. I pick up the volume of Wordsworth from the bedside table and open it at random at *Tintern Abbey* and begin to read aloud. Perhaps something will register. He may get some comfort . . . When I get to

> These beauteous forms,
> Through a long absence, have not been to me
> As is a landscape to a blind man's eye:
> But oft, in lonely rooms, and mid the din
> Of towns and cities, I have owed to them,
> In hours of weariness, sensations sweet,
> Felt in the blood, and felt along the heart

I look up from the book and down at Uncle Frank. He is staring hard at me with his eyebrows raised as if he is trying to say something. I lean across. 'What is it, Uncle Frank? Do you want to tell me something?'

He gurgles for a few seconds and suddenly the words come . . . 'There's something I want . . . something I want . . .'

'Yes, Uncle Frank. What is it?'

'Your father . . . Your father . . .'

'Yes, Uncle Frank. What is it?'

Alas, his voice degenerates to mere gurgling again. What is it he wants to tell me? That he hates Father? That Father brought on the stroke, that Father has killed him? That Father is not my father? It's no good. He can't get the words out and I return to *Tintern Abbey*. When I next look up he is staring blankly. I continue with the poem:

> . . . and this prayer I make
> Knowing that Nature never did betray
> The heart that loved her . . .

I stop again. He wants to say something. 'Are you listening, Uncle Frank?'

'Yes.'

'What have I just read?'

'Words . . . Words . . . Words . . .'

'Yes . . . Now what was it you wanted to tell me about my father?'

'Your father . . . Yes . . . Your father . . . I don't . . . I can't remember . . . can't think,' and he taps his head with his hand, conjoined as it is with a plastic tube. I continue:

> and in after years,
> When these wild ecstasies shall be matured
> Into a sober pleasure, when thy mind
> Shall be a mansion for all lovely forms,
> Thy memory be as a dwelling-place
> For all sweet sounds and harmonies . . .

He has fallen asleep. A flow of dribble is running down his chin and has soaked an area of the pillow. I take a tissue from the box at the side and wipe him.

Mother and Uggers are back. She looks at me as if to ask whether it is in order to go to him. I nod and watch as she kisses the sleeping form goodbye and then we set off to find the car which is some twenty minutes' walk away. No bad thing, as far as my driving is concerned.

'Is there any more booze?' says Uggers, when we have been home ten minutes.

'We've run out.'

'Disaster. Let's see Deirdre at the pub,' and off we go. Deirdre started work there as a barmaid only today. It seems a lifetime away. She and Uggers seem to be settling in and have shown no sign of departing. I don't really mind. In fact, although I like to make a fuss and have reservations about having my loneliness wrested from me, on balance I am pleased. At the moment I don't think I could face life on my own. Something else has come to light . . . At the pre-wedding lunch, Netta happened to mention James . . . It prompted me to ask her exactly what had gone on between them . . . *Well, she said, it was all a long time ago, and yes, to tell you the truth I did have quite a crush on him, and yes we did go so far as to go to bed with each other once, but it wasn't very successful. You don't mind, do you?* When I relate this to Uggers he smiles wanly and suggests another drink.

Before we go to bed we plan an outing. We are going to walk to Halnaker Mill and will set off at dawn, hangovers and all. They think I need comforting. They are humouring me. What a day it has been. What a ghastly day.

CHAPTER 26 · A Mourning . . .

As USUAL, I slept in the spare bed that night. And not well. At first there was a lot of noise from the neighbouring room. Eventually Uggers settled down to read his cricket book, no doubt. I know his habits of old. I was tossing and turning for ages, and suffering from the thirst you get when you've had too much to drink. I'd just dropped off when there was a colossal crash from the next room. I got up to make some tea. Uggers came out to join me. 'Tom,' he said, sucking in his lower lip, 'the bed's broken. I don't know how it happened. It must be the wave principle, the Doppler effect. The idea of a wedding seems to have spiced Deirdre up a treat. It's all right, we'll sleep on the mattress.'

If a resident of Blanc Hall had looked out from a window on the north side of the house early next morning he might have distinguished a motley crew assembling in the grey light. Uggers, bearded and seventeen stone, Deirdre, five foot nothing topped with a schoolboy crop of blonde hair, and me, lean, birthmarked and carrying a heavy pine stick I'd found under the Roman bridge at Steinpass. I also had an old army bag over one shoulder. The army bag contained a map and two hip flasks of whisky.

'This is like an outing from a lunatic asylum,' said Uggers.

We set off at a good pace past the Manor, through the village and across the fields that lead to the woods. In parts they have a forlorn air since the Great Storm, particularly in winter. The pillars of the temple are down. A patchy mist hung over the river, but in places we could see that it was black and frosty on the far side. The downs were invisible: nothing but a haze of ghostly bracken and purple fields. As we dropped into the lane beyond the wood we could hear the clatter of hoofs and found ourselves hemmed in by a string of racehorses out for their morning exercise. There must have been thirty or more coming towards us out of the mist, snorting and steaming. Looking back over the hill we had just crossed we could see the light turning bluer and bluer and the ploughed fields more and more orange, and it was day.

An hour later we were on the back of the downs and suddenly, there it was on the horizon, Halnaker Mill. I raised the Austrian stick and pointed.

'Tilting at windmills?' said Uggers. 'Some more brandy?' We stopped and I got out the hip flask for the third time that morning. Brandy, whisky, it was all the same to him.

'In my country, Uncle, we have real mountains,' said the dwarf. 'Is that the Cathedral?' She pointed to the great spire rising from the mist. I nodded. 'ABC,' she said.

'What do you mean, ABC?' I said coming out of a trance.

'That's what we say when we go on the tour. Another bloody castle, another bloody church, another bloody cathedral. Pass the hip flask, Uncle. No, Uncle, I'm only joking. I think it's great, I really do. Hey, Uncle, you look really crook. Are you going to be okay?'

'Me? Oh, I shall be all right. I'm starting my new lecturing job soon.'

'Uncle'll be fine,' said Uggers. 'He's looking forward to it. Think of all those girls.'

'Think of me in the pin-striped dawn,' I said, 'setting off for my first day in a world of strident feminists and political correctness.' And, I thought, if you're religious, pray. Pray for the soul of Thomas Lamb.

As we walked on, through what to me was a holy land-scape, Deirdre prattled on artlessly about her ancestors and her travels. Uggers even tried her on capitals; what is the capital of France, that sort of thing. She did surprisingly well, but then, as she explained, in New Zealand where she came from, they have the best educational system in the world, with more universities than they knew what to do with.

We had lost the path and were heading in a straight line for the famous landmark. The mill was stark and beautiful on the skyline, and the closer we came, the more isolated it seemed. When we were only a few hundred yards away we reached a barbed wire fence. I scrambled through like a madman and ran towards the mill waving my heavy stick, bag flapping at my side. The lovers followed in more stately fashion. There is no door. I went in. A hollow shell of brick and stone. When my eyes had adjusted to the light I saw the graffiti: *so-and-so loves so-and-so*, and the expletives, the oaths, the promises, the dates. And then I saw something I had written there a long time ago. I thought it had lasted rather well: *Netta ti amo.*

Early next morning when I was still in bed I heard the telephone ringing. As there was a receiver in my former bedroom, Uggers called out to say he'd got it. Then he appeared in the doorway stark naked. 'It's all right, it's all right. Uncle Frank's dead.' He said it as if I might have made some kind of scene. The good die young. Uncle Frank had made eighty-six.

I went straight over to Mother's and we had some toast and tea in the kitchen before setting off for the hospital. When we got inside, Mother turned to me and said, 'Do you mind if I go in alone?' I paced about like an expectant father until she returned. She was very controlled. She looked as if she'd just stepped out of the fruit cage.

There were things to do. We walked over to the Register Office, scene of Netta's recent happy event, and registered Uncle Frank's death, and from there we walked on to an undertakers, where we were shown a catalogue of coffins without prices. The bereaved were no doubt intended to say 'that looks nice' about the highly polished expensive jobs without realising what they were doing. 'We'll take the cheapest one, so long as it's made of real wood,' said Mother.

'Mahogany?' said the undertaker's assistant.

'Pine,' said Mother, and named the day.

'Let's have something to eat at Ninny's Tomb,' said Mother. 'I don't want to go back to an empty house without fortifying myself first, and somehow it seems appropriate,' and to Ninny's Tomb we went. Deirdre introduced herself to Mother. They got on famously.

'What a charming girl,' said Mother. 'It's a pity you couldn't have found yourself someone like that. The trouble with you is that you're too stuffy. I suppose you think that no one but Netta's good enough for you? Stop looking so priggish. That's one of your problems. You keep expecting other people to be perfect. People who are perfect are always frightfully dull.'

After lunch I drove Mother back to Coniston and went back to collect Uncle Frank's things. Somehow we had forgotten to take them with us. I suppose Mother had thought it unseemly to remove them whilst he was lying in state. I saw the nurse and told her the purpose of the visit. She confirmed that Uncle Frank had been moved, and that I could go along to the room. She told me I wouldn't find his pyjama trousers because she didn't like to think of him going off without anything – it didn't seem right somehow.

In his place on the bed were a few possessions for which I was obliged to sign; some stained clothes including the top half of his pyjamas, a book of wildflowers, and old Wordsworth, and I put them in a plastic bag which the nurse had given me. Uncle Frank had become his belongings.

CHAPTER 27 · . . . *Or a Funeral*

WE BURIED UNCLE Frank at the village church where he had played the organ for thirty years (until his final row with Travis-Blean) and where James and I had accompanied him most Sundays as boys.

Gathering outside to wait for the hearse when I arrived with Uggers were Birgit and the doctor, old Travis-Blean, who had decently agreed to turn out for the occasion, and a dozen or so parish faces, including the usual old biddies who regard a funeral as fine entertainment. Uggers and Deirdre were there too, looking concerned, although Uggers had complained that he had not been feeling too good. 'These sort of upsets affect me,' he said. Sensitive chap, Uggers.

Just as the hearse pulled up outside (there were no limousines) a car appeared behind it and the driver honked the horn, and put his head out of the open window. I could see the black and white college scarf, but at first I couldn't believe my eyes. 'Am I in time?' said Father. The congregation showed some interest. For several seconds I stood there gaping. How typical of him to upstage Uncle Frank.

'Aren't you going to help me out?' he called, as the coffin was being removed from the hearse. 'I've brought the wheelchair. It's in the boot. Will you get it for me?'

Birgit pushed her way forward like a bull emerging from a crowd of heifers. 'Toby. How wonderful to see you. How long has it been?' Birgit in black is the only person I know who is capable of reducing Father to silence. 'Help your father out of the car, Thomas, for the love of God. He looks thoroughly spannered.'

The procession was lined up waiting to go into the church as I manoeuvred Father into his wheelchair, and we followed behind. 'I'll just slip in at the back,' said Father. Such self-effacement. I left him there and sat in the front row on the outside next to Mother. She looked, if anything, mildly amused.

I heard Father's distinctive cough at the announcement

of *Fight the Good Fight*, and as we began to sing the famous hymn, the pall-bearers wheeled round stamping their boots in almost military style and carried out the coffin.

I was instructed to push Father to the graveside; he wasn't going to miss anything. He has developed an operatic whisper and I'm sure everyone heard him ask me if that wasn't Aunt Mary's grave they had opened for him. There is a shortage of space in the churchyard and Mr Knight had to re-open the grave and bury him on top of her. Aunt Mary would, I think, have appreciated the irony, though I doubt whether it would have appealed to James, buried six plots away. Now Uncle Frank too is rolled round in earth's diurnal course with rocks and stones and trees.

After Father had been loaded into the car, Mother got in with him and I walked back to Coniston alone with Uggers and Deirdre. The elms are gone of course, and the hornbeam came down in the Great Storm. Only the yew and the sycamore remain.

I could hear the buzz of talk and the sound of Father's laugh before I opened the door, and when I got in I saw my parents engrossed in conversation. Mother had pulled up a stool and was perched next to Father's wheelchair, filling his glass from a bottle on the floor. Birgit was handing round sandwiches.

I wandered lonely into the garden. I was in an odd mood and felt a sense of unreality, almost of dislocation. I had nothing to say to anyone. I wanted to talk to Mother, that was all, but she was far too busy talking to Father. I couldn't help thinking about Uncle Frank, lying in his cheap pine box on top of Aunt Mary, and wondering whether her own coffin had quite rotted by now. Presumably Uncle Frank had gone to eternal rest wearing the bottom half of his striped pyjamas. Surely he should have had old William and his book of wildflowers for company as he voyaged through those strange seas? And would the PCC allow us to put a brass plate on the organ even though he did fall out with Travis-Blean? *Seated one day at the organ, he was weary and ill at ease.* Would he find the lost chord, I wondered, or would the pearly gates be forever closed against him?

When Uggers, Deirdre and I left for home, Father was still there and was showing no sign of wanting to leave. 'Still not working? I expect you've got time on your hands. Does that New Zealand girl belong to the bearded fellow? I thought she was quite attractive. I was thinking of asking her up for sherry but I thought you might not like it if I did. I was always a martyr to my sense of honour. There's some business I'd like to discuss with you. Come up for a meal if you like. Tuesday evening? I'll ring to confirm, just in case anything crops up, and bring some steak. I could do with some red meat. Puts lead in the pencil, as Henry used to say.'

CHAPTER 28 · *The Light*
of Common Day

I T WAS ABOUT seven o'clock when I pulled into the side turning by Father's block of flats and ran up the three flights of stairs clutching a carrier bag containing fillet steak, Jersey potatoes, avocados and parsley, together with some domestic items ordered by the invalid earlier in the day. I felt more out of breath at the top than I would care to admit. Father had recently installed an entryphone. I pressed the button. The usual sound of rasping microphone was followed by a frail 'Come in,' and I pushed open the door. The same old smells, coffee, bleach and Brasso. 'ARRGH, I had a bad night. All my joints are aching. Even my wrists are giving trouble now. The specialist said it's the frame.'

'The zimmerframe?'

He nodded. 'The pressure of the hands carrying all this weight,' and he looked down at his body as if it wasn't really anything to do with him, 'and I bruised my chest quite nastily this morning.'

'How did you do that?'

'My wig fell off when I leant out of the window to look at the paper boy and it got lodged on the drain-pipe. You know I've got one of those things from the hospital for pulling up my socks, with a sort of pincer at the end, well, I had to lean right out and I must have pressed my chest against the catch. Thank God he didn't see me and there was no one else around. At my time of life appearance is all. Oh, have you seen my new wheelchair?' He pressed a button and the SuperCruiser rocketed forward in the direction of the sherry decanter. He poured himself a glass, put the machine into reverse gear and shot back to his corner.

'I couldn't get the hundred and fifty watt bulb you asked for, so I got a hundred watts instead.'

'Sorry,' he said waving one hand dismissively. 'That's no use to me. You'll have to take it back with you.'

'But –'

'If I order a pound of beef I don't expect to be given a pair of rollerskates.' It was going to be one of those nights. Father took a sip of sherry. 'Did I ever tell you how I missed the best time of my life?'

'May I have a beer, Father?'

'I may have my faults but I'm not an ungenerous host. You'll find one in the kitchen. And bring some crisps.' He continued to talk as I disappeared into the kitchen. 'You were always such a prude. A cold fish.' I could sense him purse his lips in disdain as he went on: 'You've never known real *passion*, I'm certain of that. When I was a subaltern in India I was, as you know, very good-looking. Henry and I had been down to the bazaar. They have marvellous perfumeries. The scents are oil-based, not spirit-based like the ones we have here so that as the evening wears on the heat brings them out. We dabbed some on our wrists and later we got rather drunk. I don't remember what happened after that but when I woke up I must admit I was *un peu mal* –'

'You had a hangover?'

'– *mal au derrière*. I had to take parade, and the Indian troops were smirking rather and giggling. I remember the Havildar-Major, a huge Sikh, twirled his moustache and gave me the sweetest smile. Of course, it occurred to me that the whole platoon might have ... well, you know. I wouldn't have blamed them. Did you see Anthony Farr on television on Friday?'

'No, it was the day of the funeral.'

'I got back just in time. I had a very good day. You should have watched it. He was excellent. You know, of course, that when I was at Magdalen he tried to nibble my ear in Blackwell's? You should read more of his books. Mind you, you don't really have a sense of history, do you? His new book – *Byron and Revolution* – is so good. Byron, now there's a poet,' and Father glanced at Henry's picture on the desk by his side. He saw me looking and pointed at the next one. 'That one's James taken on the Devil's Bridge at Murano. Though of course you were there, I believe. I think he benefited from our relationship, don't you?'

'James?'

'He had such sensitivity and strength of character. And of course he was very good-looking.' The SuperCruiser shot forward again and Father refilled his glass.

'I don't suppose you've ever thought that if you'd left us alone, James would still be alive.'

'All the time. I bought him that motorbike.'

'He said his grandparents paid for it.'

'Did he? Well, it wasn't true, I bought it. His grandparents were notoriously mean. Henry always said that if you wanted to see them scramble you just had to drop sixpence on the floor. That's how Henry got them to break open the trust fund when he wanted to buy the Aston. He sent Nicholas up to explain that there was something in it for them. By the way, in case you think I may have bumped off your Uncle Frank, I think I should point out that it was hardly my fault that the old duffer chose to look out of the window as I was making my way back to the car. There was nothing I could have done. I didn't know he'd had a seizure until your mother telephoned me. The funeral has prompted me to do some thinking. I may believe myself to be immortal, but there are people who disagree. It's time I re-made my will. Is there anything in particular you want? I've given you Clotworthy,' and he gesticulated vaguely in the direction of a large oval of darker wallpaper which marked the place where the portrait had hung. I noticed one or two other dark patches. Father was liquidating his stock. 'I thought, perhaps, my second best wig.'

'If you're not going to be using it, I'd prefer the shooting-stick umbrella.'

'Really? If you want it you can take it now. I won't be needing it. Henry gave it to me when I lost my first one — it fell off a chair at a restaurant in Venice and dropped into the Grand Canal. Mind you, I had to pay for it in the end. I had to settle a number of his outstanding bills. Did you know Henry killed a man with it?'

I shook my head. I hadn't heard *this* one before.

'I was chatting to a young soldier under the arches one night . . . he seemed such a nice boy, when a couple of his pals came up from the underground and started cutting up a bit rough. They were going to roll me, as they call it in the trade. Henry just happened to come round the corner in time. We'd planned to dine at the Ritz. He shouted at them. As you know he had an air of authority; he was not a person to cross. It seems I'd dropped the umbrella-stick in the course of being set upon and the next thing I knew two of them were running for their lives down Piccadilly and the one I'd been speaking to was lying on the ground. Henry was a big man and he'd felled him with one blow to the head. Of course he used to practise fighting with a Samurai sword. He was quite an expert. "Come on, old man," said Henry, "this is no time for lingering," and we were on the escalator in a few seconds. I read in the newspaper next day that a soldier had been found dead.'

'Is that why Henry had to disappear?'

'Disappear?' said Father. 'Henry is dead. If you are going to take the umbrella-stick do look after it. You're so careless with your things, and I'm rather fond of it, you know. Back to business. There'll be a small bequest to Nicholas, if he survives me. He fancied you like mad when you were seventeen. I can't think why. Said he wanted to kiss you all over. I've decided to leave the rest to your mother. I've put the flat up for sale. I'm thinking of moving in with her.'

'With *Mother?*'

'Don't look so surprised. I've always liked your mother. What could be more natural? I did marry her, you know. We shared the matrimonial bed. Now back to business. I am appointing you as my executor. You can have a trifle for your services . . . You know I've never seen James's grave before. I felt very moved in the churchyard. That boy meant the world to me. More than anyone.'

'More than Henry?'

'Oh yes. There wasn't the physical side of things with Henry. You've never known what it is to love. To love with passion, I mean.'

'What do you mean "the physical side"? Are you trying to tell me . . .?'

Father gave me the Clotworthy look before continuing. 'Don't be so naïve. How old are you? Nearly fifty? Surely you knew. He stayed at the flat . . . we went to Vienna . . . you remember, when you had that girl at the campsite. What was her name?'

'Trudi.'

'How clever of you to remember. It was James's idea that we asked you to come away with us . . . I wasn't sure it was a good one . . . you did get in the way a bit.'

'Father . . . I'm sorry but I want to get this straight. Are you saying that you and James had sex?'

'Of course we did. The first time was in Vienna. It was marvellous. He was such an affectionate boy.'

'In Vienna? But you picked up a tart for him!'

'Oh yes, so I did. I didn't think it would do him any harm. I don't know how he would have turned out in the end. I think a young man owes it to himself to try everything, don't you? What's the matter? Oh, you're such a prude. Now what about something to eat?'

I felt completely at a loss. I was reeling. I had lost my bearings. Father was moving in with Mother? Impossible. Father and the platoon was one thing, but Father and *James*? Surely not. Was there no end to his depravity? And he was so flippant about it. I went into the kitchen. This really was the end. And yet there I was beating the steak and scrubbing the potatoes like a dutiful daughter. It was too much. I felt my mind go into a different gear. The gun. While Father was issuing instructions from afar I went through the bedroom to the hall and opened the second drawer of the chest. I found the pistol in the old place under his boxer shorts. As I was checking the magazine I thought back to that night so long ago when Netta might have killed me with this same gun. Between thinking a thing and doing it lies a tremendous gulf . . .

'I don't suppose you'll want much wine if you're driving. There's a bottle of Bulgarian open in the kitchen. You can open a decent bottle if you really want to, but I don't want it wasted.'

I chopped the avocados and tomatoes, sprinkled on the parsley and added some Balsamic vinegar. Uggers had brought this back from Italy. It had been his contribution to household expenses. 'And bring some mustard.' 'Right you are, Father,' I said, putting the gun into my jacket pocket. 'Just coming. I hope you've got a hearty appetite.' 'I told you I'm not feeling too well. Arrgh. I'll have mine on the tray. Turn on the recorder, will you? I've got a tape of *Don Giovanni*. You've forgotten the mustard.' For a man who wasn't feeling too good, he was certainly attacking the steak with vigour. *Don Giovanni* . . . Clotworthy . . . the old photo of Henry, James on the Devil's Bridge . . . this flat. I slipped my hand into my pocket and took hold of the gun. I felt the safety catch with my thumb. Now? Or shall I save it for later?

'The steak's quite good. It was a little tough last time you came, which is why I asked you to beat it. In the old days you didn't have to beat fillet steak. I'm not sure that I like the salad. Are you using a new kind of dressing? Pour me another glass, will you? I'm not supposed to drink with the tablets, but if it's forced on me . . . Henry always said if rape's inevitable lie back and enjoy it.'

Was this my cue? Was this the moment?

'Strawberries to follow, did you say? I'll have some sugar on mine. I know you don't care for it.'

'Where is the sugar?'

'In the kitchen.' I stayed put. 'Anything wrong?'

'The sugar, Father?'

'It's in the tin.' The kitchen is a problem. All the surfaces are covered with jars and tins. I found a jar containing white crystals, and took off the lid to taste since it could have been salt, or cyanide. He was sitting with his back to the kitchen. I had the bowl of strawberries in one hand and the gun in the other. I held it to the back of his head and pulled the trigger . . .

. . . or did I? Looking back over the events of that evening I couldn't be sure.

'Uggh. What on earth did you put on my strawberries?'

'Isn't it sugar?'

'Saccharin.'

I took the bowl of strawberries back to the kitchen and rinsed them.

'The sugar's in the tin on the second shelf of the cupboard on your left.'

I opened a tin marked 'Celery Salt'. Yes. That was the sugar. 'I can still taste the saccharin. Coffee? I hope you brought some fresh beans with you, and why are you playing about with my gun? I took the firing pin out a long time ago, when I had that Swiss boy staying. He had a violent streak, you know, but the face of an angel.'

When I went out of the door of Father's flat, later that night, he smiled sweetly and asked, 'Did you really try to assassinate me?'

'I'm not sure,' I replied.

'You always were vague. I hope you did. Yours wasn't the first attempt on my life. I wonder if it'll be the last.'

CHAPTER 29 · *The Vision Splendid*

IX MONTHS AFTER the events just described, when I had settled in, after a fashion, to my new job, I found myself giving a series of refresher lectures for solicitors. These took place at a London hotel, and when not actually lecturing I had time to wander off on frolics of my own. Father had moved in with Mother at Easter. His damaged leg had been giving trouble and he had spent several days in a hospital in London while tests were carried out. The verdict of the experts was that the bone had rotted away in parts to such a degree that the leg would have to be amputated. This was something Father had always dreaded, but now that the time had come, he seemed to take the news pretty well. I had arranged to see him for a beer at the venue of his choice at one-thirty. He was due at the hospital at three. The operation was to be carried out the next day.

After a hard morning performing for the benefit of the lower branch of the legal profession I caught the tube to Covent Garden and headed for St Martin's Lane. I had been to this particular haunt of Father's on a previous occasion and I knew what to expect. As I swung through the doors and went down the steps the throb of nineties rock hit me. I looked around and took in a number of solitary males, most of them middle-aged, wearing leather jackets and with cropped hair and little moustaches. There was a huddle of pin-striped businessmen at the bar, and enthroned at a table in the far corner was Father.

'You found your way here. I was sure you'd get lost. Get yourself a beer,' he said. 'I've got one. I don't want to drink too much because of the tablets.' At least I think that's what he said because the music was so loud it was impossible to hear. I queued at the bar and got a beer.

'How are you, Father? BOOM BOOM BOOM. You

got up to London safely? How was the journey? Any adventures?'

GISH GISH GISH

'Terry met me at Victoria.'

BOOM BOOM BOOM

'Yes?'

GISH GISH CRRUMMP

'He's such a nice lad. So good-looking. And very obliging.'

BOO . . . BOO . . . GISH

'You didn't . . .?'

BOO BOOM

Father nodded . . . 'Very quick. Very successful . . . He's picking me up later.'

CRRASSSH

My set speech. It was too late to change. 'I've got six weeks' holiday soon. I wondered if you'd like me to take you to Venice after the operation, to convalesce.' BOOM BOOM. 'I could wheel you about . . .'

'Ha-ha . . . Venice . . . BOO BOO BAM . . . How kind . . . BOOM . . . inconvenience you . . . BAM BAM . . . other arrangements . . . BOOM GISH . . . Nicholas . . . Ha-ha . . . CRRUMPPP.'

I said what I hoped would be a temporary farewell to Father and took my last look at his left leg.

'Don't worry about me,' he said. 'I'm immortal.'

I told no one that I was going to Venice during the same week in August as Father. I knew Nicholas York was not fit enough to push a wheelchair very far, and Venice is not the easiest of places for such a conveyance. I was curious. And I like going to Venice anyway.

From the airport I took a water taxi, and for the price of a modest seat at the opera saw those visionary things and lovely forms, those towers, domes and temples in the diffused golden light of a Turner. It surprised the boatman when I asked to get out at the Fishmarket. '*Pescheria?*' he said. Given the chance I like to astonish.

There are other cities, but for me, if all the others go under

and Venice survives, it will be enough to justify two thousand
years of civilisation. Decaying, enchanting, vulgar, splendid and
magnificent, for me, it remains unequalled. Venice . . . city of
my conception.

I wandered about at random visiting my old haunts. I had,
of course, been hoping to bump into Father, but I knew from
forty-three years of experience that if I tried too hard nothing
would come of it. If anything was going to happen it would
happen of its own accord. All I could do was to be around at
the right time.

On my last day, I went to Torcello for a solitary lunch.
Then I took the vaporetto to the Fondamente Nuove and ambled
back to the seedy *pensione* by way of San Zanipolo. I like to
pay my respects to Colleoni, the Clotworthy of the equestrian
world. Venice . . . sunbaked brick, crumbling stucco, lapping
water . . .

That night, after a light supper at a restaurant near the
Fenice, I headed for St Mark's. It's the best time to see it,
when the air is cool and the Piazza uncrowded and the café
orchestras compete with each other as you stroll between them.
On the clock side they were playing the ubiquitous *Moonlight*
and on the other side I was pleased to recognise the famous
aria from *Gianni Schicchi*. Very appropriate as it happened. The
music was bouncing around the Piazza as I wandered towards
the Correr when I stopped dead and found myself staring in
the direction of Florian's. At a table near the musicians was
a wheelchair. Father was enthroned. Sitting beside him were
two old men.

I edged closer and recognised a ravaged version of Nicholas
York. The third man was looking away from me and I couldn't
see his face. I moved towards the Correr and doubled back
inside the arcade towards the floodlit violinist. There they
were, laughing and talking, Father, Nicholas York and,
quite unmistakably in spite of the dark glasses, Henry
Usher. They didn't see me and I walked on. The whole
thing seemed so unreal that I didn't know how to react.
At last I had tracked them down! What was I to do
next? I was pondering this question and turned to await
inspiration at a corner of St Mark's by my old porphyry

friends the Tetrarchs. Alas, at that moment, the combination of the rich food I had enjoyed that day, and the shock of seeing my father with his cronies, brought about a turn of its own, a comic turn, and I was forced, in Cervantes' immortal phrase, to do that thing which no one could do for me.

By the time I had returned to the Piazza, the objects of my curiosity had disappeared. I shot off in pursuit. There was no sign of them by the Basilica or the Campanile, no sign of them under the clock or by the lions. They were not down by the Grand Canal, nor inside the arcade. I ran down the narrow alleys towards the Monaco. Yes, there they were, climbing into a gondola! Father was already on board, seated in the wheelchair looking towards the front. Presumably he and his throne had been lifted in as a piece. It certainly made an impressive spectacle.

'Follow that gondola,' I barked at a comatose gondolier, and after some very unEnglish gesticulating and pointing, the fellow got the message and away we slid, through the choppy waters of the Grand Canal. I could just make out the outline of my quarry as it bounced along some distance in front of us, and glanced up at Father's old enemy, the moon. My skilful pilot swung our ancient craft into one of the many watery channels that feed the great artery of the city, then into another even narrower.

'*Deh vieni alla finestra . . .*' The tuneful voice of a tenor, presumably from one of those six-packs of gondolas stuffed full of tourists, drifted over the water. Soft spray, the warm air of an August night, shadow and light flickering on the water. I was almost forgetting myself. Another lurch and my guide murmured something incomprehensible. They had pulled up ahead!

'*Lente, lente,*' I said. '*Arrêtez, attendez . . . Bleibe!*'

'I wait,' he said, in what I took to be a deliberately infuriating tone. As we bounced in the wake of a passing motor taxi, I could see the old fellows stumbling out of the gondola – first the large form of the vanished viscount, Henry Usher, then the thinner outline of the disgraced former Cabinet Minister, Nicholas York, and finally, to the distant accompaniment of

Don Giovanni, I saw my father lifted ashore. 'Ha-ha.' It was him all right. At last!

My gondola slipped into the berth of its predecessor just as Henry's back disappeared inside the heavy door. I handed over a wad of notes and staggered on to the slippery steps. What if the door was locked? Unless I was prepared to swim for it I might be forced to wait here all night. Still, it would give Father and his cronies a shock in the morning! The gondola drifted away as I turned the heavy knob, and I found myself in pitch darkness on a flight of stairs. There was no turning back now.

I opened another door at the top of the stairs. The *piano nobile*. I looked around me; two huge chandeliers overhead, a grand piano, a harpsichord, a room sparsely furnished with good heavy pieces, with some fine oil paintings and tapestries. This was the room I had been inside with James, when was it, 1967, 1968? Just three months before he died? Voices! Father glided in, propelled by Henry and followed by Nicholas. Ah! here they were, the good companions, the triumvirate. I waited like a statue.

'Thomas,' said Father from his wheelchair. 'How clever of you to find us. I always thought you had no sense of direction. You know Nicholas, I believe. Allow me to introduce you to Henry.'

'I've run you to earth at last,' I said, and I heard the chandeliers rattle at the sound of my voice.

'Don't look so pleased with yourself,' said Father. 'You might be sorry. Henry might shoot you, or I might. Henry is not a man to cross.'

I bowed.

'We've met before,' said the impressive-looking man with the perceptible dent in his forehead, 'or at least we've cast eyes on each other. Twice, I believe.'

'Yes . . . I . . .'

'I must apologise for my lack of civility on that occasion at Steinpass. I knew who you were, of course. I'd seen you in this very room not so long before.'

'Good evening,' said Nicholas York. 'We haven't met for, how long is it? Twenty years? . . . Henry, won't you offer our young friend a drink?' Young friend. You can always tell a politician.

'Nicholas,' I said, 'you do realise it's August. It's social death to be seen in Venice in August. You told me so yourself.'

'Then we mustn't tell anyone, must we? . . . Henry, some champagne for Thomas, our night visitor.'

'Of course, of course, I'm forgetting myself,' and the big man loped across the room to a door, from which he emerged a few seconds later clutching a magnum of champagne. He untwisted the wire and popped the cork. I approached him and took a glass.

'To secrecy!' said our host, raising his glass.

'To immortality!' said Father.

'To immorality!' said Nicholas York.

Never before had I tasted such delicious champagne. It was liquid enchantment, an elixir, and here I was drinking it with Father and his dangerous and exotic companions. Yes I, the birthmarked son, the Venetian cousin, the by-blow, had tracked them down, had hunted them to their palatial lair, and had now, by force, by right of conquest, taken my place amongst them.

'Do you live here all the time?' I lamely asked my host.

'More than I did formerly.'

'Since you left the castle at Steinpass?'

'I don't know why I was so alarmed at seeing you. Perhaps I should have brazened it out. But I had a lot to lose.' The man's voice was powerful, yet melodious, with just a hint of the Clotworthy drawl.

'You mean you were afraid of things catching up with you?'

'Of course. Why else does one disappear?'

'What have you been doing all this time?'

'Thomas,' interrupted Father, 'didn't your mother ever tell you that it's rude to ask questions?'

'How are the young to learn, if they don't ask?' said Nicholas, who had been out on the balcony. He looked frail but his eyes were merry.

'If you spawn a child you don't think you owe it anything, Father? You think you've done your bit?'

'I think I've done more than my bit, as you put it. You were never what I would call a rewarding child.'

'Unlike James.'

'Some more champagne?' The big man came to my side with the bottle. Even at his age I'd be wary of taking him on.

'Thank you. It's delicious. Nineteen forty-nine. The year of my conception.'

'By rights it should have gone off by now, but somehow, like us, it seems to have survived more or less intact.'

'Ha-ha.'

'Forty-nine. Yes, it was a good year for us . . . one of the best . . .' added Nicholas.

The three men exchanged glances.

'It was the year when two of you went to bed with my mother. It has even been suggested that you', I nodded in the direction of Henry, 'might be my father.' He looked amused.

'Any one of us could be, actually,' said Father.

'What do you mean?' I said, aware that I was looking stupidly at him. And I couldn't help remembering that Father had told me that when I was seventeen Nicholas had wanted to *kiss me all over*.

'Well, to be quite honest,' said Nicholas, 'I'm not altogether sure that what Toby said is right. You see your mother and Mary were twins, and it must be said that they were very naughty girls as well as being very pretty. I did think I'd been to bed with Dorothy once but she refused to confirm or deny it, so I'm afraid it remains a rumour. You'd have to check with her. But I don't really think I could be your father, dear boy, do you?'

'We drew lots as to which of us was to accept responsibility,' said Father. 'I was the unlucky one. I was always a martyr to my sense of honour.'

'Why don't you come out on the balcony with me for a moment?' said Henry. 'I'll bring the champagne. Play, Nicholas. Sing, Toby.'

The piano struck up a tune I had heard in that room a long time ago:

> He sobbed and he sighed, and a gurgle he gave,
> Then he plunged himself into the billowy wave,
> And an echo arose from the suicide's grave –
> Oh willow, titwillow, titwillow!

We stepped outside into the warm night air and leant against the balustrade, looking down at the dark water. He took out a gold cigarette-case and offered me a cigarette. I declined of course. He took one and struck a match. The tobacco had a distinctive smell. 'Are you sure you won't have one?' I shook my head. He took a long drag before continuing. 'Now that things have come into the open, Thomas, I hope you will be kind enough to visit us again, when you're expected. You don't have to come when Toby is here. It's always difficult to talk with him around. But I must have your word as a gentleman to keep my existence a secret.'

'But why did you disappear?'

'I had any number of reasons. I had run out of cash, I killed a soldier in Piccadilly who was trying to rob Toby. And besides, I was bored . . .'

'Were you a spy?'

'A spy? Surely not.'

'Did you claim on the insurance?'

'That would have been a criminal offence,' he said, and smiled. 'Any more questions?'

'Would you mind telling me the identity of the lady who was here when James and I dropped in that time?'

He looked suddenly very sad. 'That was Jane. She was the daughter of a Rajah and an English dancer. She looked Italian. Venetians thought she was from Rome. She had a wonderful grasp of languages . . . She died last year. She's buried at San Michele, the cemetery island.' He turned away and took another drag of his cigarette. Except for the sound of a distant motor launch and the singing within, all was quiet. Then he continued, 'Until I met Jane, I didn't think I was the marrying kind. Come to that, I didn't think marriage was for Toby either, but I gather he's gone back to his wife of long ago . . . I liked your mother, you know, and her sister. They were delightful girls. I might almost have married Mary. I adored her but I couldn't have faced a life of poverty. I first met Jane when she was nineteen. Her husband had just died in a motor-racing accident. He was a Venetian count; he left her well provided for.'

'The palazzo?' I asked. He nodded. 'I saw her grave when I was last in Venice,' I said, 'in October. I followed Father from Steinpass. I saw him sitting in a taxi holding on to his hair. He was on his way back to the airport.'

'It seems you would have made a good spy yourself, Thomas. I really am rather impressed. You must have just missed us. I think it was the day before Toby left that we went to see the grave. He and Jane had always got on famously. She didn't stand any nonsense. She used to give him permission to speak . . . *And now, Toby, may we have one of your stories?*' He laughed at the recollection, shaking his head sadly. I could see that he had loved her. His face was a mixture of dark and light, of savagery and sensibility. He may have been a killer, a follower of the Divine Marquis, and a part-time sodomite, but he was nonetheless a man of feeling, a man of discernment, more colourful than evil, I liked to think, although, no doubt, more bad than good.

'You're not married, Thomas?' I shook my head. 'Have you ever tried it?'

'No,' I answered and thought of Netta's new ménage. I wondered how they were getting on. I glanced at my companion who was gazing at the black water below and asked, 'Did you finish your memoirs?' He swung round to face me so suddenly that I flinched but in a second he had composed his features once more. The dent in the head was somehow appropriate for this giant. 'I found the exercise book in the castle . . . I liked the bit where you said you wished your father had been a Gloucester Old Spot.'

'When it's finished I'll let you read it.'

'Will you come back?'

'Come back?'

'To England. You could claim your inheritance, your title . . .'

'Kinkering Kongs,' boomed the man who had engendered James my lost brother, and possibly me too. Then he looked at me and whispered, 'I think we should join the others, don't you?' He tossed the burning stub of his cigarette over the balcony and we watched it fall into the water. 'Shall we go inside?'

We drank champagne. We sang. Father even talked of having a Requiem Mass for his leg. He said that he had an artificial one on order, as if it had been a York ham from Harrods. When he'd got used to it he'd be able to use the umbrella-stick once more. If he couldn't get a new one, would I care to return the original?

For the first time in years, I found I was enjoying myself. To talk, to drink, to forget . . . Maybe that was the secret. I felt I had unravelled the major part of the mystery. Only one minor point, relatively speaking, remained to be clarified.

At about two in the morning Henry called from the balcony. 'Ah, here is your gondola. Nicholas must have summoned it . . . It is rather late. Here is my address. I'm sure you won't lose it. You will note that I'm known as plain Mr Unstead.'

I was being dismissed. Still, unless the old devil chose to disappear again, I knew where to find him.

'When we first knew each other,' said Nicholas, 'I remember you telling Toby that there had never been a plain Mr Usher.'

'That was before the fall,' said Father, adding for my benefit, 'a book by an American, you know.'

'Thank you, Father. Oh, that reminds me, before I go will you tell me, to the best of your knowledge, which one of you is my father?' There was a moment's silence as the three of them exchanged glances. Then Henry said,

'We can't. We don't know.'

'And you wouldn't approve of blood tests, DNA and all that,' added Father.

'Did you really draw lots . . .?'

'Of course not,' said Nicholas.

'Fortunately we're all high-nosed Romans,' said Henry, raising an eyebrow. I knew he was making mock of Father. We both laughed. Nicholas laughed. Father looked cross.

'You return home in the morning?' he said, turning to me as I bade them farewell.

'Yes, and you?'

'Oh, in a few days, if I live that long.'

'But you're immortal, Father, you've said so yourself.' I bowed, went through the door and made my way down the stone steps to the waiting gondola. '*Pescheria*,' I ordered. 'I know, Excellency,' said the worthy gondolier. At least I think that's what he said as he shoved us off; I had drunk rather a lot. Father, Nicholas and Henry waved from the balcony. We turned into a little canal and the palace and its extraordinary inhabitants, one of whom was surely my father, disappeared from view.

With hardly a sound the gondolier propelled our craft along those haunted black canals. Venice was silent. It had never seemed more beautiful. As I clambered out by the deserted fish market I remember thinking that the full moon over the Rialto looked too operatic to be real. And then I staggered back to the seedy *pensione* in which I had been conceived.